Praise for Ed McBa

D1536466

"Raw and realistic…The bad guys are very bad, and the good guys are better." —*Detroit Free Press*

"Ed McBain's 87th Precinct series…simply the best police procedurals being written in the United States." —*Washington Post*

"The best crime writer in the business." —*Houston Post*

"Ed McBain is a national treasure." —*Mystery News*

"It's hard to think of anyone better at what he does. In fact, it's impossible."—Robert B. Parker

"I never read Ed McBain without the awful thought that I still have a lot to learn. And when you think you're catching up, he gets better."
—Tony Hillerman

"McBain is the unquestioned king…light years ahead of anyone else in the field." —*San Diego Union-Tribune*

"McBain tells great stories." —Elmore Leonard

"Pure prose poetry…It is such writers as McBain who bring the great American urban mythology to life." —*The London Times*

"The McBain stamp: sharp dialogue and crisp plotting."
—*Miami Herald*

"You'll be engrossed by McBain's fast, lean prose." —*Chicago Tribune*

"McBain redefines the American police novel…he can stop you dead in your tracks with a line of dialogue." —*Cleveland Plain Dealer*

"The wit, the pacing, his relish for the drama of human diversity [are] what you remember about McBain novels." —*Philadelphia Inquirer*

"McBain is a top pro, at the top of his game." —*Los Angeles Daily News*

TRICKS

TRICKS

AN 87TH PRECINCT NOVEL

ED McBAIN

Text copyright © 1987 Hui Corporation
Republished in 2011
All rights reserved.

Printed in the United States of America.

Published by Thomas & Mercer
P.O. Box 400818
Las Vegas, NV 89140

ISBN-13: 9781612181882
ISBN-10: 1612181880

This is for Russell Wm. Hultgren

The city in these pages is imaginary.
The people, the places are all fictitious.
Only the police routine is based on established
investigatory technique.

The pair of them came down the street streaming blood.

No one paid any attention to them.

This was the city.

The taller of the two wore a bloodstained blue bathrobe. Blood appeared to be oozing from a half-dozen crosshatched wounds on his face. His hands were covered with blood. The striped pajama bottoms that showed beneath the hem of the robe were spattered with blood that seemed to have dripped from an open wound in his belly, where a dagger was plunged to the hilt.

The shorter person, a girl—although it was difficult to tell from the contorted mask of her face—wore only a paisley-patterned nightgown and high-heeled, pink pom-pommed bedroom slippers. Her garments screamed blood to the unusually mild October night. An ice pick was stuck into her chest, the handle smeared with blood. Blood was matted in her long stringy hair, bright red blood stained her naked legs, and her ankles, and the backs of her hands, and her narrow chest where it showed above the top of the yoke-necked nightgown.

She couldn't have been older than twelve.

The boy with her was perhaps the same age.

They were both carrying shopping bags that seemed stained with blood as fresh as that of their wounds. There could have been something recently severed from a human body inside each of those bags. A hand perhaps. Or a head. Or perhaps the bags had become blood-soaked only from proximity to their own bodies.

They came running up the street as though propelled by the urgency of their wounds.

"Let's try here," the boy said.

Several teeth appeared to be missing from his mouth. The black gaps were visible when he spoke. A thin line of red painted a trail from his lower lip to his chin. The flesh around his right eye was discolored red and black and blue and purple. He looked as if someone had beaten him severely before plunging the dagger into his belly.

"This one?" the girl asked.

They stopped before a street-level door.

They knocked frantically on the door.

It opened.

"Trick or treat!" they shouted in unison.

It was 4:10 P.M. on Halloween night.

The 4:00-to-midnight shift at the 87th Precinct was only ten minutes old.

"Halloween ain't what it used to be," Andy Parker said.

He was sitting behind his desk in the squadroom, his feet up on the desk, his chair tilted dangerously, as if burdened by the weight of the shoulder holster slung over its back. He was wearing rumpled trousers, an unpressed sports jacket, unshined black shoes, dingy white socks, and a wash-and-wear shirt with food stains on it. He had got his haircut at a barber's college on the Stem. There was a three-day-old beard stubble on his face. He was talking to Hawes and Brown, but they were not listening to him. That didn't stop Parker.

"What it is, Devil's Night steals from it," he said, and nodded in agreement with his observation.

At their own desks, the other detectives kept typing.

"Years ago," Parker said, "*tonight* was when the kids raised hell. Nowadays, you got church dances, you got socials at the Y, you got all kinds of shit to keep the kids out of trouble. So the kids figure, Okay, they want us to be good on Halloween, so we'll pick another night to behave like little bastards. So they invented Devil's Night, which was last night, when we got all the windows busted and the eggs thrown."

Across the room, the typewriters kept clacking.

"You guys writing books or what?" Parker asked.

No one answered him.

"I'm gonna write a book one of these days," Parker said. "Lots of cops write books, they make a fortune. I had plenty experience, I could prolly write a terrific book."

Hawes looked up for a moment, and then scratched at his back. He was sunburned and peeling. He had returned only Monday morning from a week's vacation in Bermuda, but his skin was still the color of his hair. Big redheaded man with a white streak in the hair over the left temple, where he'd once been slashed. He had not yet told Annie Rawles that he'd spent some very pleasant hours with a girl he'd met down there on the pink sands.

"This guy Wamburger in LA, he used to be a cop," Parker said, "I think with Hollywood Division. He writes these big best sellers, don't he? This other guy, Kornitch, he writes them, too, he used to be a cop in New York. Ain't nobody who didn't used to be a cop can write books sound real about cops. One of these days, I'm gonna write a big fuckin' best seller, I'll go live on a yacht in the south of France. Get these naked broads diving off the boat while I sit there doing nothing."

"Like now," Brown said.

"Yeah, bullshit, I already finished my work," Parker said. "This shift's been too fuckin' quiet. Whose idea was it to put on extra men, anyway?"

"The lieutenant's."

"So what's the use of seven guys when nothin's happening? Who's on, anyway? And where the fuck are they?"

"Cruising," Hawes said. "Out there looking for trouble."

He was thinking he himself would be looking for trouble if he told Annie what had happened in Bermuda, even though his arrangement with her was a loose one. Separate apartments, occasional conjugal visits, like they gave prisoners down in Mexico. Anyway, he'd *asked* Annie to come with him to Bermuda, hadn't he? Annie said her vacation wasn't till February. He asked her to change her vacation. She said she had to be in court all that week. She also said she hated Bermuda. He went down alone. Met this girl who practiced law in Atlanta. She'd taught him some legal tricks.

"It's so quiet, you could hear a pin drop," Parker said. "I coulda been home sleeping."

"Instead of sleeping here," Brown said, and went to the water cooler. He was a hefty, muscular black man, standing some six feet four inches tall and weighing 220 pounds. There was a glowering look on his face as he pulled a paper cup from the holder and then stabbed at the faucet button. He always looked glowering, even when he was smiling. Brown could get an armed robber to drop his piece just by glowering at him.

"Who's sleeping?" Parker said. "I'm resting, is all. I already finished my work."

"Then why don't you start writing your book?" Hawes said.

"You could write all about how Halloween ain't what it used to be," Brown said, crumpling the paper cup and going back to his desk.

"It ain't," Parker agreed.

"You could write about it's so quiet on Halloween, your hero has nothing to do," Hawes said.

"That's the truth," Parker said. "This phone ain't rung once since I come in."

He looked at the phone.

It did not ring.

"I'll bet that bothers you a lot," Brown said. "The phone not ringing."

"Nothing to do," Hawes said.

"No ax murders out there," Brown said.

"I had an ax murder once," Parker said, "I could maybe write about that."

"It's been done," Hawes said.

"Be a big fuckin' best seller."

"I don't think it was."

" 'Cause maybe a cop didn't write it. You got to be a cop to write best sellers about cops."

"You got to be an ax murderer to write best sellers about ax murders," Brown said.

"Sure," Parker said, and looked at the phone again.

"You got nothing to do," Hawes said, "whyn't you go down the hall and shave?"

"I'm working on my *Miami Vice* look," Parker said.

"You look like a bum," Brown said.

"I *am* a bum," Parker said.

"You got to be a bum to write best sellers about bums," Brown said.

"Tell that to Kennedy," Hawes said.

"Teddy? I didn't know he wrote books," Parker said. "What does he write about? Senators?"

"Go shave," Hawes said.

"Or go write a book about a barber," Brown suggested.

"I ain't a barber," Parker said.

He looked at the phone again.

"You ever see it this quiet?" he asked.

"I never even *heard* it this quiet," Brown said.

"Me, neither," Parker said. "It's like a paid vacation."

"Like always," Brown said.

"I once had a lady choked to death on a dildo," Parker said. "Maybe I could write about that. I had a lot of cases I could write about."

"Maybe you could write about the case you're working now," Brown said.

"I ain't working nothing right now."

"No kidding?"

"I finished all my work. Everything wrapped up till the phone rings."

"Maybe the phone's out of order," Hawes said.

"You think so?" Parker said, but he made no move to lift the receiver and listen for a dial tone.

"Or maybe none of the bad guys are doing anything out there," Brown said.

"Maybe all the bad guys went south for the winter," Hawes said, and thought again about Bermuda, and wondered if he should come clean with Annie.

"Fat chance," Parker said. "This weather? I never seen an October like this in my entire life. I once had a case, this guy strangled his wife with the telephone cord. I'll bet I could write about that."

"I'll bet you could."

"Hit her with the phone first, knocked her cold. Then strangled her with the cord."

"You could call it *Long Distance*," Brown said.

"No, he was standing close to her when he done it."

"Then how about *Local Call*?"

"What's wrong with *Sorry, Wrong Number*?" Parker asked.

"Nothing," Hawes said. "That's a terrific title."

"Or I could write about this guy got drowned in the bathtub. His wife drowned him in the bathtub. That was a good case."

"You could call it *Glub*," Brown said.

"*Glub* ain't a best-selling title," Parker said. "Also, she cut off his cock. The water was all red with his blood."

"Why'd she do that?" Brown asked, truly interested now.

"He was fuckin' around with some other broad," Parker said. "You shoulda seen the guy, he was a tiny little runt. His wife came in while he was taking a bath, she shoved him under the water, good-bye, Charlie. Then she cuts off his cock with his own straight razor, throws it out the window."

"The razor?"

"No, the cock. Hit an old lady walking by in the street. Hit her right on top of the head, knocked this plastic flower off her hat. She bends down to pick up the flower, she sees the cock laying on the sidewalk. Right away she wonders who she can sue. She picks it up, runs to her lawyer with it. Goes running down the street with this cock in her fist, in this city nobody even blinked."

"Carella and I once worked a case," Hawes said, "where this guy cut off another guy's hands."

"Why'd he do that?"

"Same reason. Love."

"That's *love*?"

"Love or money," Hawes said, and shrugged. "The only two reasons there are."

"Plus your lunatics," Brown said.

"Well, that's a whole 'nother ball game," Parker said. "Your lunatics. I once had a lunatic, he killed four priests before we caught up with him. We ast him why he was killing priests. He told us his father was a priest. How could that be, his father a priest?"

"Maybe his mother was a nun," Brown said.

"No, his mother was a registered nurse. Fifty years old, but gorgeous. Peaches Muldoon, her name was. Her square handle, I mean it, she was from Tennessee. Told me her son was nuts for sure, and she was glad I nailed him. Peaches Muldoon. A red-head. A real racehorse."

"Who'd *she* say the father was?"

"Her brother," Parker said.

"Nice case," Hawes said.

"Yeah. Maybe I oughta write about that one."

"You're not a priest."

"Sometimes *I feel* like a priest," Parker said. "You know the last time I got laid? Don't ask."

"Maybe you oughta go look up Peaches," Brown suggested.

"She's prolly dead by now," Parker said, giving the idea serious consideration. "This was maybe ten years ago, this case."

"She'd be sixty by now," Hawes said.

"If she ain't dead, yeah. But sixty ain't old, you know. I laid a lot of sixty-year-old broads. They have lots of experience, they know what they're doing."

He looked at the phone again.

"Maybe I *will* go shave," he said.

The two women knew each other well.

Annie Rawles was a detective/1st working out of the Rape Squad.

Eileen Burke was a detective/2nd who worked out of Special Forces.

They were in Annie's office discussing murder.

The clock on the wall read 4:30 P.M.

"Why'd they drag *you* in?" Eileen asked.

"My experience with decoys," Annie said. "I guess Homicide's getting desperate."

"Who caught the squeals?"

"Guy named Alvarez at the Seven-Two."

"In Calm's Point?"

"Yes."

"All three?"

"All three."

"Same area of the precinct?"

"The Canal Zone, down by the docks. You'd think you were in Houston."

"I've never been to Houston."

"Don't go."

Eileen smiled.

She was five feet nine inches tall, with long legs, good breasts, flaring hips, flaming red hair, and green eyes. There was no longer a scar on her left cheek. Plastic surgery had taken care of that. But Annie wondered if there were still internal scars.

"You don't have to take this one," she said. "I know it's short notice."

"Well, tell me some more," Eileen said.

"Or it can wait till *next* Friday. Shit, Homicide only called me an hour ago. Told me Alvarez wasn't making any headway, maybe the spic needed a helping hand. Homicide's words, not mine."

"Good old Homicide," Eileen said, and shook her head knowingly.

She wondered if Annie had doubts about her handling this one. She hadn't handled a really difficult one since the accident. Calling it an "accident" made it easier to think about. An accident was something that could happen to anyone. Something that needn't necessarily happen again. An accident wasn't a rapist slashing open your left cheek and then taking you by force.

Annie was watching her.

Eyes the color of loam behind glasses that gave her a scholarly look, black hair cut in a wedge, firm cupcake breasts on a slender body. About the same age as Eileen, a bit shorter. As hard and as brilliant as a diamond. Annie used to work out of Robbery, where she'd blown away two guys holding up a midtown bank. Blew them out of the air. If she hadn't been frightened by two seasoned hoods facing a max of twenty, would she have any sympathy for a decoy cop running scared?

Well, I've been on the job, Eileen thought, I'm *not* running scared.

But she was.

"When was the first one?" she asked.

"The tenth. A Friday night, full moon. Alvarez thought maybe a loony. Then the second one turned up a week later, the seventeenth. And another one last Friday night."

"Always Friday night, huh?"

"So far."

"So tonight's Friday, so Homicide wants a decoy."

"So does Alvarez. I spoke to him right after I got the call. He sounds smart as hell, but so far he hasn't got a place to hang his hat."

"What's his thinking on it?"

"You don't know the Zone, huh?"

"No."

"Then you missed what I was saying about Houston."

"I guess so."

"There's an area bordering the Ship Canal down there, it's infested with hookers and dope. Sleaziest dives I've ever seen in my life. The docks on the Calm's Point Canal run a close second."

"Are they hookers then? The victims?"

"Yes. Hookers."

"All three?"

"One of them only sixteen years old."

Eileen nodded.

"What'd he use?" she asked.

Annie hesitated.

"A knife," she said.

And suddenly it all played back again in Eileen's head...

Her hand going for the Browning .380 automatic tucked into her boot, Don't force me to cut you, *the pistol coming free of its holster, moving into firing position—and he slashed her face. Sudden fire blazed a trail across her cheek She dropped the gun at once. Good girl, he said. And slashed her pantyhose and the panties underneath...*

And...

And thrust the cold flat side of the knife against her...against her...

"Want me to cut you here, too?"

She shook her head.

No, please, *she thought.*

And mumbled the words incoherently, No, please, and said them aloud at last, "No, please. Please. Don't...cut me again. Please."

"Want me to fuck you instead?"

"Don't cut me again."

Annie was watching her intently.

"Slit their throats with a knife," she said.

Eileen was covered with cold sweat.

"So...I...I guess they want me to play hooker, is that it?" she said.

"That's it."

"New girl in town, huh?"

"You've got it."

"Cruising? Or have they set up...?"

"They're planting you in a place called Larry's Bar. On Fairview and East Fourth."

Eileen nodded.

"Tonight, huh?"

"Starting around eight."

"That's early, isn't it?"

"They want to give him enough rope."

"Where do I check in?"

"The Seven-Two. You can change there."

"Into what? The hookers today look like college girls."

"Not the ones working the Canal Zone."

Eileen nodded again.

"Has Alvarez picked my backups?"

"One. A big beefy guy named..."

"I want at least two," Eileen said.

"I'm your other one," Annie said.

Eileen looked at her.

"If you want me."

Eileen said nothing.

"I'm not afraid of using the piece," Annie said.

"I know you're not."

"But if you'd feel better with another man..."

"Nothing's going to make me feel better," Eileen said. "I'm scared shitless. You could back me with the Russian army, and I'd still be scared."

"Then don't do it," Annie said.

"Then when do I stop being scared?" Eileen asked.

The room went silent.

"Homicide asked me to get the best decoy I knew," Annie said softly. "I picked you."

"Thanks a lot," Eileen said.

But she smiled.

"You *are*, you know."

"I *was*."

"*Are*," Annie said.

"Sweet talker," Eileen said.

And smiled again.

"So…it's up to you," Annie said, and looked up at the clock. "But you've got to let me know right away. They want everything in place by eight tonight."

"Who's this big beefy guy?"

"His name's Shanahan. Irish as Paddy's underwear, six feet tall, weighs at least two hundred pounds. I wouldn't want to meet him in a dark alley, believe me."

"I *would*," Eileen said. "I'd like an hour with him before I hit the street. Can he be in the squadroom by seven?"

"You'll do it then?"

"Only 'cause you're the other backup," Eileen said, and smiled again.

But she was trembling inside.

"This guy who killed them," she said. "Do they have any idea what he looks like?"

"Alvarez says he's got some statements that seem to jibe. But who knows what he'll look like tonight? If he comes in at all."

"Terrific," Eileen said.

"One thing for sure, though."

"Yeah?"

"He's passing himself off as a trick."

The saw ripped through wood, ripped through flesh and bone along the middle of the wooden box and the middle of the woman. Blood gushed from the track the saw made, following the sharp teeth. The saw itself was bloody when at last he withdrew it from box and woman. He looked up at the wall clock. 5:05 P.M. He nodded in grim satisfaction.

And lifted the lids on both sides of the box.

And the woman stepped out in one piece, grinning, and held her arms over her head, and the audience began to applaud and cheer.

"Thank you, thank you very much," the man said, bowing.

The audience was composed mostly of boys and girls between the ages of thirteen and eighteen because the performance was being held at the high school on North Eleventh. The principal of the school, Mr. Ellington, beamed contentedly. Hiring the magician had been his idea. A way to keep these restless teenagers happy and occupied for an hour or so before they hit the streets. He would make a little speech after the performance was over, which should be any minute now. He would tell them all to go home and have a good dinner and then put on their costumes and go out for a safe and sane Halloween in the secure knowledge that among the rights granted in a democracy was freedom of assembly—like the assembly they'd had this evening—and also freedom of assembly in the streets, but *not* the freedom to perform malicious mischief, definitely not. That would be his pitch. The kids, grateful for an hour's entertainment, would—he hoped—follow his directives. No one from Herman Raucher High would become involved in vandalism tonight. Nossir.

He watched now as the magician's assistant rolled the wooden box off the stage. She was a good-looking blonde, in her late twenties Ellington guessed, wearing a sequined costume that exposed to good advantage her long, long legs and her exuberant breasts. Ellington noticed that most of the boys in the auditorium could not take their eyes off the assistant's long legs and the popping tops of her creamy white breasts. He himself was having a little difficulty doing that. She was back on stage now, wheeling a tall box. A vertical one this time. The magician—whose name was Sebastian the Great—was wearing tails and a top hat. Ellington looked up at the clock. This was probably the closing number of the act. He hoped so because he wanted to make his little speech and get the kids the hell out of here. He had promised Estelle he would stop by on the way home from school. Estelle was the lady he stopped by to see every Wednesday and Friday afternoon, when his wife thought he had meetings with the staff. Estelle's legs weren't as long, nor were her breasts as opulent as those on the magician's assistant, but then again Estelle was forty-seven years old.

"Thank you, kids," Sebastian the Great said, "thank you. Now I know you're all anxious to get out there in the streets for a safe and sane Halloween, and so I won't keep you much longer. Ah, thank you, Marie," he said to his assistant.

Her name's Marie, Ellington thought, and wondered what her last name was, and wondered if she was listed in the phone book.

"You see here a little box—well, not so little because I'm a pretty tall fellow—which I'm going to step into in just a moment… thank you, Marie, you can go now, you've been very helpful, let's have a nice round of applause for Marie, kids."

Marie held her hands up over her head, legs widespread, big smile on her mouth, and the kids applauded and yelled, especially the boys, and then she did a cute little sexy turn and went strutting off the stage in her high heels.

"That's the last you'll see of Marie tonight," Sebastian said.

Shit, Ellington thought.

"And in just a few minutes, you'll see the last of me, too. What I'm going to do, kids, I'm going to step inside this box…"

He opened the door on the face of the box.

"And I'm going to ask you all to count to ten…out loud… one, two, three, four, and so on—you all know how to count to ten, don't you?"

Laughter from the kids.

"And I'm going to ask your principal, Mr. Ellington, to come up here—Mr. Ellington, would you come up here now, please?— and when you reach the number ten, he's going to open the door of this box, and Sebastian the Great will be gone, kids, I will have disappeared, vanished, poof! So…ah, good, Mr. Ellington, if you'll just stand here beside the box, thank you. That's very good." He took off his top hat. Stepping partially into the box, he said, "I'm going to say good-bye to you now…"

Applause and cheering from the kids.

"Thank you, thank you," he said, "and I want to remind you again to please have a safe and sane Halloween out there. Now the minute I close this door, I want you to start counting out loud. And when you reach ten, Mr. Ellington will open the door and I'll be gone but not forgotten. Mr. Ellington? Are you ready?"

"Ready," Ellington said, feeling like an asshole.

"Good-bye, kids," Sebastian said, and closed the door behind him.

"One!" the kids began chanting. "Two! Three! Four! Five! Six! Seven! Eight! Nine! Ten!"

Ellington opened the door on the box.

Sebastian the Great had indeed vanished.

The kids began applauding.

Ellington went to the front of the stage, and held up his hands for silence.

He would have to remind the kids not to try sawing anybody in half, because that had been only a trick.

The station wagon pulled up to the curb in front of the liquor store on Culver and Ninth. The big woman behind the wheel was a curly-haired blonde in her late forties, wearing a blue dress with a tiny white floral print, a cardigan sweater over it. A kid was sitting beside her on the front seat. Three more kids were in the back of the car. The kids looked perhaps eleven or twelve years old, no older than that.

They threw open the doors and got out of the car.

"Have fun, kids," the blonde behind the wheel said.

The kids were all dressed like robbers.

Little black leather jackets, and little blue jeans, and little white sneakers, and little billed caps on their little heads, and little black masks over their eyes. They were all carrying shopping bags decorated with little orange pumpkins. They were all holding little toy pistols in their little hands. They went across the sidewalk in a chattering little excited group, and one of them opened the door to the liquor store. The clock on the wall behind the counter read 5:15 P.M. The owner of the store looked up the moment the bell over the door sounded.

"Trick or treat!" the little kids squealed in unison.

"Come on, kids, get out of here," the owner said impatiently. "This is a place of business."

And one of the little kids shot him in the head.

Parker had shaved and was back in the squadroom, rummaging through the file cabinets containing folders for all the cases the detectives had successfully closed. In police work, there was no such thing as a solution. You never *solved* a case, you closed it out. Or it remained *open,* which meant the perpetrator was already in Buenos Aires or Nome, Alaska, and you'd *never* catch him. The Open File was the graveyard of police detection.

ED McBAIN

"I feel like a new man," Parker said. In fact, he looked like the same old Parker, except that he had shaved. "Muldoon," he said, "Muldoon, where are you, Muldoon?"

"You really gonna call a sixty-year-old lady?" Brown asked.

"Peaches Muldoon, correct," Parker said. "If she was well preserved at fifty, she's prolly still got it all in the right places. Where the fuck's the file?"

"Look under Aging Nurses," Hawes said.

"Look under Decrepit Broads," Brown said.

"Yeah, bullshit, wait'll you see her picture," Parker said.

The clock on the squadroom wall read 5:30 P.M.

"Muldoon, here we go," Parker said, and yanked a thick file from the drawer.

The telephone rang.

"Who's catching?" Parker asked.

"I thought you were," Brown said.

"Me? No, no. You're up, Artie."

Brown sighed and picked up the phone.

"87th Squad," he said, "Brown."

"Artie, this is Dave downstairs."

Sergeant Murchison, at the muster desk.

"Yeah, Dave."

"Adam Four just responded to a 10-20 on Culver and Ninth. Liquor store called Adams Wine and Spirits."

"Yeah?"

"They got a homicide there."

"Okay," Brown said.

"You got some people out, don't you?"

"Yes."

"Who? Can you take a look for me?"

Brown reached across the desk for the duty chart.

"Kling and Carella are riding together," he said. "Meyer and Genero are out solo."

"Any idea which sectors?"

"No."

"Okay, I'll try to raise them."

"Keep in touch."

"Will do."

Brown hung up.

"What?" Hawes asked.

"Homicide on Culver. There goes the neighborhood."

The telephone rang again.

"Take a look at this picture," Parker said, coming over to Brown's desk. "You ever see a body like this one?"

"87th Squad, Hawes."

"Look at those tits," Parker said.

"Hello, who am I talking to, please?" a woman's voice asked.

"Detective Hawes."

"Legs that won't quit," Parker said.

"My husband's gone," the woman said.

"Yes, ma'am," Hawes said, "let me give you the number for—"

"My name is—"

"It'll be best if you call Missing Persons, ma'am," Hawes said. "They're specially equipped to deal with—"

"He disappeared here in *this* precinct," the woman said.

"Still…"

"Does that look like a fifty-year-old broad?" Parker asked.

The telephone rang again. Brown picked up.

"87th Squad, Brown," he said.

"Artie? This is Genero."

"Yeah?"

"Artie, you won't believe this."

"What won't I believe?" Brown asked. He looked up at Parker, covered the mouthpiece, and whispered, "Genero."

Parker rolled his eyes.

"It happened again," Genero said.

"My name is Marie Sebastiani," the woman on Hawes's phone said. "My husband is Sebastian the Great."

Hawes immediately thought he was talking to a bedbug.

"Ma'am," he said, "if your husband's really gone..."

"I'm at this restaurant, you know?" Genero said. "On Culver and Sixth?"

"Yeah?" Brown said.

"Where they had the holdup last night? I stopped by to talk to the owners?"

"Yeah?"

"My husband is a magician," Marie said. "He calls himself Sebastian the Great. He's disappeared."

Good magician, Hawes thought.

"And I go out back to look in the garbage cans?" Genero said. "See maybe somebody dropped a gun in there or something?"

"Yeah?" Brown said.

"I mean he's *really* disappeared," Marie said. "Vanished. I went out back of the high school where he was loading the car, and the car was gone, and so was Frank. And all his tricks were dumped in the driveway like—"

"Frank, ma'am?"

"My husband. Frank Sebastiani. Sebastian the Great."

"It happened again, Artie," Genero said. "I almost puked."

"What happened again?"

"Maybe he just went home, ma'am," Hawes said.

"No, we live in the next state, he wouldn't have left without me. And his stuff was all over the driveway. I mean, expensive *tricks*."

"So what are you saying, ma'am?"

"I'm saying somebody must've stolen the car and God knows what he did to Frank."

"Artie?" Genero said. "Are you with me?"

"I'm with you," Brown said, and sighed.

"It was in one of the garbage cans, Artie."

"What was in one of the garbage cans?"

"Which high school is that, ma'am?" Hawes asked.

"Herman Raucher High. On North Eleventh."

"Are you there now?"

"Yes. I'm calling from a pay phone."

"You stay right there," Hawes said, "I'll get somebody to you."

"I'll be waiting out back," Marie said, and hung up.

"Artie, you better come over here," Genero said. "The Burgundy on Culver and Sixth."

"What is it you found in—"

But Genero had already hung up.

Brown slipped into his shoulder holster.

Hawes clipped his holster to his belt.

Parker picked up the telephone receiver.

"Peaches Muldoon, here I come," he said.

5:40 P.M. on Halloween night, the streets dark for almost an hour now, the city off daylight savings time since the twenty-sixth of the month. All the little monsters and goblins and devils and bats out in force, carrying their shopping bags full of candy from door to door, yelling "Trick or treat!" and praying no one would give them a treat with a double-edged razor blade in it.

Brown looked at his watch.

Along about now, his wife, Caroline, would be taking Connie around. His eight-year-old daughter had previewed her costume for him last night. She'd looked like the most angelic witch he'd ever seen in his life. All next week, there'd be sweets to eat. The only people who profited from Halloween were the candy makers and the dentists. Brown was in the wrong profession.

He had chosen to walk to the Burgundy Restaurant on Culver and Sixth. It wasn't too far from the station house, and a cop—if Genero could be considered one—was already on the scene.

The night was balmy.

God, what an October this had been.

Leaves still on the trees in the park, dazzling yellows and reds and oranges and browns, daytime skies a piercing blue, nighttime skies pitch-black and sprinkled with stars. In a city where itchy citizens took off their overcoats far too early each spring, it now seemed proper and fitting that there was no need to put them on again quite yet. He walked swiftly toward Culver, turning to glance at ET hurrying by with Frankenstein's monster on one side and Dracula on the other. Smiling, he turned the corner onto Culver and began walking toward Sixth.

Genero was waiting on the sidewalk outside the restaurant.

He looked pale.

"What is it?" Brown asked.

"Come on back," Genero said. "I didn't touch it."

"Touch what?" Brown asked. But Genero was already walking up the alleyway on the right-hand side of the restaurant.

Garbage cans flanked either side of the restaurant's back door, illuminated by an overhead floodlight.

"That one," Genero said.

Brown lifted the lid on the can Genero was pointing to.

The bloody upper torso of a human body was stuffed into the can, on top of a green plastic garbage bag.

The torso had been severed at the waist from the rest of the body.

The torso had no arms.

And no head.

"Why does this always happen to me?" Genero asked God.

"I once found a hand in an airlines bag," Genero said.

"No shit?" Monoghan asked without interest.

Monoghan was a Homicide cop. He usually worked in tandem with his partner Monroe, but there had been two homicides in the Eight-Seven tonight, a few blocks apart from each other, and Monoghan was here behind the restaurant on Culver and Sixth, and Monroe was over at the liquor store on Culver and Ninth. It was a shame; Monoghan without Monroe was like a bagel without lox.

"Cut off at the wrist," Genero said. "I almost puked."

"Yeah, a person could puke, all right," Monoghan said.

He was looking down into the garbage can where the bloody torso still rested on the green plastic bag.

"Nothing but a piece of fresh meat here," he said to Brown.

Brown had a pained look in his eyes. He merely nodded.

"ME on the way?" Monoghan asked.

"Called him ten minutes ago."

"You won't need an ambulance for this one," Monoghan said. "All you'll need is a shopping bag."

He laughed at his own little witticism.

He sorely missed Monroe.

"Looks like a man, don't it?" he said. "I mean, no knockers, all that hair on the chest."

"This hand I found," Genero said, "it was a man's, too. A great big hand. I nearly puked."

There were several uniformed cops in the alley now, and a couple of technicians sniffing around the back door of the restaurant, and a plainclothes lady cop from Photo taking her Polaroids. Crime Scene signs already up, even though this *wasn't* a crime scene in the strictest sense of the word, in that the crime had almost certainly taken place elsewhere. All they had here was the detritus of a crime, a piece of fresh meat—as Monoghan had called it—lying in a garbage can, the partial remains of what had once been a human being. That and whatever clues may have been left by the person who'd transported the torso to this particular spot.

"It's amazing the number of dismembered stiffs you get in this city," Monoghan said.

"Oh, boy, you're telling *me*?" Genero said.

Monoghan was wearing a black homburg, a black suit, a white shirt, and a black tie. His hands were in his jacket pockets, only the thumbs showing. He looked like a sad, neat undertaker. Genero was trying to look like a hip big-city detective disguised as a college boy. He was wearing blue slacks and a reindeer-patterned sweater over a sports shirt open at the throat. Brown penny loafers. No hat. Curly black hair, brown eyes. He resembled a somewhat stupid poodle.

Monoghan looked at him.

"You the one found this thing here?" he asked.

"Well, yes," Genero said, wondering if he should have admitted this.

"Any other parts in these other garbage cans?"

"I didn't look," Genero said, thinking one part had been plenty.

"Want to look now?"

"Don't get prints on any of those garbage-can lids," one of the techs warned.

Genero tented a handkerchief over his hand and began lifting lids.

There were no other parts.

"So all we got here is this chest here," Monoghan said.

"Hello, boys," the ME said, coming up the alley. "What've we got here?"

"Just this chest here," Monoghan said, indicating the torso.

The ME peeked into the garbage can.

"Very nice," he said, and put down his satchel. "Did you want me to pronounce it dead, or what?"

"You could give us a postmortem interval, that'd be helpful," Monoghan said.

"Autopsy'll give you that," the ME said.

"Looks of this one," Monoghan said, "somebody already *done* the autopsy. What'd he use, can you tell?"

"Who?" the ME said.

"Whoever cut him up in pieces."

"He wasn't a brilliant brain surgeon, I can tell you that," the ME said, looking at the torn and jagged flesh where the head, arms, and lower torso had been.

"So what was it? A cleaver? A hacksaw?"

"I'm not a magician," the ME said.

"Any marks, scars, tattoos?" Brown asked quietly.

"None that I can see. Let me roll it over."

Genero noticed that the ME kept referring to it as "it."

The ME rolled it over.

"None here, either," he said.

"Nothing but a piece of fresh meat," Monoghan said.

Hawes was wearing only a lightweight sports jacket over a shirt open at the throat, no tie, no hat. A mild breeze riffled his red hair; October this year was like springtime in the Rockies. Marie Sebastiani seemed uncomfortable talking to a cop. Most honest citizens did; it was the thieves of the world who felt perfectly at home with law-enforcement officers.

Fidgeting nervously, she told him how she'd changed out of her costume and into the clothes she was now wearing—a tweed jacket and skirt, a lavender blouse, and high-heeled pumps—while her husband, Sebastian the Great, a.k.a. Frank Sebastiani, had gone out behind the high school to load the car with all the *little* tricks he used in the act. And then *she'd* gone out back to where she was supposed to meet him, and the car was gone, and he was gone, and his tricks were scattered all over the driveway.

"By *little* tricks…" Hawes said.

"Oh, you know, the rings, and the scarves, and the balls, and the birdcage…well, all this stuff all over the place here. Jimmy comes with the van to pick up the boxes and the bigger stuff."

"Jimmy?"

"Frank's apprentice. He's a jack of all trades, drives the van to wherever we're performing, helps us load and unload, paints the boxes when they need it, makes sure all the spring catches are working properly…like that."

"He dropped you both off today, did he?"

"Oh, yes."

"And helped you unload and all?"

"Same as always."

"And stayed for the performance?"

"No, I don't know where he went during the performance. Probably out for a bite to eat. He knew we'd be done here around five, five-thirty."

"So where is he now? Jimmy?"

"Well, I don't know. What time do you have?"

Hawes looked at his watch.

"Five after six," he said.

"Gee, I don't know *where* he is," Marie said. "He's usually very punctual."

"What time *did* you get done here?" Hawes asked.

"Like I said, around five-fifteen or so."

"And you changed your clothes..."

"Yes. Well, so did Frank."

"What does he wear on stage?"

"Black tie and tails. And a top hat."

"And he changed into?"

"Is this important?"

"Very," Hawes said.

"Then let me get it absolutely correct," Marie said. "He put on a pair of blue slacks, and a blue sports shirt, no pattern on it, just the solid blue, and blue socks, and black shoes, and a...what do you call it? Houndstooth, is that the weave? A sort of jagged little black and blue weave. A houndstooth sports jacket. No tie."

Hawes was writing now.

"How old is your husband?" he asked.

"Thirty-four."

"How tall is he?"

"Five-eleven."

"Weight?"

"One-seventy."

"Color of his hair?"

"Black."

"Eyes?"

"Blue."

"Does he wear glasses?"

"No."

"Is he white?"

"Well, of *course*," Marie said.

"Any identifying marks, scars, or tattoos?"

"Yes, he has an appendectomy scar. And also a meniscectomy scar."

"What's that?" Hawes asked.

"He had a skiing accident. Tore the cartilage in his left knee. They removed the cartilage—what they call the meniscus. There's a scar there. On his left knee."

"How do you spell that?" Hawes asked. "Meniscectomy?"

"I don't know," Marie said.

"On the phone, you told me you live in the next state..."

"Yes, I do."

"Where?"

"Collinsworth."

"The address?"

"604 Eden Lane."

"Apartment number?"

"It's a private house."

"Telephone number, area code first?"

"Well, I'll give you Frank's card," she said, and dug into her shoulder bag and came up with a sheaf of cards. She took one from the stack and handed it to Hawes. He scanned it quickly, wrote both the home and office phone numbers onto his pad, and then tucked the card into the pad's flap.

"Did you try calling home?" he asked.

"No. Why would I do that?"

"Are you sure he didn't go home without you? Maybe he figured this Jimmy would pick you up."

"No, we were planning on eating dinner here in the city."

"So he wouldn't have gone home without you."

"He never has."

"This Jimmy...what's his last name?"

"Brayne."

"Brain? Like in somebody's head?"

"Yes, but with a Y."

"B-R-A-Y-N?"

"With an E on the end."

"B-R-A-Y-N-E?"

"Yes."

"James Brayne."

"Yes."

"And his address?"

"He lives with us."

"Same house?"

"A little apartment over the garage."

"And *his* phone number?"

"Oh, gee," she said, "I'm not sure I remember it."

"Well, try to remember," Hawes said, "because I think we ought to call back home, see if either of them maybe went back there."

"They wouldn't do that," Marie said.

"Maybe they got their signals crossed," Hawes said. "Maybe Jimmy thought your husband was going to take the stuff in the car..."

"No, the big stuff won't fit in the car. That's why we have the van."

"Or maybe your husband thought you were getting a ride back with Jimmy..."

"I'm sure he didn't."

"What kind of a car was your husband driving?"

"A 1984 Citation. A two-door coupe."

"Color?"

"Blue."

"License-plate number?"

"DL 74-3681."

"And the van?"

"A '79 Ford Econoline."

"Color?"

"Tan, sort of."

"Would you know the license-plate number on that one?"

"RL 68-7210."

"In whose name are the vehicles registered?

"My husband's."

"Both registered across the river?"

"Yes."

"Let's find a phone, okay?" Hawes said.

"There's one inside," she said, "but calling them won't do any good."

"How do you know?"

"Because Frank wouldn't have dumped his tricks all over the driveway this way. These tricks cost money."

"Let's try calling them, anyway."

"It won't do any good," Marie said. "I'm telling you."

He dialed Sebastiani's home and office numbers, and got no answer at either. Marie at last remembered the number in the room over the garage, and he dialed that one, too. Nothing.

"Well," he said, "let me get to work on this. I'll call you as soon as—"

"How am I going to get home?" Marie asked.

They always asked how they were going to get home.

"There are trains running out to Collinsworth, aren't there?"

"Yes, but—"

"I'll drop you off at the station."

"What about all those tricks outside in the driveway?"

"Maybe we can get the school custodian to lock them up someplace. Till your husband shows up."

"What makes you think he'll show up?"

"Well, I'm sure he's okay. Just some crossed signals, that's all."

"I'm not sure I want to go home tonight," Marie said.

"Well, ma'am…"

"I think I may want to…could I come to the police station with you? Could I wait there till you hear anything about Frank?"

"That's entirely up to you, ma'am. But it may take a while before we—"

"And can you lend me some money?" she asked.

He looked at her.

"For dinner?"

He kept looking at her.

"I'll pay you back as soon as…as soon as we find Frank. I'm sorry, but I've only got a few dollars on me. Frank was the one they paid, he's the one who's got all the money."

"How *much* money, ma'am?"

"Well, just enough for a hamburger or something."

"I meant how much money does your husband have on him?"

"Oh. Well, we got a hundred for the job. And he probably had a little something in his wallet, I don't know how much."

Which lets out robbery, Hawes thought. Although in this city, there were people who'd slit your throat for a nickel. He suddenly wondered how much money he himself was carrying. This was the first time in his entire life that a victim had asked him for a loan.

"I'm sort of hungry myself," he said. "Let's find the custodian and then go get something to eat."

Monroe looked bereft without Monoghan.

The clock on the liquor-store wall read 6:10 P.M.

He was standing behind the cash register, where the owner of the store had been shot dead a bit more than an hour earlier. The body was already gone. There was only blood and a chalked outline on the floor behind the counter. The cash register was empty.

"There was four of them," the man talking to Meyer said.

Meyer had been cruising the area when Sergeant Murchison raised him on the radio. He had got here maybe ten minutes after it was all over, and had immediately radioed back with a confirmed DOA. Murchison had informed Homicide, so here was Monroe, all alone, and looking as if he'd lost his twin brother. He was wearing a black homburg, a black suit, a white shirt, and a black tie. His hands were in his jacket pockets, only the thumbs showing. He looked like a sad, neat undertaker. Meyer wondered where Monoghan was. Wherever he was, Meyer figured he'd be dressed exactly like Monroe. Even if he was home sick in bed, he'd be dressed like Monroe.

Meyer himself was wearing brown slacks, a brown cotton turtleneck, and a tan sports jacket. He thought he looked very dapper tonight. With his bald head and his burly build, he figured he looked like Kojak, except more handsome. He was sorry Kojak was off the air now. He'd always felt Kojak gave bald cops a good name.

"Little kids," the man said.

This was the third time he'd told Meyer that four little kids had held up the liquor store and shot the owner.

"What do you mean, little kids?" Monroe asked from behind the cash register.

"Eleven, twelve years old," the man said.

His name was Henry Kirby, and he lived in a building up the street. He was perhaps sixty, sixty-five years old, a thin, graying man wearing a short-sleeved sports shirt and wrinkled polyester slacks. He'd told first Meyer and then Monroe that he was coming to the store to buy a bottle of wine when he saw these little kids running out with shopping bags and guns. Monroe still couldn't believe it.

"You mean *children*?" he said.

"Little kids, yeah," Kirby said.

"Grade-schoolers?"

"Yeah, little kids."

"Prepubescent twerps?" Monroe said.

He was doing okay without Monoghan. Without Monoghan, he was being Monoghan and Monroe all by himself.

"Yeah, little kids," Kirby said.

"What were they wearing?" Meyer said.

"Leather jackets, blue jeans, sneakers, and masks."

"What kind of masks?" Monroe asked. "Like these monster masks? These rubber things you pull over your head?"

"No, just these little black masks over their eyes. Like robbers wear. They were robbers, these kids."

"And you say there were four of them?"

"Four, right."

"Ran out of the store with shopping bags and guns?"

"Shopping bags and guns, right."

"What kind of guns?" Monroe asked.

"Little guns."

"Like .22s?"

"I'm not so good at guns. These were little guns."

"Like Berettas?"

"I'm not so good at guns."

"Like little Brownings?"

"I'm not so good at guns. They were little guns."

"Did you hear any shots as you approached the store?" Meyer asked.

"No, I didn't. I didn't know Ralph was dead till I walked inside."

"Ralph?" Monroe said.

"Ralph Adams. It's his store. Adams Wine and Spirits. He's been here in this same spot for twenty years."

"Not no more," Monroe said tactfully.

"So where'd these kids go when they came out of the store?" Meyer asked.

He was thinking this sounded like Fagin's little gang. The Artful Dodger, all that crowd. A cop he knew in England had written recently to say his kids would be celebrating—if that was the word for it—Halloween over there this year. Lots of American executives living in England, their kids had introduced the holiday to the British. Just what they need, Meyer thought. Maybe next year, twelve-year-old British kids'd start holding up liquor stores.

"They ran to this car parked at the curb," Kirby said.

"A vehicle?" Monroe said.

"Yeah, a car."

"An automobile?"

"A car, yeah."

"What kind of car?"

"I'm not so good at cars."

"Was it a big car or a little car?"

"A regular car."

"Like a Chevy or a Plymouth?"

"I'm not so good at cars."

"Like an Olds or a Buick?"

"A regular car, is all."

"They all got in this car?" Meyer asked.

"One in the front seat, three in the back."

"Who was driving?"

"A woman."

"How old a woman?"

"Hard to say."

"What'd she look like?"

"She was a blonde."

"What was she wearing?"

"I really couldn't see. It was dark in the car. I could see she was a blonde, but that's about all."

"How about when the kids opened the doors?" Monroe asked. "Didn't the lights go on?"

"Yeah, but I didn't notice what she was wearing. I figured this was maybe a carpool, you know?"

"What do you mean?"

"Well, the kids were all about the same age, so they couldn't all be *her* kids, you know what I mean? So I figured she was just driving maybe her own kid and some of his friends around. For Halloween, you know?"

"You mean the kid's mother was a wheelman, huh?"

"Well…"

"For a stickup, huh? A wheelman for four eleven-year-olds."

"Or twelve," Kirby said. "Eleven or twelve."

"These kids," Meyer said, "Were all of them boys?"

"They were *dressed* like boys, but I really couldn't say. They all went by so fast. Just came running out of the store and into the car."

"Then what?" Monroe asked.

"The car pulled away."

"Did you see the license plate?"

"I'm not so good at license plates," Kirby said.

"Was it you who called the police?" Meyer asked.

"Yes, sir. I called 911 minute I saw Ralph laying dead there behind the counter."

"Did you use this phone here?" Monroe asked, indicating the phone alongside the register.

"No, sir. I went outside and used the pay phone on the corner."

"Okay, we've got your name and address," Monroe said, "we'll get in touch if we need you."

"Is there a reward?" Kirby asked.

"For what?"

"I thought there might be a reward."

"We're not so good at rewards," Monroe said. "Thanks a lot, we'll be in touch."

Kirby nodded glumly and walked out of the store.

"Halloween ain't what it used to be," Monroe said.

"You just got yourself another backup," Kling said.

"No," Eileen said.

"What do you mean no? You're going into one of the worst sections in the city—"

"Without you," she said.

"—looking for a guy who's already killed..."

"Without *you,* Bert."

"Why?"

They were in an Italian restaurant near the Calm's Point Bridge. It was twenty minutes past 6:00; Eileen had to be at the Seven-Two in forty minutes. She figured five minutes over the bridge, another five to the precinct, plenty of time to eat without hurrying. She probably shouldn't be eating, anyway. In the past, she'd found that going out hungry gave her a fighter's edge. Plenty of time to eat *after* you caught the guy. Have two martinis after you caught him, down a sirloin and a platter of fries. After you caught him. If you caught him. Sometimes you didn't catch him. Sometimes he caught you.

She was carrying her hooker threads and her hardware in a tote bag sitting on the floor to the left of her chair. Kling was sitting opposite her, hands clasped on the tabletop, leaning some-what forward now, blond hair falling onto his forehead, intent look in his eyes, wanting to know why she didn't need a tagalong boyfriend tonight.

"Why do you think?" she asked.

The chef had overcooked the spaghetti. They'd specified *al dente* but this was the kind of dive where the help thought Al Dente was some guy with Mafia connections.

"I think you're crazy is what I think."

"Thanks."

"Damn it, if I can throw some extra weight your way…"

"I don't want you throwing anything my way. I've got a guy who's twice your size and a woman who can shoot her way out of a revolution. That's all I need. Plus myself."

"Eileen, I won't get in your way. I'll just—"

"No."

"I'll just be there if you need me."

"You really don't understand, do you?"

"No, I don't."

"You're not just another cop, Bert."

"I know that."

"You're my…"

She debated saying "boyfriend" but that sounded like a teen-ager's steady. She debated saying "lover" but that sounded like a dowager's kept stud. She debated saying "roommate" but that sounded like you lived with either another woman or a eunuch. Anyway, they weren't actually living together, not in the same apartment. She settled for what had once been a psychologist's term, but which had now entered the jargon as a euphemism for the guy or girl with whom you shared an unmarried state.

"You're my SO," she said.

"Your what?"

"Significant Other."

"I should hope so," Kling said. "Which is why I want to—"

"Listen, are you dense?" she asked. "I'm a cop going out on a job. What the hell's the matter with you?"

"Eileen, I…"

"Yes, *what*? Don't you think I can cut it?"

She had chosen an unfortunate word.

Cut.

She saw the look on his face.

"That's just what I mean," she said.

"What are you talking about?"

"I'm not going to get cut again," she said, "don't worry about it."

He looked at her.

"This time I shoot to kill," she said.

He took a deep breath.

"This spaghetti tastes like a sponge," she said.

"What time are you due there?"

"Seven."

He looked up at the clock.

"Where are they planting you?"

"A bar called Larry's. On Fairview and East Fourth."

"This guy Shanahan, is he any good?"

"I hope so," she said, and shoved her plate aside. "Could we get some coffee, do you think? And how come you're chalking off Annie?"

"I'm not—"

"I'd trade a hundred Shanahans for Annie."

"Calm down, Eileen."

"I'm calm," she said icily. "I just don't like your fucking attitude. You want to hand wrestle me? Prove you can go out there tonight and do the job better than I can?"

"Nobody said—"

"I can do the job," she said.

He looked into her eyes.

"I can do it," she said.

He didn't want to leave the parts where they'd be found too easily, and yet at the same time he didn't want to hide them so well that they wouldn't be discovered for weeks. This was tricky business here. Putting the pieces of the jigsaw in different places, making sure he wasn't spotted while he was distributing the evidence of bloody murder.

He'd dropped the first one behind a restaurant on Culver, near Sixth, figuring they'd be putting out more garbage when they closed tonight, hoping they'd discover the upper torso then and immediately call the police. He didn't want to scatter the various parts in locations too distant from each other because he wanted this to remain a strictly local matter, one neighborhood, one precinct, *this* precinct. At the same time, he couldn't risk someone finding any one of the parts so quickly that there'd be police crawling all over the neighborhood and making his job more difficult.

He wanted them to put it all together in the next little while.

Two, three days at the most, depending on how long it took them to find the parts and make identification.

By then, he'd be far, far away.

He cruised the streets now, driving slowly, looking for prospects.

The other parts of the body—the head, the hands, the arms, the lower torso—were lying on a tarpaulin in the trunk.

More damn kids in the streets tonight.

Right now, only the little ones were out. In an hour or so, you'd get your teenyboppers looking for trouble, and later tonight you'd get your older teenagers, the ones *really* hoping to do damage.

Kick over a garbage can, find a guy's arm in it. How does that grab you, boys?

He smiled.

Police cars up ahead, outside a liquor store.

Bald guy coming out to the curb, studying the sidewalk and then the street.

Trouble.

But not *his* trouble.

He cruised on by.

Headed up to the Stem, made a right turn, scanning the storefronts. Kids swarming all over the avenue, trick or treat, trick or treat. Chinese restaurant there on the right. All-night supermarket on the corner. Perfect if there was a side alley. One-way side street, he'd have to drive past, make a right at the next corner, and then another right onto Culver, come at it from there. Stopped for the red light at the next corner, didn't want some eager patrolman pulling him over for a bullshit violation. Made the right turn. Another light on Culver. Waited for that one to change. Turned onto Culver, drove up one block, made another right onto the one-way street. Drove up it slowly. Good! An alley between the corner supermarket and the apartment house alongside it. He drove on by, went through the whole approach a second time. Guy in an apron standing at the mouth of the alley, lighting a cigarette. Drove by again. And again. And again and again until the alley and the sidewalk were clear. He made a left turn into the alley. Cut the ignition, yanked out the keys. Came around the car. Unlocked the trunk. Yanked out one of the arms. Eased the trunk shut. Walked swiftly to the nearest garbage can. Lifted the lid. Dropped the arm in it. Left the lid slightly askew on top of the can. Got back in the car again, started it, and backed slowly out of the alley and into the street.

Two down, he thought.

The police stations in this city all looked alike. Even the newer ones began looking like the older ones after a while. A pair of green globes flanking the entrance steps, a patrolman standing on duty outside in case anybody decided to go in with a bomb. White numerals lettered onto each of the globes: 72. Only the numbers changed. Everything else was the same. Eileen could have been across the river and uptown in the Eight-Seven.

Scarred wooden entrance doors, glass-paneled in the upper halves. Just inside the doors was the muster room. High desk on the right, looked like a judge's bench, waist-high brass railing some two feet in front of it, running the length of it. Sergeant sitting behind it. On the wall behind him, photographs of the mayor and the police commissioner and a poster printed with the Miranda-Escobedo warnings in English and in Spanish. Big American flag on the wall opposite the desk. Wanted posters on the bulletin board under it. She flashed her shield at the sergeant, who merely nodded, and then she headed for the iron-runged steps at the far end of the room.

Rack with charging walkie-talkies on the wall there, each unit stenciled PROPERTY OF 72ND PRECINCT. Staircase leading down to the holding cells in the basement, and up to the Detective Division on the second floor, hand-lettered sign indicating the way. She climbed the steps, apple green walls on either side of her, paint flaking and hand-smudged. She was wearing sensible, low-heeled walking shoes, a cardigan sweater over a white cotton blouse, and a brown woolen skirt. The hooker gear was still in the tote bag, together with her hardware.

Down the corridor past the Interrogation Room, and the Clerical Office, and the men's and women's toilets, and the locker rooms, through a wide doorway, and then to the slatted wooden rail divider with green metal filing cabinets backed up against it on the inside. Stopped at the gate in the railing. Flashed the potsy again at the guy sitting behind the closest desk.

"Eileen Burke," she said. "I'm looking for Shanahan."

"You found him," Shanahan said, and got to his feet and came around the desk, hand extended. He was not as big as Annie had described him, five-eleven or so, maybe 170 pounds, 180. Eileen wished he were bigger. Black hair and blue eyes, toothy grin, what Eileen's father used to call a black Irishman. "Mike," he said, and took her hand in a firm grip. "Glad to have you with us. Come on in, you want some coffee?"

"Sounds good," she said, and followed him through the gate in the railing and over to his desk. "Light with one sugar."

"Coming right up," he said, and went to where a Silex pot of water was sitting on a hot plate. "We only got instant," he said, "and that powdered creamer stuff, but the sugar's real."

"Good enough," she said.

He spooned instant coffee and creamer into a cup, poured hot water over it, spooned sugar into it with the same white plastic spoon, stirred it, and then carried the cup back to his desk. She was still standing.

"Sit down, sit down," he said. "I'll buzz Lou, tell him you're here."

He looked up at the clock.

Ten minutes to 7:00.

"I thought you and Annie might be coming over together," he said, and picked up the phone receiver. "Good lady, Annie, I used to work with her in Robbery." He stabbed at a button on the base of the phone, waited, and then said, "Lou? Eileen Burke's here, you want to come on back?" He listened. "No, not yet." He looked at the clock again. "Uh-huh," he said. "Okay, fine." He put the receiver back on the cradle. "He'll be right here," he said to Eileen. "He's down the hall in Clerical, thought you might want to look over the reports on the case. We been working it together, Lou and me, not that we're getting such hot results. Which is why Homicide's on our backs, huh?"

She registered this last silently. She did not want a backup harboring a grudge over Homicide's interference. Some cops treated a tough case as if it were a sick child. Nurse it along, take its temperature every ten minutes, change the sheets, serve the hot chicken soup. Anybody else went near it, watch out. She hoped that wasn't the situation here. She wished the Seven-Two had *asked* for assistance, instead of having it dumped on them.

"How's the coffee?" Shanahan asked.

She hadn't touched it. She lifted the cup now. Squadroom coffee cups all looked alike. Dirty. In some squadrooms, the detectives had their initials painted on the cups, so they could tell one dirty cup from another. She sipped at the coffee. The imprint of her lipstick appeared on the cup's rim. It would probably still be there a month from now.

"Okay?" he said.

"Yes, fine," she said.

"Ah, here's Lou," he said, looking past her shoulder toward the railing. She turned in the chair just in time to see a slight, olive-complexioned man coming through the gate. Small mustache under his nose. Thick manila file folder in his right hand. Five-nine, she estimated. Moved like a bullfighter, narrow shoulders and waist, delicate hands. But you could never tell. Hal Willis at the Eight-Seven was only five-eight and he could throw any cheap thief on his ass in three seconds flat.

"Burke?" he said. "Nice to see you." No trace of an accent. Second-or third-generation American, she guessed. He extended his hand. Light, quick grip, almost instant release. No smile on his face. "Lou Alvarez," he said. "Glad to have you with us, we can use the help."

Party manners? Or a genuine welcome? She wished she knew. It would be her ass on the line out there tonight.

"I've got the file here," he said, "you might want to take a look at it while we're waiting for Rawles." He looked up at the clock. Still only five minutes to 7:00, but he nodded sourly. Was this an indication that he thought all women were habitually late? Eileen took the manila folder from him.

"You can skip over the pictures," he said.

"Why?"

Alvarez shrugged.

"Suit yourself," he said.

She was looking at the photographs when Annie walked in.

"Hi," Annie said, and glanced up at the clock.

7:00 sharp.

"Hello, Mike," she said, "how's The Chameleon these days?"

"*Comme-çi comme-ça,*" Shanahan said, and shook her hand.

"We used to call him The Chameleon," she explained to Eileen, and then said, "Annie Rawles," and offered her hand to Alvarez.

"Lou Alvarez."

He took her hand. He seemed uncomfortable shaking hands with women. Eileen was suddenly glad it would be Shanahan out there with her tonight.

"Why The Chameleon?" she asked.

"Man of a thousand faces," Annie said, and looked at the photograph in Eileen's hand. "Nice," she said, and grimaced.

"Never mind the pictures," Alvarez said, "the pictures can't talk. We got statements in there from a couple of girls working the Zone, they give us a pretty good idea who we're looking for. Homicide's been pressuring us on this from minute one. That's 'cause the mayor made a big deal in the papers about cleaning up the Zone. So Homicide dumps it on us. You help us close this one out," he said to Eileen, "I'll personally give you a medal. Cast it in bronze all by myself."

"I was hoping for gold," Eileen said.

"You'd better take a look at those other pictures," Shanahan said.

"She don't have to look at them," Alvarez said.

"Which ones?" Eileen asked.

"You trying to spook her?"

"I'm trying to prepare her."

"She don't have to look at the pictures," Alvarez said.

But Eileen had already found them.

The earlier photographs had shown slashed faces, slit throats. These showed rampant mutilation below.

"Used the knife top and bottom," Shanahan said.

"Uh-huh," Eileen said.

"Slashed the first girl in a doorway two blocks from the bar."

"Uh-huh."

"Second one in an alleyway on East Ninth. Last one on Canalside."

"Uh-huh."

"What I'm saying is watch your step," Shanahan warned. "This ain't your garden variety weirdo jumpin' old ladies in the park. This is a fuckin' animal, and he means business. You get in the slightest bit of trouble, you holler. I'll be there in zero flat."

"I'm not afraid to holler," Eileen said.

"Good. We ain't trying to prove nothing here, we only want to catch this guy."

"I'm the one who catches him," Alvarez said, "I'll cut off his balls."

Eileen looked at him.

"What'd these other girls tell you?" Annie asked.

She did not want Eileen to keep studying those pictures. Once around the park was once too often. She took them from her hand, glanced at them only cursorily, and put them back into the folder. Eileen looked up at her questioningly. But Alvarez was already talking.

"You familiar with the Canal Zone, you know most of the girls work on the street," he said. "A car pulls up, the girl leans in the window, they agree on a price, and she does the job while the trick drives them around the block. It's Have Mouth, Will Travel, is what it is. But there's a bar near the docks where you get a slightly better-class hooker. We're talking comparative here. None of these girls are racehorses."

"What about this bar?" Annie said.

"It's called Larry's, on Fairview and East Fourth. The girls working the cars go in there every now and then, shoot up in the toilet, fix their faces, whatever. But there's also some girls a little younger and a little prettier who hang out there looking for tricks. Again, we're talking comparative. The girls on the meat rack outside get only five bucks for a handjob and ten for a blowjob. The ones working the bar get double that."

"The point is," Shanahan said, "the three girls he ripped were working the bar."

"So that's where you're planting me," Eileen said.

"Be safer all around," Alvarez said.

"I'm not looking for safe," she said, bristling.

"No, and you're not a real hooker, either," Alvarez said, bristling himself. "You stand out there on the street, you keep turning down tricks, the other girls'll make you for fuzz in a minute. You'll be standing out there all alone before the night's ten minutes old."

"Okay," she said.

"I want this guy," he said.

"So do I."

"Not the way I want him. I got a daughter the age of that little girl in there," he said, wagging his finger at the folder.

"Okay," Eileen said again.

"You work the bar," Alvarez said, "you get a chance to call your own shots. You played hooker before?"

"Yes."

"Okay, so I don't have to tell you how to do your job."

"That's right, you don't."

"But there are some mean bastards down there in the Zone, and not all of them are looking to carve you up. You better step easy all around. This ain't Silk Stocking work."

"None of it is," Eileen said.

They both glared at each other.

"What'd they say about him?" Annie asked, jumping in.

"What?" Alvarez said.

Still angry. Figuring Homicide had sent him an amateur. Figuring she'd be spotted right off as a plant. Fuck you and your daughter both, Eileen thought. I know my job. And it's still *my* ass out there.

"These girls you talked to," Annie said. "What'd they say?"

"What?"

"About the guy, she means," Shanahan said. "This ain't gospel, Annie, this is maybe just hookers running scared, which they got every right to be. But on the nights of the murders, they remember a guy sitting at the bar. Drinking with the victims. The three he ripped. Same guy on three different Friday nights. Big blond guy, six-two, six-three, maybe two hundred pounds, dressed different each time, but blending in with everybody else in the joint."

"Meaning?"

"Meaning Friday-night sleaze. No uptown dude looking for kicks."

"Do you get any of those?" Eileen asked.

"Now and then," Shanahan said. "They don't last long in the Zone. Hookers ain't the only predators there. But this guy looked like one of the seamen off the ships. Which don't necessarily mean he *was,* of course."

"Anything else we should know about him?"

"Yeah, he had them in stitches."

"What do you mean?"

"Kept telling them jokes."

Eileen looked at him.

"Yeah, I know what you're thinking," Shanahan said. "A stand-up comic with a knife."

"Anything else?"

"He wears eyeglasses," Alvarez said.

"One of the girls thinks he has a tattoo on his right hand. Near the thumb. She's the only one who mentioned it."

"What kind of tattoo?"

"She couldn't remember."

"How many girls did you talk to?"

"Four *dozen* altogether," Alvarez said, "but only two of them gave us a handle."

"What time was this?" Annie asked. "When they saw him at the bar with the victims?"

"Varied. As early as nine, as late as two in the morning."

"Gonna be a long night," Annie said, and sighed.

Shanahan looked up at the clock.

"We better work out our strategy," he said. "So we can move when he does. Once he gets Eileen outside…"

He let the sentence trail.

The clock ticked into the silence of the squadroom.

"Do they know you down there in the Zone?" Eileen asked.

Shanahan looked at her.

"Do they?"

"Yes, but—"

"Then what the hell…?"

"I'll be—"

"What good's a backup who—"

"You won't recognize me, don't worry."

"No? What does the bartender say when you walk in? Hello, Detective Shanahan?"

"Six-to-five right this minute, you won't know me when I walk in," Shanahan said.

"Don't take the bet," Annie said.

"Will I know you if I have to holler?"

"You'll know me then. Because I'll be there."

"You're on," Eileen said. "But if I make you, I go straight home. I walk out of there and go straight home. Understood?"

"I'd do the same. But you won't know me."

"I hope not. I hope I lose the bet."

"You will," Annie promised.

"I didn't like your shooting him," the blonde at the wheel of the station wagon said. "That wasn't at all necessary, Alice."

Alice said nothing.

"You fire the guns in the air to scare them, to let them know you mean business, that's all. If that man you shot is dead, the rest of the night could be ruined for us."

Alice still said nothing.

"The beauty part of this," the blonde said, "is they never expect lightning to strike twice in the same night. Are you listening, kiddies?"

None of the kids said a word.

The digital dashboard clock read 7:04.

"They figure you do a stickup, you go home and lay low for a while. That's the beauty part. We play our cards right tonight, we go home with forty grand easy. I mean, a Friday night? Your liquor stores'll be open, some of them, till midnight, people stocking up for the weekend. Plenty of gold in the registers, kids, there for the taking. No more shooting people, have you got that?"

The kids said nothing.

The eyes behind the masks darted, covering both sides of the avenue. The slits in the masks made all the eyes look Oriental, even the blue ones.

"Especially you, Alice. Do you hear me?"

Alice nodded stiffly.

"There she is," the blonde said, "number two," and began easing the station wagon in toward the curb.

The liquor store was brightly lighted.

The lettering on the plate-glass window read FAMOUS BRANDS WINE & WHISKEY.

"Have fun, kids," the blonde said.

The kids piled out of the car.

"Trick or treat, trick or treat!" they squealed at an old woman coming out of the liquor store.

The old woman giggled.

"How *cute!*" she said to no one.

Inside the store, the kids weren't so cute.

The owner had his back to them, reaching up for a half-gallon of Johnny Walker Red.

Alice shot him at once.

The thirty-year-old account executive standing in front of the counter screamed.

She shot him, too.

The kids cleaned out the cash register in less than twelve seconds. One of them took a fifth of Canadian Club from the shelves. Then they ran out of the store again, giggling and yelling, "Trick or treat, trick or treat!"

"Hello, Peaches?" the man on the telephone said.

"Yes?"

"I've been trying to reach you all day. My secretary left your number, but she didn't say which agency you're with."

"Agency?"

"Yes. This is Phil Hendricks at Camera Works. We're shooting some stuff next week, and my secretary thought you might be right for the job. How old are you, Peaches?"

"Forty-nine," she said without hesitation. Lying a little. Well, lying by eleven years, but who was counting?

"That's perfect," he said, "this is stuff for the Sears catalogue, a half-dozen mature women modeling housedresses. If you'll give me the name of your agency, I'll call them in the morning."

"I don't have an agency," Peaches said.

"You don't? Well, that's strange. I mean…well, how long have you been modeling?"

"I'm not a model," Peaches said.

"You're not? Then how'd my secretary…?"

There was a long, puzzled silence on the line.

"This *is* Peaches Muldoon, isn't it?" he said.

"Yes," she said, "but I've never…"

"349-4040?"

"That's the number. But your secretary must've…"

"Well, here's your name and number right here in her handwriting," he said. "But you say you're not a model?"

"No, I'm an RN."

"A what?"

"A registered nurse."

"Then how'd she…?"

Another puzzled silence.

"Have you ever *thought* of modeling?" he asked.

"Well…not seriously."

"Because maybe you mentioned to someone that you were looking for modeling work, and this got to my secretary somehow. That's the only thing I can figure."

"What's your secretary's name?"

"Linda. Linda Greeley."

"No, I don't know anyone by that name."

"*Did* you mention to someone that you might be interested in modeling?"

"Well…you know…people are always telling me I should try modeling, but you know how people talk. I never take them seriously. I mean, I'm not a kid anymore, you know."

"Well, forty-nine isn't exactly *ancient*," he said, and laughed.

"Well, I suppose not. But people try to flatter you, you know. I'm not really beautiful enough to do modeling. There's a certain type, you know. For modeling."

"What type *are* you, Peaches?" he asked.

"Well, I don't know how to answer that."

"Well, how tall are you, for example?"

"Five-nine," she said.

"How much do you weigh?"

"I could lose a little weight right now," she said, "believe me."

"Well, there isn't a woman on earth who doesn't think she could stand to lose a few pounds. How much *do* you weigh, Peaches?"

"A hundred and twenty," she said. Lying a little. Well, lying by ten pounds. Well, twenty pounds, actually.

"That's not what I'd call *obese*," he said. "Five-nine, a hundred-twenty."

"Well, let's say I'm…well…zoftig, I guess."

"Are you Jewish, Peaches?"

"What?"

"That's a Jewish expression, zoftig," he said. "But Muldoon isn't Jewish, is it?"

"No, no. I'm Irish."

"Red hair, I'll bet."

"How'd you guess?" she asked, and laughed.

"And isn't that a faint Southern accent I detect?"

"I'm from Tennessee originally. I didn't think it still showed."

"Oh, just a trace. Which is why zoftig sounded so strange on your lips," he said. "Well, I'm sorry you're not a model, Peaches, truly. We're paying a hundred and twenty-five a hour, and we're shooting something like two dozen pages, so this could've come to a bit of change. Do you work full time as a nurse?"

"No. I do mostly residential work."

"Then you might be free to…"

He hesitated.

"But if you're not experienced…"

He hesitated again.

"I just don't know," he said. "What we're looking for, you see, is a group of women who are mature and who could be accepted as everyday housewives. We're not shooting any glamour stuff here, no sexy lingerie, nothing like that. In fact…well, I don't really know. But your inexperience might be a plus. When you say you're a zoftig type, you don't mean…well, you don't look *too* glamorous, do you?"

"I wouldn't say I look glamorous, no. I'm forty-nine, you know."

"Well, Sophia Loren's what? In her fifties, isn't she? And she certainly looks glamorous. What I'm saying is we're not looking for any Sophia Lorens here. Can you imagine Sophia Loren in a housedress?" he said, and laughed again. "Let me just write down your dimensions, okay? I'll discuss this with the ad agency in the morning, who knows? You said five-nine…"

"Yes."

"A hundred and twenty pounds."

"Yes."

"What are your other dimensions, Peaches? Bust size first."

"Thirty-six C."

"Good, we don't want anyone who looks *too*, well…you get some of these so-called *mature* models, they're big-busted, but very flabby. You're not flabby, are you?"

"Oh, no."

"And your waist size, Peaches?"

"Twenty-six."

"And your hips?"

"Thirty-six."

"That sounds very good," he said. "Are your breasts firm?" he asked.

"What?"

"Your breasts. Forgive me, but I know the ad agency'll want to know. They've had so many of these so-called mature models who come in with breasts hanging to their knees, they're getting a little gun-shy. Are your breasts good and firm?"

Peaches hesitated.

"What did you say your name was?" she asked.

"Phil Hendricks. At Camera Works. We're a professional photography firm, down here on Hall Avenue."

"Could I have your number there, please?"

"Sure. It's 847-3300."

"And this is for the Sears catalogue?"

"Yes, we begin shooting Monday morning. We've already signed two women, both of them in their late forties, good firm bodies, one of them used to model lingerie in fact. Do me a favor, will you, Peaches?"

"What's that?" she said.

"Is there a mirror in the room there?"

"Yes?"

"Does the phone reach over there? To where the mirror is?"

"Well, it's right there on the wall."

"Stand up, Peaches, and take a look at yourself in that mirror."

"Why should I do that?"

"Because I want an objective opinion. What are you wearing right now, Peaches?"

"A blouse and a skirt."

"Are you wearing shoes?"

"Yes?"

"High-heeled shoes?"

"Yes?"

"And a bra? Are you wearing a bra, Peaches?"

"Listen, this conversation is making me a little nervous," she said.

"I want your objective opinion, Peaches."

"About what?"

"About whether your breasts are good and firm. Can you see yourself in the mirror, Peaches?"

"Listen, this is really making me *very* nervous," she said.

"Take off your blouse, Peaches. Look at yourself in your bra, and tell me…

She hung up.

Her heart was pounding.

A trick, she thought. He tricked me! How could I have been so dumb? Kept *talking* to him! Kept *believing* his pitch! Gave him all the answers he…

How'd he know my first name?

I'm listed as P. Muldoon, how'd he…?

The answering machine. Hi, this is Peaches, I can't come to the phone just now. Of course. Said he'd been trying to reach me all day. Hi, this is Peaches, I can't come to the phone just now. Got the Muldoon and the number from the phone book, got my first name from the answering…

Oh, God, my *address* is in the book, too!

Suppose he *comes* here?

Oh dear God…

The telephone rang again.

Don't answer it, she thought.

It kept ringing.

Don't answer it.

Ringing, ringing.

But Sandra's supposed to call about the party.

Ringing, ringing, ringing.

If it's him again, I'll just hang up.

She reached out for the phone. Her hand was trembling. She lifted the receiver.

"Hello?" she said.

"Peaches?"

Was it him again? The voice didn't sound quite like his.

"Yes?" she said.

"Hi, this is Detective Andy Parker. I don't know if you remember me or not, I'm the one who locked up your crazy—"

"Boy, am I glad to hear from *you!*" she said.

"How about that?" Parker said, putting up the phone. "Remembered me right off the bat, told me to hurry on over!"

"You're unforgettable," Brown said. He was at his desk, typing a report on the torso they'd found behind the Burgundy Restaurant. Genero was looking over his shoulder, trying to learn how to spell dismembered.

The squadroom was alive with clattering typewriters.

Meyer sat in his dapper tan sports jacket typing a report on the kids who'd held up the liquor store and killed the owner.

Kling was at his own desk, typing a follow-up report on a burglary he'd caught three days ago. He was thinking about Eileen. He was thinking that right about now Eileen was in Calm's Point, getting ready to hit the Zone. He was thinking he might just wander over there later tonight. He looked up at the clock. 7:15. Maybe when he got off at midnight. See what was happening over there. She didn't have to know he was there looking around. A third backup never hurt anybody.

"So," Parker said, "if nobody needs me here, I think I'll mosey on over."

"Nobody needs you, right," Meyer said. "We got two homicides here, nobody needs you."

"Tell me the truth, Meyer," Parker said. "You think those two homicides are gonna be closed out tonight? In all your experience, have you ever closed out a homicide the same day you caught it? Have you?"

"I'm trying to think," Meyer said.

"In all my experience, that never happened," Parker said. "Unless you walk in and there's the perp with a smoking gun in his hand. Otherwise, it takes weeks. Months sometimes. Sometimes *years.*"

"Sometimes *centuries*," Brown said.

"So what's your point?" Meyer said.

"My point is…*here's* my point," he said, opening his arms wide to the railing as Carella came through the gate. "Steve," he said, "I'm very glad to see you."

"You are?" Carella said.

He was a tall slender man with the build and stance of an athlete, brown hair, brown eyes slanting slightly downward to give his face a somewhat Oriental look. Tonight he was wearing a plaid sports shirt under a blue windbreaker, light cotton corduroy trousers, brown loafers. He went directly to his desk and looked in the basket there for any telephone messages.

"How's it out there?" Brown asked.

"Quiet," Carella said. "You got back okay, huh?" he asked Kling.

"I caught a taxi."

Carella turned to Parker. "Why are you so happy to see me?" he asked.

" 'Cause my colleague, Detective Meyer Meyer there, sitting at his desk there in his new jacket and his bald head, is eager to crack a homicide he caught, and he needs a good partner."

"That lets me out," Carella said. "What kind of homicide, Meyer?"

"Some kids held up a liquor store and shot the owner."

"Teenagers?"

"Eleven-year-olds."

"No kidding?"

"You gotta get yourself some lollipops," Brown said, "bait a trap with them."

"So is everybody all paired up nice now?" Parker asked. "You got Genero…"

"Thanks very much," Brown said.

"Meyer's got Steve…"

"I only stopped by for some coffee," Carella said.

"And I got Peaches Muldoon."

"Who's that?"

"A gorgeous registered nurse who's dying to see me."

"Sixty years old," Brown said.

"That's an old *lady*!" Genero said, shocked.

"Tell him."

"You ever date a nurse?" Parker said.

"Me?" Genero said.

"You, you. You ever date a nurse?"

"No. And I never dated a sixty-year-old lady, either."

"Tell him," Brown said.

"There is nothing like a nurse," Parker said. "It's a fact that in the book business if you put the word nurse in a title, you sell a million more copies."

"Who told you that?"

"It's a fact. A publisher told me that. In this office where they stole all his typewriters, this was maybe a year ago. A nurse in the title sells a million more copies."

"I'm gonna write a book called *The Naked and the Nurse*," Brown said.

"How about *Gone with the Nurse*?" Meyer said.

"Or *Nurse-twenty-two*?" Carella said.

"Kid around, go ahead," Parker said. "You see me tomorrow morning, I'll be a wreck."

"I think you'd better stick around," Brown said. "Cotton's all alone out there."

"Bert can go hold his hand, soon as he finishes writing his book there."

"What book?" Kling asked, looking up from his typewriter.

"Me," Parker said, "I'm gonna go do a follow-up on a homicide investigation."

"Ten years old," Brown said.

"I thought you said eleven," Carella said, puzzled.

"The homicide. Ten years ago. He arrested a nut was killing priests. The nurse is his mother."

"The *kids* are eleven years old," Meyer said. "The ones who did the liquor store guy. Or twelve."

"That's what I thought," Carella said. He still looked puzzled.

"Any further objections?" Parker asked.

They all looked at him sourly.

"In that case, gentlemen, I bid you a fond adoo."

"You gonna leave a number where we can reach you?" Brown asked.

"No," Parker said.

The phone rang as he went through the gate and out into the corridor.

Watching him go, Brown shook his head and then picked up the phone receiver.

"87th Squad, Brown."

"Artie, this is Dave downstairs," Murchison said. "You're handling that body in the garbage can, ain't you?"

"*Piece* of a body," Brown said.

"Well, we just got another piece," Murchison said.

Hawes had to keep telling himself this was strictly business.

Bermuda had been one thing, Bermuda was a thousand miles away, and besides he'd asked Annie to go along with him. This was another thing. This was the big bad city, and Annie lived here and besides he had a date with her tomorrow night, and furthermore Marie Sebastiani was married.

As of the moment, anyway.

The possibility existed that her husband had run off on his own to get away from her, though why anyone would want to abandon a beautiful, leggy blonde was beyond Hawes. If that's what had happened, though—Sebastian the Great tossing his junk all over the driveway and then taking off in the Citation—then maybe he was gone forever, in which case Marie wasn't as married as she thought she was. Hawes had handled cases where a guy went out for a loaf of bread and never was heard from since. Probably living on some South Sea island painting naked natives.

One case he had, the guy told his wife he was going down for a *TV Guide*. This was at 8:00. The wife sat through the 11:00 news, and then the Johnny Carson show, and then the late movie, and still no hubby with the *TV Guide*. Guy turned up in California six years later, living with two girls in Santa Monica. So maybe Sebastian the Great had pulled the biggest trick of his career, disappearing on his wife. Who knew?

On the other hand, maybe the lady's concern was well founded. Maybe somebody had come across Frank Sebastiani while he was loading his goodies in the car, and maybe he'd zonked the magician and thrown his stuff out of the car and took off with the car and the magician both. Dump the magician later on, dead or alive, and sell the car to a chop shop. Easy pickings on a relatively quiet Halloween night. It was possible.

Either way, this was strictly business.

Hawes wished, however, that Marie wouldn't keep touching him quite so often.

The lady was very definitely a toucher, and although Hawes didn't necessarily buy the psychological premise that insisted casual body contact was an absolute prerequisite to outright seduction, he had to admit that her frequent touching of his arm or his shoulder or his hand was a bit unsettling. True enough, the touching was only to emphasize a conversational point—as when she told him again how grateful she was that he was taking her to dinner—or to indicate this or that possible restaurant along the Stem. He had parked the car on North Fifth, and they were walking westward now, heading downtown, looking for a place to eat. At 7:35 on a Friday night there were still a lot of restaurants open, but Marie had told him she felt like pizza and so he chose a little place just south of the avenue, on Fourth. Red-checkered tablecloths, candles in Chianti bottles, people waiting in line for tables. Hawes rarely pulled rank, but now he casually mentioned to the hostess that he was a detective working out of the Eight-Seven and he hadn't had anything to eat since he came on at 4:00.

"This way, officer," the hostess said at once, and led them to a table near the window.

As soon as the hostess was gone, Marie said, "Does that happen all the time?"

"Does what happen?"

"The royal treatment."

"Sometimes," Hawes said. "You sure you only want pizza? There's plenty other stuff on the menu."

"No, that's what I really feel like. Cheese and anchovies."

"Would you like a drink?" he asked. "I'm on duty, but…"

"Do you really honor that?"

"Oh, sure."

"I'll just have beer with the pizza."

Hawes signaled to the waiter, and then ordered a large pizza with cheese and anchovies.

"Anything to drink?" the waiter asked.

"A draft for the lady, a Coke for me."

"Miller's or Michelob?"

"Miller's," Marie said.

The waiter went off again.

"This is really very nice of you," Marie said, and reached across the table to touch his hand briefly. A whisper touch. There, and then gone.

"As soon as we get back to the squadroom," Hawes said, "I'll call Auto again, see if they turned up anything on either of the vehicles."

He had made a call to Auto Theft from the custodian's office at the high school, reporting both the Citation and the Econoline, but he knew what the chances were of finding either vehicle tonight. He didn't want to tell her that.

"That would be a start," she said. "If they found the cars."

"Oh, sure."

A pained look crossed her face.

"I'm sure he's okay," Hawes said.

"I hope so."

"I'm sure."

He wasn't at all sure.

"I just keep thinking something terrible has happened to him. I keep thinking whoever stole the car…"

"Well, you don't know that for a fact," Hawes said.

"What do you mean?"

"Well, that the car was stolen."

"It's gone, isn't it?"

"Yes, but…"

He didn't want to tell her that maybe her husband had driven off on his own, heading for the wild blue yonder. Let the lady enjoy her pizza and her beer. If her husband had in fact abandoned her, she'd learn it soon enough. If he was lying dead in an alley someplace, she'd learn that even sooner.

He didn't bring up Jimmy Brayne again until after they'd been served.

She was digging into the pizza as if she hadn't eaten for a week. She ate the way that woman in the *Tom Jones* movie ate. Licked her lips, rolled her eyes, thrust pizza into her mouth as if she were making love to it. Come on, he thought. Strictly business here.

"He's normally reliable, is that right?" he said.

"Who?"

"Jimmy Brayne."

"Oh, yes. Completely."

"How long has he been working for you?"

"Three months."

"Started this July?"

"Yes. We did the act at a big Republican picnic on the Fourth. That was the first time Jimmy helped us."

"Carrying the stuff over in the van…"

"Yes."

"Picking it up later."

"Yes."

"Did he know where he was supposed to pick you up tonight?"

"Oh, sure. He dropped the stuff off at the school, of course he knew."

"Helped you unload it?"

"Yes."

"When was that? What time?"

"We got there about three-fifteen."

"Drove into the city together?"

"Frank and I were following the van."

"And Jimmy left the school at what time?"

"As soon as everything was on stage."

"Which was when?"

"Three-thirty, a quarter to four?"

"And he knew he was supposed to come back at five-thirty?"

"Yes."

"Is it possible he went someplace with your husband?"

"Like where?"

"For a drink or something? While you were changing?"

"Then why was all the stuff on the sidewalk?"

"It's just that…well, *both* of them disappearing…"

"Excuse me," the waiter said. "Officer?"

Hawes looked up.

"Officer, I hate to bother you," the waiter said. "Yes?"

"Officer, there's somebody's arm in one of the garbage cans out back."

It was ten minutes to 8:00 on the face of the clock on the locker-room wall.

They could have been teenagers swapping stories about their boyfriends.

Nothing in their conversation indicated they were going out hunting for a killer.

"Maybe I should've gone down later," Annie said. "The trial ended on Wednesday, I could've gone down then." She stepped into her short skirt, pulled it over her blouse and pantyhose, zipped up the side, fastened the button at the waist. "Trouble is, I wasn't sure I *wanted* to go."

"But he asked you, didn't he?" Eileen said.

"Sure, but…I don't know. I got the feeling he was just going through the motions. I'll tell you the truth, I think he wanted to go down there alone."

"What makes you think so?" Eileen asked.

She was wearing a low-cut blouse, and a wraparound skirt as short as Annie's, fastened on the right-hand side with a three-inch-long ornamental safety pin. The pin would be a last-ditch weapon if she needed it. If she needed it, she would poke out his eyes with it.

She was sitting on the bench in front of the lockers, pulling on high-heeled boots with floppy tops. A holster was strapped to her ankle inside the right boot. The pistol in the holster was a .25-caliber Astra Firecat automatic, with a two-and-a-half-inch barrel. It weighed a bit les than twelve ounces. Six-shot magazine, plus one in the firing chamber. She would pump all seven slugs into his face if she had to. There was a six-shot, .44-caliber Smith & Wesson hammerless revolver in her handbag. Plus a switchblade knife. Rambo, she thought. But it won't happen to me again. She was wearing two pairs of panties under her pantyhose. Her psychological weapons.

"I just…I don't know," Annie said. "I think Cotton's trying to end it, I just don't know."

She reached into the locker for her handbag, took out her cosmetics kit.

Eileen was standing now, looking down into the boots.

"Can you see this gun?" she asked.

Annie came over to her, lipstick in her hand. She looked down into the floppy top of the boot on Eileen's right foot.

"You might want to lower the holster," she said. "I'm getting a glimpse of metal."

Eileen sat again, rolled down the boot top, unstrapped the holster, lowered it, strapped it tight again.

"Maybe you should've gone down there, had it out with him," she said.

"Well, that would've ended it for sure. A man doesn't want a showdown on his vacation."

"But if he *wants* to end it…"

"I'm not sure of that."

"Well, what makes you think he *might* want to?"

"We haven't made love in the past two weeks."

"Bert and I haven't made love since the rape," Eileen said flatly, and stood up and looked down into the boots again.

"I'm…sorry," Annie said.

"Maybe that'll change tonight," Eileen said.

And Annie suddenly knew she was planning murder.

The old lady's name was Adelaide Davis, and she had seen the kids going into the liquor store on Culver and Twelfth. She was now standing outside on the sidewalk with Carella and Meyer. Inside the store, two ambulance attendants were hoisting the body of the owner onto a stretcher. Monroe was watching the operation, his hands in his jacket pockets. A tech from the Mobile Lab unit was dusting the register for fingerprints. The ME was kneeling over the second body. One of the attendants said, "Up," and they both lifted the stretcher and then stepped gingerly around the ME and the other body.

A crowd had gathered on the sidewalk. This was still only 8:00 on a balmy Friday night, a lot of people were still in the streets. The ambulance attendants went past Mrs. Davis and the two detectives. Mrs. Davis watched them as they slid the stretcher into the ambulance. She watched them as they carried another stretcher back into the store. Patrolmen were shooing back the crowd now, making sure everyone stayed behind the barriers. Mrs. Davis felt privileged. Mrs. Davis felt like a star. She could see some of her neighbors in the crowd, and she knew they envied her.

"I can't believe this," she said. "They looked so cute."

"How many were there, ma'am?" Carella asked.

Mrs. Davis liked Carella. She thought he was very handsome. The other detective was bald, she had never favored bald men. Wait'll she told her daughter in Florida that she'd witnessed a murder—*two* murders—and had talked to detectives like on television.

"Oh, just a handful of them," she said.

"How many would you say?" Meyer asked.

"Well, they went by very fast," she said. "But I'd say there were only four or five of them. They all jumped out of the station wagon and ran into the store."

"It was a station wagon, huh? The vehicle?"

"Oh, yes. For certain."

"Would you know the year and make?"

"I'm sorry, no. A blue station wagon."

"And these kids ran out of it with guns in their hands, huh?"

"No, I didn't see any guns. Just the shopping bags."

"No guns," Carella said.

"Not until they got inside the store. The guns were in the shopping bags."

"So when they got inside the store, these little boys pulled the guns and—"

"No, they were little girls."

Meyer looked at Carella.

"Girls?" he said.

"Yessir. Four or five little girls. All of them wearing these long dresses down to their ankles and little blond wigs. They looked like little princesses."

"Princesses," Carella said.

"Yes," Mrs. Davis said. "They had on these masks that covered their entire faces, with sort of Chinese eyes on them—slanted, you know—well, maybe Japanese, I guess. Well, like *your* eyes," she said to Carella. "Slanted, you know?"

"Yes, ma'am."

"And rosy cheeks painted on the masks, and bright red lips, and I think little beauty spots near the mouth. They were absolutely beautiful. Like little Chinese princesses. Or Japanese. Except that they were blonde."

"So they had on these Chinese-looking masks..."

"Or Japanese..."

"Right," Meyer said, "and they were wearing blond wigs..."

"Yes, curly blond wigs. Like Little Orphan Annie, except she's a redhead."

"Curly blond wigs, and long dresses."

"Yes, like gowns. They looked like darling little princesses."

"What kind of shoes, ma'am?" Carella asked.

"Oh. I don't know. I didn't notice their shoes."

"They weren't wearing *sneakers*, were they?"

"Well, I really couldn't see. The gowns were very long."

The ambulance attendants were coming out with the second body now. The ME was still inside, talking to Monroe. Mrs. Davis looked down at the body as it went past. Before tonight, she had never seen a dead body except in a funeral home. Tonight, she'd just seen two of them close up.

"So they ran into the store," Carella said.

"Yes, yelling 'Trick or treat.' "

"Uh-huh," Carella said. "And pulled the guns…"

"Yes. And shot Mr. Agnello and the man who was in the store with him."

"Shot them right off?" Meyer said.

"Yes."

"Didn't say it was a stickup or anything, just started shooting."

"Yes. Mr. Agnello and the man with him."

"What happened next, ma'am? In the store. Did you keep watching?"

"Oh, yes. I was scared to death, but I kept watching."

"Did you see them clean out the cash register?"

"Yes. And one of them took a bottle of whiskey from the shelf."

"Then what?"

"They came running out. I was standing over there, to the left, over there, I'm not sure they saw me. I guess maybe they would've shot me, too, if they'd seen me."

"You were lucky," Carella said.

"Yes, I think I was."

"What'd they do then?" Meyer asked.

"They got back in the station wagon, and the woman drove them off."

"There was a woman driving the car?"

"Yes, a blonde woman."

"How old, would you know?"

"I really couldn't say. A sort of heavyset woman, she might've been in her forties."

"By heavyset…"

"Well, sort of stout."

"What was she wearing, would you remember?"

"I'm sorry."

Monroe was coming out of the liquor store.

"This the witness here?" he asked.

"A very good witness," Carella said.

"Well, thank you, young man," Mrs. Davis said, and smiled at him. She was suddenly glad she hadn't told him she'd wet her pants when she saw those little girls shooting Mr. Agnello.

"So what've we got here?" Monroe said. "An epidemic of kindergarten kids holding up liquor stores?"

"Looks that way," Carella said. "Where's your partner?"

"Who the hell knows where he is?" Monroe said. "Excuse me, lady."

"Oh, that's perfectly all right," she said. This was just like cable television, with the cursing and all. She couldn't wait to phone her daughter and tell her about it.

"Same kids, or what?" Monroe asked.

"What?" Mrs. Davis said.

"Excuse me, lady," Monroe said, "I was talking to this officer here."

"Little girls this time," Meyer said. "But it sounds like the same bunch. Same blonde driving the car."

"Nice lady, that blonde," Monroe said. "Driving kids to stick-ups. What kind of car, did you find out?" He turned to Carella. "What it is, the fart at the other store couldn't…excuse me, lady."

"Oh, that's perfectly all right," she said.

"A blue station wagon," Meyer said.

"You happen to know what year and make, lady?"

"I'm sorry, I don't."

"Yeah," Monroe said. "So all we got is the same big blonde driving four kids in a blue station wagon."

"That's about it," Meyer said.

"There wasn't homicides involved here, I'd turn this over to Robbery in a minute. You better give them a buzz, anyway."

"I already did," Meyer said. "After the first one."

One of the techs ambled out of the store.

"Got some bullets here," he said. "Who wants them?"

"What do they look like?" Monroe asked.

The technician showed him the palm of his hand. A white cloth was draped over it, and four spent bullets rested on it.

".22s maybe," he said, and shrugged.

Mrs. Davis leaned over to look at the technician's palm.

"So, okay, lady," Monroe said, "you got any further business here?"

"Cool it," Carella said.

Monroe looked at him.

"I'll have one of our cars drop you home, Mrs. Davis," Carella said.

"A taxi service, they run up here," Monroe said to the air.

"Cool it," Carella said again, more softly this time, but somehow the words carried greater menace.

Monroe looked at him again and then turned to Meyer.

"Bag them bullets and get them over to Ballistics," he said. "Call Robbery and tell them we got another one."

"Sounds like good advice," Meyer said.

Monroe missed the sarcasm. He glared again at Carella, and then walked to where his car was parked at the curb.

Wait'll I tell my daughter! Mrs. Davis thought. A ride in a police car!

The patrolmen riding Charlie Four were approaching the corner of Rachel and Jakes, just cruising by, making another routine run of the sector when the man riding shotgun spotted it.

"Slow down, Freddie," he said.

"What do you see, Joe?"

"The van there. Near the corner."

"What about it?"

Joe Guardi opened his notebook. "Didn't we get a BOLO on a Ford Econoline?" He snapped on the roof light, scanned the notebook. "Yeah, here it is," he said. In his own handwriting, he saw the words "BOLO tan '79 Ford Econoline, RL 68-7210. Blue '84 Citation, DL 74-3681." The word BOLO stood for Be On the Lookout.

"Yeah," he said again. "Let's check it out."

The two men got out of the car. They flashed their torches over the van. License plate from the next state, RL 68-7210.

They tried the door closest to the curb.

Unlocked.

Freddie slid it all the way open.

Joe came around to the passenger side of the van. He slid the door open there, leaned in, and thumbed open the glove compartment.

"Anything?" Freddie asked.

"Looks like a registration here."

He took the registration out of a clear-plastic packet containing an owner's manual and a duplicate insurance slip.

The van was registered to a Frank Sebastiani whose address was 604 Eden Lane in Collinsworth, over the river.

The movie had let out at 7:00, and they had stopped for a drink on the Stem later. They had begun arguing in the bar, in soft, strained voices, almost whispers, but everyone around them knew they were having a fight because of the way they leaned so tensely over the small table between them. At first, the fight was only about the movie they'd seen. She insisted it had been based on a novel called *Streets of Gold,* by somebody or other, and he insisted the movie'd had nothing whatever to do with that particular novel, the movie was an original. "Then how come they're allowed to use the same title?" she asked, and he said, "They can do that 'cause you can't copyright a title. They can make the shittiest movie in the world if they want to, and they can call it *From Here to Eternity* or *The Good Earth* or even *Streets of Gold,* like they did tonight, and nobody in the world can do a damn thing about it." She glared at him for a moment, and then said, "What the hell do you know about copyright?" and he said, "A hell of a lot more than you know about *anything,*" and by now they were really screaming at each other in whispers, and leaning tensely over the table, eyes blazing, mouths drawn.

They were still arguing on the way home.

But by now the argument had graduated to something more vital than an unimportant little novel called *Streets of Gold* or a shitty little movie that hadn't been based upon it.

They were arguing about sex, which is what they almost always argued about. In fact, maybe that's what they'd really been arguing about back there in the bar.

It was almost 8:30 but the streets were already beginning to fill with teenagers on the prowl. Not all of them were looking for trouble. Many of them were merely seeking to let off adolescent energy. The ones out for fun and games were wearing costumes that weren't quite as elaborate as those the toddlers and later the teenyboppers had worn. Some of the teenage girls, using the excuse of Halloween to dress as daringly as they wished, walked the streets looking like hookers or Mata Haris or go-go dancers or sexy witches in black with slits up their skirts to their thighs.

Some of the teenage boys were dressed like combat marines or space invaders or soldiers of fortune, most of them wearing bandoliers and carrying huge plastic machine guns or huge plastic death-ray guns. But these weren't the ones looking for trouble. The ones looking for trouble weren't dressed up for Halloween. They wore only their usual clothing, with perhaps a little blackening on their faces, the better to melt into the night. These were the ones looking to smash and to burn. These were the ones who had caused Lieutenant Byrnes to double-team his detectives tonight. Well, *almost* double-team them. Seven men on instead of the usual four.

The arguing couple came up the street toward the building where they lived, passing a group of teenage girls dressed like John Held flappers, sequined dresses with wide sashes, long cigarette holders, beaded bands around their foreheads, giggling and acting stoned, which perhaps they were. The couple paid no attention to them. They were too busy arguing.

"What it is," he said, "is there's never any spontaneity to it."

"Spontaneity, sure," she said. "What you mean by spontaneity is jumping on me when I come out of the shower..."

"There's nothing wrong with—"

"When I'm all clean."

"When do you *want* to make love?" he asked. "When you're all dirty?"

"I sure as hell don't want to get all *sweaty* again after I've just taken a shower."

"Then how about *before* you take your shower?"

"I don't like to make love when I feel all sweaty."

"So you don't like to do it when you're sweaty and you don't like to do it when you're *not* sweaty. When *do* you...?"

"You're twisting what I'm saying."

"No, I'm not. The point I'm trying to make—"

"The point is you're a sex maniac. I'm trying to cook, you come up behind me and shove that humongous thing at me—"

"I don't see anything wrong with spontaneous—"

"Not while I'm cooking!"

"Then how about when you're *not* cooking? How about when I get home, and we're having a martini, how about…?"

"You know I like to relax before dinner."

"Well, what the hell is making love? *I* find making love relaxing, I have to tell you. If *you* think making love is some kind of goddamn strenuous *obstacle* course…"

"I can't enjoy my cocktail if you're pawing me while I'm trying to re—"

"I don't consider *fondling* you *pawing* you."

"You don't know how to be gentle. All you want to do is jump on me like a goddamn *rapist!*"

"I do not consider passion *rape!*"

"That's because you don't know the difference between making love and—"

"Okay, what's this all about? Tell me what it's all about, okay? Do you want to quit making love *entirely*? You don't want to do it *before* your shower, you don't want to do it *after* your shower, you don't want to do it while we're *drinking* or while you're *cooking* or while we're watching television, or when we wake up in the morning, when the hell *do* you want to do it, Elise?"

"When I feel like doing it. And stop shouting!"

"I'm not *shouting*, Elise! When do you want to do it? Do you *ever* want to do it, Elise?"

"Yes!" she shouted.

"When?"

"Right now, Roger, okay? Right here, okay? Let's do it right here on the sidewalk, okay?"

"Fine by me!"

"You'd do it, too, wouldn't you?"

"Yes! Right here! *Anywhere!*"

"Well, I wouldn't! You'd have done it at the goddamn *movies* if I'd let you."

"I'd have done it in the bar, too, if you hadn't started *arguing* about that dumb movie!"

"You'd do it in church!" she said. "You're a maniac, is what you are."

"That's right, I'm a maniac! You're driving me crazy is why I'm a maniac!"

They were entering their building now. He lowered his voice.

"Let's do it in the elevator, okay?" he said. "You want to do it in the elevator?"

"No, Roger, I don't want to do it in the goddamn elevator."

"Then let's take the elevator up to the roof, we'll do it on the roof."

"I don't want to do it on the goddamn roof, either."

He stabbed angrily at the elevator button.

"Where *do* you want to do it, Elise? *When* do you want to do it, Elise?"

"Later."

"When later?"

"When Johnny Carson goes off."

"If *we* were on television," he said, "and Johnny Carson was watching *us*," he said, "and he had a big hard-on—"

"We happen to *live* here, Roger."

"—do you think Johnny Carson would wait till *we* were off to do it? Or would Johnny Carson…?"

"I don't care what Johnny Carson would do or wouldn't do. I don't even *like* Johnny Carson."

"Then why do you want to wait till he's off?"

The elevator doors opened.

At first they thought it was a stuffed dummy. The lower half of a scarecrow or something. Blue pants, blue socks, black shoes, black belt through the trouser loops. A Halloween prank. Some kids had tossed half a stuffed dummy into the elevator.

And then they realized that a jagged, bloody edge of torn flesh showed just above the dummy's waist, and they realized that they were looking at the lower torso of a human being and Elise screamed and they both ran out of the lobby and out of the building and up to the pay phone on the corner, where Roger breathlessly dialed 911.

The cruising cops in Boy Two responded within three minutes.

One of the cops got on the walkie-talkie to the Eight-Seven.

The other cop, although he should have known better, went through the stiff's trousers and found a wallet in the right hip pocket.

Inside the wallet, which he also shouldn't have touched, he found a driver's license with a name and an address on it.

"Well, here's who he is, anyway," he said to his partner.

"What this is," Parker said, "you had an obscene phone call, is what this is."

"That's what I figured it was," Peaches said.

She still looked pretty good. Maybe like a woman in her early fifties. Good legs—well, the legs never changed—breasts still firm, hair as red as he remembered it, maybe with a little help from Clairol. Wearing a simple skirt and blouse, high-heeled shoes. Legs tucked up under her on the couch. He was glad he'd shaved.

"They're not all of them what you think they're gonna be," Parker said. "I mean, they don't get on the phone and start talking dirty right away—well, some of them do—but a lot of them have a whole bagful of tricks, you don't realize what's happening till you already got you doing things."

"That's *just* what happened," Peaches said. "I didn't realize what was going on. I mean, he gave me his *name* and…"

"Phil Hendricks, right?" Parker said. "Camera Works."

"Right. And his address and his phone number…"

"Did you try calling that number he gave you?"

"Of *course* not!"

"Well, I'll give it a try if you like, but I'm sure all that was phony. I had a case once, this guy would call numbers at random, hoping to get a babysitter. He'd finally get a sitter on the phone, tell her he was doing research on child abuse, smooth-talked these fifteen-, sixteen-year-old girls into slapping around the babies they were sitting."

"What do you mean?"

"He'd tell them how important it was in their line of work to guard against their own tendencies, everybody has such tendencies—this is him talking—and child abuse is an insidious thing. And he'd have them interested and listening, and he'd say, 'I know you yourself must have been tempted on many an occasion to slap the little kid you're sitting, especially when he's acting up,' and the fifteen-year-old sitter goes, 'Oh, boy, you said it,' and he goes, 'For example, haven't you been tempted at least once tonight to smack him around?' and she goes, 'Well…' and he goes, 'Come on, tell me the truth, I'm a trained child psychologist,' and before you know it, he's got her convinced that the best way to *curb* these tendencies is to *release* them, you know, in a therapeutic manner, slap the kid gently, why don't you go get the kid now? And she runs to get the kid and he tells her to give the kid a gentle slap, and before you know it he's got her beating the daylights out of the kid while he's listening and getting his kicks. That was this one case I had, I may write a book about it one day."

"That's fascinating," Peaches said.

"Another case I had, this guy would look in the paper for ads where people were selling furniture. He was looking for somebody selling a kid's bedroom set, you know? Getting rid of the kiddy furniture, replacing it with more mature stuff. He knew he'd

get either a youngish mother or a teenage girl on the phone—
it's usually the girls who want their furniture changed when they
get into their teens. And he'd start talking to them about the furniture, either the mother if she was home, or the teenage girl if
the mother was out, and while he was talking to them, because it
would be a long conversation, you know, what kind of bed is it,
and how's the mattress, and how many drawers in the dresser, like
that, while he was on the phone he'd be…well…"

"He'd be masturbating," Peaches said.

"Well, yes."

"Do you think the man who called me tonight was masturbating while he talked to me?"

"That's difficult to say. From what you told me, he either *was*
already, or was leading up to it. He was trying to get you to talk
about your body, you see. Which is still very nice, by the way."

"Well, thank you," Peaches said, and smiled.

"Sounds to me like that's what would've set him off. Getting
you to strip in front of the mirror there. You'd be surprised how
many women go along with something like that. He hooks them
into thinking they've got a shot at modeling—there isn't a woman
alive who wouldn't like to be a model—and then he gets them
looking at themselves while he does his number."

"That's when I began to realize," Peaches said.

"Sure."

"When he told me to take off my blouse."

"Sure. But lots of women don't realize even then. You'd be surprised. They just go along with it, thinking it's legit, never guess-
ing what's happening on the other end."

"I'm afraid he might come here," Peaches said.

"Well, these guys don't usually do that," Parker said. "They're
not your rapists or your stranglers, usually. Don't quote me on

that, you got all *kinds* of nuts out there. But usually your telephone callers aren't your violent ones."

"Usually," Peaches said.

"Yes," Parker said.

"Because he has my address, you see."

"Um," Parker said.

"And my name is on the mailbox downstairs. With the apartment number."

"I know. I saw it when I rang the bell. But that says P. Muldoon."

"Sure, but that's what's in the phone book, too. P. Muldoon."

"Well, I doubt he'll be coming around here. He may not even call again. What I'd do, though, if I was you, I'd change that message on your answering machine. Lots of single girls, they do these fancy messages, music going in the background, they try to sound sexy, it makes the caller think he's got some kind of swinger here. Better to just put a businesslike message on the machine. Something like, 'You've reached 123-4567,' and then, 'Please leave a message when you hear the beep.' Strictly business. You don't have to explain that you can't come to the phone because everybody *knows* they caught the machine. And of course you shouldn't say, 'I'm out just now,' or anything like that, because that's an invitation to burglars."

"Yes, I know."

"The point is most people today are familiar with answering machines, they *know* they're supposed to leave a message when they hear the beep, so you don't have to give them a whole list of instructions, and you don't have to sound cute, either. Your friends hear that cute little message a coupla hundred times, they want to shoot you. An obscene caller hears that cute little message, he figures he's got a live one, and he'll keep calling back till he can get you talking."

"I see," Peaches said.

"Yeah," Parker said. "Do you have any male friends who can record a message for you?"

"Well…"

"Because that's usually the best thing. That way any nut who's running his finger down the book for listings with only a first initial, he comes across P. Muldoon, he gets a man's voice on the answering machine, he figures he got a Peter Muldoon or a Paul Muldoon, but not a Peaches Muldoon. He won't call back. So that's a good way to go unless you're afraid it'll scare off any men who may be calling you legitimately. That's up to you."

"I see," Peaches said.

"Yeah," Parker said. "Now with this guy who called you tonight, he already knows there's a Peaches Muldoon living here, and he already got you going pretty far with his little routine, so he may call you back. What we'll do if he keeps calling you, we'll put a trap on the line…"

"A trap?"

"Yeah, so we can trace the call even if he hangs up. You've got to let me know if he calls again."

"Oh, I *will*," Peaches said.

"So that's about it," Parker said. "Though maybe he won't call again."

"Or come here."

"Well, like I said, I don't think he'll do that. But you know how to reach me if he does."

"I really appreciate this," Peaches said.

"Well, come on, I'm just doing my job."

"Are you on duty right now?" she asked.

"Not exactly," he said.

"Wanna come to party?" she said.

Marie Sebastiani was showing them another card trick.

"What we have is three cards here," she said. "The ace of spades, the ace of clubs, and the ace of diamonds." She fanned the cards out, the ace of diamonds under the ace of spades on the left and the ace of clubs on the right. "Now I'm going to put these three aces face down in different parts of the deck," she said, and started slipping them into the deck.

Five detectives were watching her.

Carella was on the phone to Ballistics, telling them he wanted a fast comeback on the bullets the techs had recovered at Famous Brands Wine & Liquors. The guy at Ballistics was giving him a hard time. He told Carella this was almost a quarter to 9:00 already, and he went off at midnight. The lab would be closed till 8:00 tomorrow morning. He was telling Carella the report could wait till then. Carella was telling him he wanted it right away. Meanwhile, he was watching Marie's card trick at the same time.

The other four detectives were either standing around Carella's desk, or else sitting on parts of it. His desk resembled a convention center. Brown was standing just to the left of Carella, his arms folded across his chest. He knew this was going to be another good trick. She had done four card tricks since Hawes came back to the squad-room with her. This was after Hawes had called Brown from a little pizza joint on North Fourth to say one of the people there had found an arm in a garbage can out back. Brown had rushed on over with Genero. Now they had three pieces. Or rather the Medical Examiner had them. The upper torso and a pair of arms. Brown was hoping the ME would be able to tell him whether or not the parts belonged to each other. If the parts didn't match, then they were dealing with maybe three separate corpses. Like the three cards Marie Sebastiani now slipped face down into various places in the deck.

"The ace of spades," she said. "The ace of diamonds." Sliding it into the deck. "And the ace of clubs."

Genero was watching the cards carefully. He felt certain he'd be able to catch the secret here, though he hadn't been able to on the last four tricks. He wondered if they were breaking some kind of regulation, having a deck of cards here in the squadroom. He was hoping the ME would call to say they were dealing with a single corpse here. Somehow, the idea of a single chopped-up corpse was more appealing than three separate chopped-up corpses.

Meyer was standing beside him, watching Marie's hands. She had long slender fingers. The fingers slipped the cards into the deck as smoothly as a drug dealer running a knife into a competitor. Meyer was wondering why those little kids had changed their clothes before pulling the second stickup. He was also wondering whether there'd be a third stickup. Were they finished for the night? Nightey-night, kiddies, beddy-bye time. Or were they just starting?

Hawes was standing closest to Marie. He could smell her perfume. He was hoping her husband had abandoned her and run off to Hawaii. He was hoping her husband would call her from Honolulu to say he had left her. This would leave a cold, empty space in Marie's bed. Her proximity now was stupefyingly intoxicating. Hawes guessed it was her perfume. He had not yet told her that the blues had located the van. No word on the Citation yet. Maybe hubby and his apprentice had flown off to Hawaii together. Maybe hubby was gay. Hawes glanced at Marie's pert little behind as she leaned over the desk to pick up the deck of cards. He was sorely tempted to put his hand on her behind.

"Who'd like to shuffle?" she asked.

"Me," Genero said. He was sure the secret of all her tricks had something to do with shuffling.

Marie handed the deck to him.

Meyer watched her hands.

Genero shuffled the cards and then handed the deck back to her.

"Okay, Detective Brown," she said. "Pick one of those three cards. Either the ace of clubs, the ace of diamonds, or the ace of spades."

"Clubs," Brown said.

She riffled through the deck, the cards face up, searching for it. When she found the ace of clubs, she pulled it out, and tossed it onto the desk. "Detective Meyer?" she said. "How about you?"

"The ace of spades," he said.

"I don't get it," Genero said.

Marie was looking through the deck again.

"Where's the trick?" Genero said. "If you're looking at the cards, of *course* you're going to find them."

"Right you are," she said. "Here's the ace of spades."

She tossed it onto the desk.

"Which card do *you* want?" she asked Genero.

"There's only one card left."

"And which one is that?"

"The ace of diamonds."

"Okay," she said, and handed him the deck. "Find it for me."

Genero started looking through the deck.

"Have you found it yet?" she asked.

"Just hold on a minute, okay?" he said.

He went through the entire deck. No ace of diamonds. He went through it a second time. Still no ace of diamonds.

"Have you got it?" she asked.

"It isn't here," he said.

"Are you sure? Take another look."

He went through the deck a third time. Still no ace of diamonds.

"But I saw you put it back in the deck," he said, baffled.

"Yes, you did," she said. "So where is it?"

"I give up, where is it?"

"Right here," she said, grinning, and reached into her blouse, and pulled the ace of diamonds out of her bra.

"How'd you do that?" Hawes asked.

"Maybe I'll tell you sometime," Marie said, and winked at him.

The telephone rang. Carella was sitting closest to it. He picked up.

"87th Squad, Carella," he said.

"Steve, this is Dave downstairs. Let me talk to either Brown or Genero, okay? Preferably Brown."

"Hold on a sec," Carella said, and extended the receiver to Brown. "Murchison," he said.

Brown took the receiver.

"Yeah, Dave?"

"I just got a call from Boy Two," Murchison said. "It looks like we maybe got an ID on that body been turning up in bits and pieces. A couple found the lower half in their building, in the elevator. *If* it's the same body. Wallet in the guy's hip pocket, driver's license in it. You better run on over there, I'll notify Homicide."

"What's the address?" Brown asked, and listened. "Got it," he said, writing. "And the couple's name?" He listened again. "Okay. And the name on the license? Okay," he said, "we're rolling." He put the receiver back on the cradle. "Let's go, Genero," he said, "the pieces are coming together. We just got ourselves the lower half. Name tag on it, this time."

"This trick is called The Mystic Prediction," Marie said, and began shuffling the cards.

"What do you mean, name tag?" Genero asked.

"The dead man's carrying a wallet," Brown said.

"How?"

"What do you mean *how*? In his *pocket* is how."

"I'm going to ask any one of you to write down a three-figure number for me," Marie said.

"You mean he's wearing pants?" Genero said.

"Unless there's a pocket sewn on his ass," Brown said.

"You mean there's *pants* on the lower half of the body?"

"Whyn't we run on over and see for ourselves, okay?"

"Who wants to write down three numbers for me?" Marie asked. "Any three numbers?"

"And his name's in the wallet?" Genero said.

"On his driver's license," Brown said. "Let's go."

Both men started for the railing. Kling was coming back from the men's room down the hall. He opened the gate and made a low bow, sweeping his arm across his body, ushering them through.

"So what's his name?" Genero asked.

"Frank Sebastiani," Brown said.

And Marie fainted into Kling's arms.

Annie Rawles was already in place when Eileen pulled up outside Larry's. The clock behind the bar, a big ornate thing rimmed with orange neon, read five minutes to 9:00. Through the plate-glass window, Annie could see the white Cadillac edging into the curb. The bartender could see it, too. They both watched with casual interest as the driver cut the engine, Annie nursing a beer, the bartender polishing glasses. The man behind the wheel of the car was big and black and wearing pimp threads.

They both watched as Eileen got out of the car on the curb side, long legs flashing and signaling, little hidden pistol tucked into one of those soft sexy boots, high-stepping her way toward the entrance door now.

Mr. Pimp leaned across the seat, rolled down the window on the curb side.

Yelled something to Eileen.

Eileen sashayed back, bent over to look in the window. Short skirt tight across her ass, flashing, advertising.

Started shaking her head, waving her arms around.

"She's givin' him sass," the bartender said.

Southern accent you could cut with a butter knife. Maybe this wasn't so far from Houston after all.

"An' he don't like it none," the bartender said.

Mr. Pimp came storming out of the car on the driver's side, walked around the car, stood yelling at her on the sidewalk.

Eileen kept shaking her head, hands on her hips.

"Won't stop sassin' him, will she?" the bartender said.

And suddenly Mr. Pimp slapped her.

"Whomp her good," the bartender said, nodding encouragement.

Eileen staggered back from the blow, her green eyes blazing. She bunched her fists and went at him as if she'd kill him, but he shoved her away, turned her toward the bar, shoved her again, toward the door of the bar this time, and then strutted back to the Caddy, lord of all he surveyed. Eileen was nursing her cheek. She glared at the Caddy as it pulled away from the curb.

Act One had begun.

Four pieces had become one piece.

Maybe.

They showed her the bundle of clothing first.

Black shoes, blue socks. Blue trousers. Black belt. White Jockey undershorts. Blood stains on the waistband of the trousers and the shorts.

"I...I think those are Frank's clothes," Marie said.

Some coins in one of the pants pockets. A quarter, two dimes, and a penny.

No keys. Neither house keys nor car keys.

A handkerchief in another pocket.

And a wallet.

Black leather.

"Is this your husband's wallet?" Brown asked.

"Yes."

Her voice very soft. As if what they were showing her demanded reverence.

In the wallet, a driver's license issued to Frank Sebastiani of 604 Eden Lane, Collinsworth. No credit cards. Voters Registration card, same name, same address. $120 in $20s, $5s, and $1s. Tucked into one of the little pockets was a green slip of paper with the words MARIE'S SIZES hand-lettered onto it, and beneath that:

Hat:	22
Dress:	8
Bra:	36B
Belt:	26
Panties:	5
Ring:	5
Gloves:	6½
Stockings:	9½ (Medium)
Shoes:	6½B

"Is this your husband's handwriting?" Brown asked.

"Yes," Marie said. Same soft reverential voice.

They led her inside.

The morgue stank.

She reeled back from the stench of human gasses and flesh.

They walked her past a stainless-steel table upon which the charred remains of a burn victim's body lay trapped in a pugilistic pose, as though still trying to fight off the flames that had consumed it.

The four pieces of the dismembered corpse were on another stainless-steel table. They were casually assembled, not quite joining. Lying there on the table like an incomplete jigsaw puzzle.

She looked down at the pieces.

"There's no question they're the same body," Carl Blaney said.

Lavender-eyed, white-smocked. Standing under the fluorescent lights, seeming neither to notice nor to be bothered by the intolerable stink in the place.

"As for identification..."

He shrugged.

"As you see, we don't have the hands or the head yet."

He addressed this to the policemen in the room. Ignoring the woman for the time being. Afraid she might puke on his polished tile floor. Or in one of the stainless-steel basins containing internal organs. Three cops now. Hawes, Brown, and Genero. Two cases about to become one. Maybe.

The lower half of the torso was naked now.

She kept looking down at it.

"Would you know his blood type?" Blaney asked.

"Yes," Marie said. "B."

"Well, that's what we've got here."

Hawes knew about the appendectomy and meniscectomy scars because she'd mentioned them while describing her husband. He said nothing now. First rule of identification, you didn't prompt the witness. Let them come to it on their own. He waited.

"Recognize anything?" Brown asked.

She nodded.

"What do you recognize, ma'am?"

"The scars," she said.

"Would you know what kind of scars those are?" Blaney asked.

"The one on the belly is an appendectomy scar."

Blaney nodded.

"The one on the left knee is from when he had the cartilage removed."

"That's what those scars are," Blaney said to the detectives.

"Anything else, ma'am?" Brown asked.

"His penis," she said.

Neither Blaney nor any of the detectives blinked. This wasn't the Meese Commission standing around the pieces of a corpse, this was a group of professionals trying to make positive identification.

"What about it?" Blaney asked.

"There should be a small...well, a beauty spot, I guess you'd call it," Marie said. "On the underside. On the foreskin."

Blaney lifted the corpse's limp penis in one rubber-gloved hand. He turned it slightly.

"This?" he asked, and indicated a birthmark the size of a pin-head on the foreskin, an inch or so below the glans.

"Yes," Marie said softly.

Blaney let the penis drop.

The detectives were trying to figure out whether or not all of this added up to a positive ID. No face to look at. No hands to examine for fingerprints. Just the blood type, the scars on belly and leg, and the identifying birthmark—what Marie had called a beauty spot—on the penis.

"I'll work up a dental chart sometime tomorrow," Blaney said.

"Would you know who his dentist was?" Hawes asked Marie.

"Dentist?" she said.

"For comparison later," Hawes said. "When we get the chart."

She looked at him blankly.

"Comparison?" she said.

"Our chart against the dentist's. If it's your husband, the charts'll match."

"Oh," she said. "Oh. Well… the last time he went to a dentist was in Florida. Miami Beach. He had this terrible toothache. He hasn't been to a dentist since we moved north."

"When was that?" Brown asked.

"Five years ago."

"Then the most recent dental chart…"

"I don't even know if there *is* a chart," Marie said. "He just went to somebody the hotel recommended. We had a steady gig at the Regal Palms. I mean, we never had *a family* dentist, if that's what you mean."

"Yeah, well," Brown said.

He was thinking Dead End on the teeth.

He turned to Blaney.

"So what do you think?" he said.

"How tall was your husband?" Blaney asked Marie.

"I've got all that here," Hawes said, and took out his notebook. He opened it to the page he'd written on earlier, and began reading aloud. "Five-eleven, one-seventy, hair black, eyes blue, appendectomy scar, meniscectomy scar."

"If we put a head in place there," Blaney said, "we'd have a body some hundred and eighty centimeters long. That's just about five-eleven. And I'd estimate the weight, given the separate sections here, at about what you've got there, a hundred-seventy, a hundred-seventy-five, in there. The hair on the arms, chest, legs, and pubic area is black—which doesn't necessarily mean the *head* hair would match it exactly, but at least it rules out a blonde or a redhead, or anyone in the brown groupings. This hair is very definitely *black*. The eyes—well, we haven't got a head, have we?"

"So have we got a positive ID or what?" Brown asked.

"I'd say we're looking at the remains of a healthy white male in his late twenties or early thirties," Blaney said. "How old was your husband, madam?"

"Thirty-four," she said.

"Yes," Blaney said, and nodded. "And, of course, identification of the birthmark on the penis would seem to me a conclusive factor."

"Is this your husband, ma'am?" Brown asked.

"That is my husband," Marie said, and turned her head into Hawes's shoulder and began weeping gently against his chest.

The hotel was far from the precinct, downtown on a side street off Detavoner Avenue. He'd deliberately chosen a fleabag distant from the scene of the crime. *Scenes* of the crime, to be more accurate. Five separate scenes if you counted the head and the hands. Five scenes in a little playlet entitled "The Magical and Somewhat Sudden Disappearance of Sebastian the Great."

Good riddance, he thought.

"Yes, sir?" the desk clerk said. "May I help you?"

"I have a reservation," he said.

"The name, please?"

"Hardeen," he said. "Theo Hardeen."

Wonderful magician, long dead. Houdini's brother. Appropriate name to be using. Hardeen had been famous for his escape from a galvanized iron can filled with water and secured by massive locks. Failure Means a Drowning Death! his posters had proclaimed. The risks of failure here were even greater.

"How do you spell that, sir?" the clerk asked.

"H-A-R-D-E-E-N."

"Yes, sir, I have it right here," the clerk said, yanking a card. "Hardeen, Theo. That's just for the one night, is that correct, Mr. Hardeen?"

"Just the one night, yes."

"How will you be paying, Mr. Hardeen?"

"Cash," he said. "In advance."

The clerk figured this was a shack-up. One-night stand, guy checking in alone, his bimbo—or else a hooker from the Yellow Pages—would be along later. Never explain, never complain, he thought. Thank you, Henry Ford. But charge him for a double.

"That'll be eighty-five dollars, plus tax," he said, and watched as the wallet came out, and then a $100 bill, and the wallet disappeared again in a wink. Like he figured, a shack-up. Guy didn't want to show even a glimpse of his driver's license or credit cards, the Hardeen was undoubtedly a phony name. Theo Hardeen? The names some of them picked. Who cared? Take the money and run, he thought. Thank you, Woody Allen.

He calculated the tax, made change for the C-note, and slid the money across the desktop. Wallet out again in a flash, money disappearing, wallet disappearing, too.

"Did you have any luggage, sir?" he asked.

"Just the one valise."

"I'll have someone show you to your room, sir," he said, and banged a bell on the desk. "Front!" he shouted. "Checkout time is twelve noon, sir. Have a nice night."

"Thank you."

A bellhop in a faded red uniform showed him to the third-floor room. Flicked on the lights in the bathroom. Taught him how to operate the window air-conditioning unit. Turned on the television set for him. Waited for the tip. Got his 50¢, looked at it on the palm of his hand, shrugged, and left the room. What the hell had he expected for carrying that one bag? Rundown joint like this—well, that's why he'd picked it. No questions asked. In, out, thank you very much.

He looked at the television screen, and then at his watch.

A quarter past 9:00.

Forty-five minutes before the 10:00 news came on.

He wondered if they'd found the four pieces yet. Or either of the cars. He'd left the Citation in the parking lot of an A & P four blocks north of the river, shortly after he'd deep-sixed the head and the hands.

Something dumb was on television. Well, *everything* on television was dumb these days. He'd have to wait till 10:00 to see what was happening, if anything.

He took off his shoes, lay full length on the bed, his eyes closed, and relaxed for the first time today.

By tomorrow night at this time, he'd be in San Francisco.

Eileen came out of the ladies' room and walked toward the farthest end of the bar, where a television set was mounted on the wall. Quick heel-clicking hooker glide, lots of ass and ankle in it. She didn't even glance at Annie, sitting with her legs crossed at the cash-register end of the bar. Two or three men sitting at tables around the place turned to look at her. She gave them a quick once-over, no smile, no come-on, and took a stool next to a guy watching the television screen. She was still fuming. In the mirror behind the bar, she could still see the flaming imprint of his hand on her left cheek. The bartender ambled over.

"Name it," he said.

"Rum-Coke," she said. "Easy on the rum."

"Comin'," he said, and reached for a bottle of cheap rum on the shelf behind him. He put ice in a glass, short-jiggered some rum over it, filled the glass with Coke from a hose. "Three bucks even," he said, "a bargain. You be runnin' a tab?"

"I'll pay as I go," she said, and reached into her shoulder bag. The .44 was sitting under a silk scarf, butt up. She took out her wallet, paid for the drink. The bartender lingered.

"I'm Larry," he said. "This's my place."

Eileen nodded, and then took a sip of the drink.

"You're new," Larry said.

"So?" she said.

"So I get a piece," he said.

"You get shit," Eileen said.

"I can't have hookers hangin' around in here 'cept I get a piece."

"Talk to Torpedo," she said.

"I don't know nobody named Torpedo."

"You don't, huh? Well, ask around. I got a feeling you won't like talking to him."

"Who's Torpedo? The black dude was slapping you around?"

"Torpedo Holmes. Ask around. Meanwhile, fuck off."

"You see the lady sittin' there at the end of the bar?" Larry said.

Eileen looked over at Annie.

"I see her."

"She's new, too. We had a nice little talk minute she come in. I'm gettin' twenty percent of her action, just for lettin' her plant her ass on that stool."

"She ain't got Torpedo," Eileen said. "You want to get off my fuckin' back, or you want me to make a phone call?"

"Go make your phone call," Larry said.

"Mister," Eileen said, "you're askin' for more shit than you're worth."

She swung off the stool, long legs reaching for the floor, picked up her bag, shouldered it, and swiveled toward the phone booth. Watching her, Annie thought God, she's good.

In the phone booth, Eileen dialed the hot-line number at the Seven-Two.

Alvarez picked up.

"Tell Robinson to get back here," she said. "The bartender's hassling me."

"You got him," Alvarez said, and hung up.

Detective/2nd Grade Alvin Robinson worked out of the Seven-Three, near the park and the County Court House. The team at the Seven-Two was certain he wouldn't be made for a cop here in the Canal Zone, and were using him tonight only to establish Eileen's credentials as a bona fide hooker. He wouldn't be part of the backup team, though Eileen might have wished otherwise. She was still annoyed that he'd hit her that hard—even though she knew he'd been going for realism—but in the Caddy on the way over he'd sounded like a tough, dependable cop who knew his business.

He walked into the bar not ten minutes after she placed her call. Eyes challenging, sweeping the room under the wide brim of his hat, everyone in the joint looking away. He did a cool pimp shuffle over to where Eileen was sitting, and put his hand on her shoulder.

"That him?" he asked, and cocked his head to where Larry was filling a jar with tomato juice. Eileen merely nodded. "You," Robinson said, and pointed his finger. "Come here."

Larry took his time ambling over.

"You givin' my fox trouble?" Robinson said.

"You got a phone in that pussy wagon of yours?" Larry said, toughing it out though he'd never seen a meaner-looking black man in his life. Everybody in the bar was looking at them now. The guys at the tables, the one who'd been watching television a minute earlier.

"I ast you a question," Robinson said.

"I read her the rules, pal," Larry said. "The same rules—"

"Don't pal *me,* pal," Robinson said. "I ain't your fuckin' pal, and I don't live by no rules. If you never heard of Torpedo Holmes, then you got some quick learnin' to do. Nobody cuts my action, man. Nobody. Less he's lookin' for some *other* kinda cut I'd be mighty obliged to supply. You got that?"

"I'm tellin' you—"

"No, you ain't *tellin'* me nothin', mister. You *list'nin'* is what you doin'." He reached into his wallet, took a frayed piece of glossy paper from it, unfolded it, and smoothed it flat on the bar. "This's from *LA Magazine,*" he said. "You recognize that picture there?"

Larry looked down at a color photograph of a big black man wearing a red silk lounge robe and grinning cockily at the camera. The room in the background was opulent. The caption under the picture read: *Thomas "Torpedo" Holmes at Home.*

Robinson thought the resemblance was a good one. But even if it hadn't been, he firmly believed that most white men—especially a redneck like this one—thought all niggers looked alike. Thomas "Torpedo" Holmes was now doing ten years at Soledad. The article didn't mention the bust and conviction, because it had been written three years earlier, when Holmes was riding too high for his own good. You don't shit on cops in print, not even in LA.

"I'm assumin' you don't know how to read," Robinson said, "so I'll fill you in fast." He snatched the article off the bar top before it got too much scrutiny, folded it, put it back into his wallet again. Eileen sat looking bored. "Now what that article says, man, is that not even LA's finest could lay a finger on me, is what that article says. An' the same applies right here in *this* city, ain't no kinda law can touch me, ain't no kinda shitty bartender—"

"I *own* this place!" Larry said.

"You list'nin' to me, man, or you runnin' off at the mouth? I'm tellin' you I don't cut my action with nobody, not the law, not nobody else runnin' girls, and most of all not *you.*"

"This ain't LA," Larry said.

"Well, no shee-it?" Robinson said.

"I mean, I got rules here, man."

"You want me to shove your rules up your ass, man? Together with that jar of tomato juice? Man, don't tempt me. This little girl here, she's gonna sit here long as she likes, you dig, man? An' if I'm happy with the service she gets, then maybe I'll drop some other little girls off every now an' then, give this fuckin' dump some class." His wallet came out again. He threw a $50 bill on the counter. "This is for whatever she wants to drink. When that's used up, I'll be back with more. You better pray I don't come back with somethin' has a sharp end. You take my meanin', man?"

Larry picked up the bill and tucked it into his shirt pocket. He figured he'd won a moral victory. "What's all this strong-arm shit?" he asked, smiling, playing to the crowd now, showing them he hadn't backed down. "We're two gentlemen here, can't we talk without threatening each other?"

"Was you threatenin' me?" Robinson said. "I didn't hear nobody threatenin' me."

"What I meant—"

"We finished here, man? You gonna treat Linda nice from now on?"

"All I said to the lady—"

"What you said don't mean shit to me. I don't want no more phone calls from her."

"I don't mind a nice-looking girl in the place," Larry said.

"Good. An' I don't mind her bein' here," Robinson said, and grinned a big watermelon-eating grin. He put his hand on Eileen's shoulder again. "Now, honey," he said, "go easy on the sauce. 'Cause Daddy got some nice candy for you when the night's done."

"See you, Torp," she said, and offered her cheek for his kiss.

Robinson gave Larry a brief, meaningful nod, and then did his cool pimp shuffle over to the door and out to the white Cadillac at the curb.

From the other end of the bar, Annie said, "I wish *I* had a man like that."

The third liquor-store holdup took place while Alvin Robinson was doing his little dog-and-pony act for the owner of Larry's Bar, but the blues didn't respond till 9:30, and Carella and Meyer didn't arrive at the scene till 9:35, by which time Robinson was already driving back toward the 73rd Precinct.

This time, nobody had been killed—but not for lack of trying. Martha Frey, the forty-year-old woman who owned and operated the store on Culver and Twentieth, told them that four of them—wearing clown suits, and pointed pom-pommed clown hats, and white clown masks with bulbous red noses and wide grinning red mouths—had started shooting the minute they walked in. She'd grabbed for her heart and fallen down behind the counter in what she hoped was a very good imitation of someone who'd been mortally wounded. It had occurred to her, while they were cleaning out the cash register, that one of them might decide to put a "coop dee gracie," as she called it, in her head while she was lying there playing possum. None of them had. She considered it a miracle that she was still alive, four little guns opening up that way, all of them at the same time. She wondered if maybe they'd hit her after all. Was it possible she was now in shock and didn't know she'd been hit? Did the detectives see any blood on her?

Meyer assured her that she was still in one piece.

"I can't believe they missed me," she said, and made the sign of the cross. "God must have been watching over me."

Either that, or they were nervous this time around, Carella thought. Three times in the space of four hours, even your seasoned pro could spook. No less a handful of grade-schoolers.

"Did you see who was driving the car?" Carella asked.

"No," Martha said. "I was tallying the register for the night. I usually close at nine on Fridays, but this is Halloween, there's lots of parties going on, people run short of booze, they make a last-minute run to the store. This was maybe twenty after when they came in."

The Mobile Lab van was pulling up outside the store.

"Techs'll be here a while," Carella said. "They'll want to see if there's anything on that register."

"There ain't anything *in* it, that's for sure," Martha said mournfully.

"Did they say anything to you?" Meyer asked. "When they came in?"

"Just 'Trick or treat!' Then they started shooting."

"Didn't say, 'This is a stickup,' anything like that?"

"Nothing."

"Hello, boys," one of the techs said. "Kiddy time again?"

"School let out again?" the other tech said.

"How about when they were cleaning out the register?" Meyer asked, ignoring them.

"One of them said, 'Hold it open, Alice.' I guess he meant the shopping bag."

"Alice?" Carella said. "A girl?"

"A woman, yes," Martha said.

Carella thought this was carrying feminism a bit too far.

"Well, this little girl—" he started to say, but Martha broke in at once.

"A *woman*," she said. "Not a little girl. These weren't *children*, Detective Carella, they were *midgets*."

He looked at her.

"I used to work the high-wire with Ringling," she said. "Broke my hip in a fall, quit for good. But I still know midgets when I see them. These were *midgets.*"

"What'd I tell you, Baz?" one of the techs said. "I shoulda taken your bet."

"Midgets," the other tech said. "I'll be a son of a bitch."

Me, too, Carella thought.

But now they knew what they were looking for.

And now they had a pattern.

Peaches and Parker were the only ones not in costume.

"What are you supposed to be?" a man dressed like a cowboy asked.

"I'm a cop," Parker said.

"I'm a victim," Peaches said.

"I'll be damned," the cowboy said.

Parker showed his shield to everyone he met.

"Looks like the real McCoy," a pirate said.

Peaches lifted her skirt and showed a silent-movie director a black-and-blue mark on her thigh.

"I'm a victim," she said.

She had got the black-and-blue mark banging against a table on her way to the bathroom one night.

The silent-movie director, who was wearing jodhpurs and carrying a megaphone, said, "That's some leg, honey. You wanna be in pictures?"

The girl with him was dressed as Theda Bara. "That's an anagram for Arab Death," she said.

Parker looked into the front of her clingy, satin, low-cut dress, and said, "You're under arrest," and showed her his shield.

In the kitchen, Dracula and Superman and Scarlett O'Hara and Cleopatra were snorting cocaine.

Parker didn't show them his shield. Instead, he snorted a few lines with them.

Peaches said, "You're kinda fun for a cop."

This was the first time in a good many years that anyone had told Parker he was kind of fun, for a cop or anything else. He hugged her close.

She went, "Oooooo."

A white man in blackface, dressed as Eddie Murphy dressed as the Detroit detective in *Beverly Hills Cop* said, "I'm a cop," and showed Parker a fake shield.

"I'll go along quietly," Parker said, and hugged Peaches again.

"Way I figure it," Kling said, "we go over there soon as we're relieved. Maybe get to the Zone around midnight, a little after."

"Uh-huh," Hawes said, and looked up at the wall clock.

Ten minutes to 10:00. Less than two hours before the relieving shift began filtering in.

"They don't even need to know we're there," Kling said. "We take one of the sedans, just cruise the streets."

They were sitting at his desk, talking in whispers. Across the room, Brown was getting a description of Jimmy Brayne. He was right now ready to bet the farm that Sebastian the Great's apprentice was the one who'd done him in and chopped him up in pieces.

"This guy's extremely dangerous," Kling said. "Juked three people already."

"And you think they may need help, huh?" Hawes said. "Annie and Eileen?"

"More the merrier," Kling said.

"White or black?" Brown asked.

"White," Marie said.

"His age?"

"Thirty-two."

"Height?"

"About six feet."

"Annie never even mentioned she was going out on this," Hawes said. "I talked to her must've been—"

"She didn't get the call from Homicide till late this afternoon. That's the thing of it, Cotton. They pulled this whole damn thing out of a Cracker Jack box."

"Weight?" Brown said.

"About a hundred and eighty? Something like that."

"Color of hair?"

"Black."

"Eyes?"

"Brown."

"I mean, would *you* go out there with only two backups?" Kling said. "Where the guy's armed with a knife, and already boxed three people?"

"Those don't sound like bad odds," Hawes said. "Three to one? All three of them loaded. Against only a knife."

"*Only,* huh? My point is, if Annie and this Shanahan guy stay too close to her," Kling said, "he won't make his move. So they have to keep their distance. But if he breaks out, who's covering the backfield?"

"Any identifying scars, marks, or tattoos?" Brown asked.

"Not that I know of."

"Any regional accent or dialect?"

"He's from Massachusetts. He sounds a little like the Kennedys."

"What was he wearing when you left the house today?"

"Let me think."

She was sitting on a bench under the squadroom bulletin board, her hands folded on her lap. Her face was still tear-stained. Brown had one foot up on the bench, a clipboard resting on his knee. He waited.

"Blue jeans," she said. "And a woolen sweater, no shirt. A V-necked sweater. Sort of rust-colored. And sneakers. And... white socks, I think. Oh, yes. He wears a sort of medallion around his neck. A silver medallion, I think he won it in a swim meet. A high school swim meet."

"Wears it all the time?"

"I've never seen him without it."

"Have you discussed this with Eileen?" Hawes asked.

"Yeah, I mentioned it at dinner," Kling said.

"Told her you want to go over there?"

"Yeah."

"To the Zone?"

"Yeah."

"What'd she say?"

"She told me she could handle it."

"But you don't think she can, huh?"

"I think she can handle it better with a few more people on the job. They shoulda known that themselves, Homicide. And also the Seven-Two. Putting two women on the street against—"

"Plus Shanahan."

"Well, I don't know this Shanahan, do you?"

"No, but—"

"For all I know—"

"But you can't automatically figure he's a hairbag."

"I don't know what he is. I *do* know he's not gonna care as much about Eileen as *I* care about her."

"Maybe that's the problem," Hawes said.

"Does he wear a wristwatch?" Brown asked.

"Yes," Marie said.

"Would you know what kind?"

"One of those digital things. Black with a black band. A Seiko, I think. I'm not sure."

"Any other jewelry?"

"A ring. He wears it on his right pinky. A little gold ring with a red stone. I don't think it's a ruby, but it looks like one."

"Is he right-handed or left-handed?"

"I don't know."

"What do you mean?" Kling said.

"I mean, why don't you leave it to them?" Hawes said.

Kling looked at him.

"They're experienced cops, all of them. If Homicide or the Seven-Two hasn't put an army out there, it's maybe 'cause they think they'll spook him."

"I don't see how two more guys is gonna make an *army*," Kling said.

"These guys can smell traps," Hawes said, "they're like animals in the jungle. Anyway, they'll be carrying walkie-talkies, won't they? Annie, Shanahan? Maybe even Eileen. There'll be RMP's cruising the Zone, they're not gonna be alone out there. Any one of 'em calls in a 10-13..."

"I don't want her getting cut again," Kling said.

"You think *she* wants to get cut again?" Hawes said.

"Tell me what happened before you left the house today," Brown said. "Was he behaving differently in any way?"

"Same as always," Marie said.

"Did he get along okay with your husband?"

"Yes. Well, he wants to be a magician, you see. He studies all the tricks the famous magicians did—Dai Vernon, Blackstone, Audley Walsh, Tommy Windsor, Houdini, Ballantine—all of them. He keeps up with all the new people, too, tries to dope out their tricks. And my husband is..."

Her face almost broke.

"My husband...was...very patient with him. Always willing to explain a sleight, or a pocket trick, or a stage illusion...helping him with his patter...taking the time to...to...show him and...and guide him. I don't know how he could've done something like this. I'll tell you the truth, Detective Brown, I'm willing to give you anything you need to find Jimmy, but I can't believe he did this."

"Well, *we* don't know that for sure, either," Brown said.

"That's just what I mean," Marie said. "I just pray to God something hasn't happened to *him,* too. I just hope somebody hasn't...hasn't killed them *both.*"

"How do *you* get along with him?" Brown asked.

"Jimmy? I think of him as a brother."

"No friction, huh? I mean, the three of you living in the same house?"

"None whatever."

"So what does that mean?" Kling asked. "You won't go with me?"

"I don't think *you* should go, either," Hawes said.

"Well, I'm going."

"She knows her job," Hawes said flatly. "And so does Annie."

"She *didn't* know her job when that son of a bitch—"

Kling caught himself. He took a deep breath.

"Take it easy," Hawes said.

"I'm going out there tonight," Kling said. "With you or without you."

"Take it easy," Hawes said again.

Brown walked over.

"Here's the way I figure it," he said to Hawes. "You caught the Missing P, I caught the pieces. Turns out it's the same case. I figure maybe Genero ought to go back to cruising, find all that trouble in the streets the loot's worried about. You and me can team up on this one, how does that sound to you?"

"Sounds good," Hawes said.

"I'll go tell Genero," Brown said, and walked off.

"You okay?" Hawes asked Kling.

"I'm fine," Kling said.

But he walked off, too.

The precinct map was spread out on the long table in the Interrogation Room. Meyer and Carella were hunched over the map. They had already asked Sergeant Murchison to run a check on any circuses or carnivals that happened to be in town. They did not think there'd be any at this time of year. In the meantime, they were trying to figure out where the midgets would hit next.

"Midgets," Meyer said, shaking his head. "You ever bust a midget?"

"Never," Carella said. "I busted a dwarf once. He was a very good burglar. Used to crawl into vents."

"What's the difference?" Meyer asked.

"A midget is a person of unusually small size, but he's physically well proportioned."

"So? Dopey and Doc were well proportioned, too."

"That's the movies," Carella said. "In real life, a dwarf has abnormal body proportions."

"Can you name all the Seven Dwarfs?" Meyer asked.

"I can't even name Snow White," Carella said.

"Go on, give it a try."

"Anyone can name the Seven Dwarfs," Carella said.

"Go ahead, name them."

"Dopey, Doc…"

"I gave you those two free."

"Grumpy, Sleepy, Sneezy…how many is that?"

"Five."

"Bashful."

"Yeah?"

"And…"

"Yeah?"

"Who's the seventh one?" Carella said.

"Nobody can name all seven of them," Meyer said.

"So tell me who he is."

"Think about it," Meyer said, smiling.

Carella hunched over the precinct map. Now the goddamn seventh dwarf would bother him all night long.

"First hit was here," he said, indicating the location on the map. "Culver and Ninth. Second one here. Still on Culver, three blocks east. Next one was Culver and Twentieth."

"They're working their way uptown on Culver."

"First one at…have you got that timetable?"

Meyer opened his notebook. "Five-fifteen," he said. "Second one at a little after seven. Third one about forty minutes ago."

"So what's the interval?"

"Five-fifteen, seven-oh-five, nine-twenty. Figure two hours, more or less."

"Time to change their costumes…"

"Or maybe we're dealing with *three* gangs here, did that occur to you?"

"There aren't that many midgets in the world," Carella said.

"You figured out the seventh dwarf yet?"

"No." He looked at the map again. "So the next one should be further uptown on Culver, and they should hit around eleven, eleven-thirty."

"*If* there's a next one."

"And unless they speed up the timetable."

"Yeah," Meyer said, and shook his head again. "Midgets. I always thought midgets were law-abiding citizens."

"Just be happy they aren't giants," Carella said.

"You got it," Meyer said.

"Huh?" Carella said.

"Happy. That's the seventh dwarf."

"Oh. Yeah."

"So what do you want to do?"

"First let's check Dave, see if he came up with any circuses or carnivals."

"That's a long shot," Meyer said.

"Then let's call Ballistics again, see if they got anything on the bullets."

"We'll maybe get a caliber and make," Meyer said, "but I don't see how that's gonna help us."

"And then I guess we better head uptown," Carella said, "case Culver, see which stores are possibles for the next hit."

"You figuring on a plant?"

"Unless there's a dozen of them."

"Well, it's getting late, there won't be many open."

Carella folded the map.

"So," he said. "Murchison first."

She was still sitting on the bench, weeping softly, when Hawes approached her.

"Mrs. Sebastiani?" he said.

Marie looked up. Face tear streaked, blue eyes rimmed with red now.

"I'm sorry to bother you," he said.

"No, that's all right," she said.

"I wanted to tell you…we found the van, but we still haven't located the Citation. You said Brayne drove the van into the city today…"

"Yes."

"So maybe the techs'll be able to lift his prints from the wheel. He hasn't got a criminal record, has he?"

"Not that I know of."

"Well, we'll run him through the computer, see what we come up with. Meanwhile, if the techs lift anything, and if we find the Citation, then maybe we'll know if he's the one who drove it away from the school. By comparing prints from the two wheels, do you see?"

"Yes. But…well, we *all* drove both cars a lot. I mean, you'll probably find my prints and Frank's together with Jimmy's. If you find any prints."

"Uh-huh, yes, that's a possibility. But we'll see, okay? Meanwhile, Detective Brown has already put out a bulletin on Brayne, and we'll be watching all railroad stations, bus terminals, airports, in case he—"

"*You'll* be watching?"

"Well, not Brown and me personally. I mean the police. The bulletin's gone out already, as I said, so maybe we'll get some results there. If he's trying to get out of the city."

"Yes," Marie said, and nodded.

"Brown and I are gonna run back to the high school, see if anybody there saw what happened in that driveway."

"Well…will anyone *be* there? I mean, won't the teachers…?"

"And the kids, yes, they'll be gone, that'll have to wait till morning. But the custodian'll be there, and maybe *he* saw something."

"Will it be the same custodian who was there this afternoon?"

"I don't know, but we're going to check it out, anyway."

"Yes, I see."

"Meanwhile, I wanted to know what *you* plan to do. Do you have any relatives or friends here in the city?"

"No."

"Then will you be going back home? I know you're short of cash…"

"Yes, but there was money in Frank's wallet."

"Well, the lab'll be running tests on the wallet and everything in it, so I can't let you have that. But if you want me to lend you train fare, or bus fare…what I'm asking is whether or not you plan on going home, Mrs. Sebastiani. Because, honestly, there's nothing more you can do here."

"I…I don't know what I want to do," she said, and began crying again, burying her face in an already sodden handkerchief.

Hawes watched her, awkward in the presence of her tears.

"I'm not sure I want to go home," she said, her voice muffled by the handkerchief. "With Frank gone…"

The sentence trailed.

She kept sobbing into the handkerchief.

"You have to go home sometime," Hawes said gently.

"I know, I know," she said, and blew her nose, and sniffed, and wiped at her eyes with the back of her hand. "There are calls I'll have to make…Frank's mother in Atlanta, and his sister…and I guess…I suppose I'll have to make funeral arrangements…oh God, how are they going to…what will they…?"

Hawes was thinking the same thing. The body was in four separate pieces. The body didn't have hands or a head.

"That'll have to wait till autopsy, anyway," he said. "I'll let you know when…"

"I thought they'd already done that."

"Well, that was a prelim. We asked for a preliminary report, you see. But the ME'll want to do a more thorough examination."

"Why?" she asked. "I've already identified him."

"Yes, but we're dealing with a murder here, Mrs. Sebastiani, and we need to know...well, for example, your husband may have been *poisoned* before the body was...well..."

He cut himself short.

He was talking too much.

This was a goddamn grieving widow here.

"There are lots of things the ME can tell us," he concluded lamely.

Marie nodded.

"So...*will* you be going home?" he asked.

"I suppose."

Hawes opened his wallet, pulled out two $20s and a $10.

"This should get you there," he said, handing the money to her.

"That's too much," she said.

"Well, tide you over. I'll give you a ring later tonight, make sure you got home okay. And I'll be in touch as we go along. Sometimes these things take a little while, but we'll be work—"

"Yes," she said. "Let me know."

"I'll have one of the cars drop you off," he said. "Will you be going home by train or...?"

"Train, yes."

She seemed numb.

"So...uh...whenever you're ready, I'll buzz the sergeant and he'll pull one of the cars off the street. I'd drive you myself, but Brown and I want to get over to the school."

Marie nodded.

And then she looked up and said—perhaps only to herself—"How am I going to live without him?"

Genero was annoyed.

He was the one who'd found the first piece of the body, and now all *four* pieces were out of his hands. So to speak. He blamed it on seniority. Both Brown and Hawes had been detectives longer than he had, and so they'd immediately taken charge of a juicy homicide. So here he was, back on the street again, cruising like a goddamn patrolman. He was more than annoyed. He was enormously pissed.

The streets at a quarter past 10:00 were still teeming with people…well, sure, who expected this kind of weather at the end of October? Guys in shirtsleeves, girls in summer dresses, everybody strolling up the avenue like it was summertime in Paris, not that he'd ever been there. Lady there on the corner with a French poodle, letting the dog poop right on the sidewalk, even though it was against the law. He wondered if he should arrest her. He considered it beneath his dignity, a detective/3rd having to arrest a lady whose dog was illegally pooping. He let the dog poop, drove on by.

Made a cursory tour of the sector.

Who else was out here?

Kling?

Came onto Culver, began heading east.

Past the first liquor store got robbed tonight, then the second one...

What had they been talking about back there in the squad-room? Meyer and Carella. Midgets? Was it possible? Midgets holding up liquor stores? Those little Munchkins from *The Wizard of Oz* holding up *liquor* stores, for Christ's sake? He didn't know what kind of a world this was getting to be. He thanked God every night before he went to sleep that he had been chosen to enforce law and order in the kind of world this was getting to be. Even if sometimes he had a good ripe murder yanked out of his hands. The only way to get ahead in the Department was to crack a good homicide every now and then. Not that it had done Carella much good, all the homicides he'd cracked. Been a detective for how many years now? Still only 2nd grade. Well, sometimes people got passed over. The meek shall inherit the earth, he thought. Still, he wished he'd had an honest crack at that homicide tonight. He was the one found the first piece, wasn't he?

Onto Mason Avenue, the hookers out in force, well, Halloween, lots of guys coming uptown to look for the Great Pumpkin. Went home with the Great Herpes and maybe the Great AIDS. He wouldn't screw a Mason Avenue hooker if you gave him a million dollars. Well, maybe he would. For a million, maybe. That one on the corner looked very clean, in fact. But you could never tell. Anyway, she was Puerto Rican, and his mother had warned him against fooling around with any girls who weren't Italian. He wondered if Italian girls ever got herpes. He was positive they never got AIDS.

Swinging north again, up one of the side streets, then onto the Stem, all gaudy and bright, he really loved this part of the...

"Boy One, Boy One..."

The walkie-talkie lying on the seat beside him. Dispatcher trying to raise...

"Boy One."

Answering.

"10-21 at 1141 Oliver, near Sixth. Apartment 42, 10-21 at 1141 Oliver, near Sixth. See the lady."

"What was that apartment again?"

"Four-two."

"Rolling."

A burglary past, couple of blocks down and to the south. No need for a detective on the scene. If it had been a 10-30, an armed robbery in progress, or even a 10-34, an assault in progress, he'd have responded along with the blues. He guessed. Sometimes it was better not to stick your nose into too many things. A 10-13— an assist officer—sure. Man called in for help, you got to the scene fast, *wherever* you were.

Ran uptown on the Stem for a couple of blocks, made a right turn at random, heading south toward the park. He'd swing onto Grover there, parallel the park for a while, then run north to the river, come back down Silvermine, take a run around the Oval, then back south on...

Up ahead.

Four teenagers.

Running into the building on the corner.

Just a glimpse of them.

Blue jeans and denim jackets.

Something in their hands.

Trouble?

Shit, he thought.

He eased the car over. No parking spaces on the street, he double-parked in front of the building and picked up the walkie-talkie.

"Eight-Seven," he said, "DD Four."

Calling home, identifying himself. One of the six unmarked sedans used by the Detective Division.

"Go ahead, Four."

"Genero," he said. "10-51, four in number, at 1217 North 11th."

"Stay in touch, Genero."

He'd identified the four teenagers as a roving band, a non-crime incident, and he hoped that was what it turned out to be. Getting out of the car, he pulled back the flap of his jacket and was clipping the walkie-talkie to his belt when a loud whooshing sound erupted from inside the building. He almost dropped the walkie-talkie. He looked up sharply. Flames! In the lobby there! And running out of the building, the four teenagers, one of them still carrying in his right hand what looked like a Molotov cocktail. Instinctively, Genero yelled, "Stop! Police!" and yanked his service revolver from its holster.

The kids hesitated for only a moment.

"Police!" he shouted again.

The one with the firebomb held a Zippo lighter to the wick and hurled the bottle at Genero.

The bottle crashed at his feet. Flames sprang up from the sidewalk. He threw both hands up to protect his face, and then immediately stepped back and brought his right hand down again, pistol level, firing into the wall of fire, through the wall of fire, two quick shots in succession.

Somebody screamed.

And suddenly they were on him. They jumped through the flames like circus performers, three of them hitting him almost simultaneously, knocking him to the pavement. He rolled away from the fire, tried to roll away from their kicks. He brought the gun hand up again, fired again, three shots gone now, heard someone grunt. Don't waste any, he thought, and one of them kicked him in the head. He went blank for an instant. His finger tightened reflexively on the trigger. The gun exploded wild, close to his own ear. He blinked his eyes. He was going. He fought unconsciousness. Someone kicked him in the shoulder, and the sharp pain rocketed into his brain and brought him back. Four shots gone, he thought. Make the next ones count. He rolled away again. He blinked them into focus. Only two of them on their feet now. The third one flat on his back near the entrance to the building. Fourth one lying on the sidewalk dangerously close to the fire. He'd hammered two of them, but there were still two to go, and only two shots left in the gun.

His heart was pounding.

But he took his time.

Waited till the lead kicker was almost on him, and then shot for his chest.

Second one right behind him, almost knocked off his feet when his buddy blew back into him. Genero fired again. Took the second one in the left shoulder, sent him spinning around and staggering back toward the wall of the building.

Genero could hardly breathe.

He got to his feet, fanned the empty gun at them.

Nobody seemed to be going anywhere.

He backed off a pace, pulled cartridges from his belt, loaded them into the cylinder, counting...four, five, six, and ready again.

"Move and you're dead," he whispered, and yanked the walkie-talkie from his belt.

Detective/3rd Grade Richard Genero had come of age on the eve of All Hallows' Day.

The school custodian who answered the night bell was the same one who'd locked Sebastian the Great's tricks in a storeroom earlier this afternoon. Peering through the grilled upper glass panel of the door at the back of the building, he recognized Hawes at once, unlocked the door, and let him in.

" 'Evening, Mr. Buono," Hawes said.

"Hey, how you doing?" Buono said.

He was a man in his late sixties, thinning gray hair, thin gray mustache over his upper lip. Pale blue eyes, somewhat bulbous nose. He was wearing coveralls. A flashlight was in one of the pockets. He clipped his ring of keys to a loop on the pocket.

"This is my partner, Detective Brown," Hawes said.

"Nice to meetcha," Buono said. "You come back for the stuff?"

"Well, no," Hawes said. "Few questions we'd like to ask you."

Buono immediately figured they knew he was stealing supplies from the classroom closets.

"Hey, sure," he said, and tried to look innocent. He locked the door behind them, and said, "Come on over the office, we can talk there. My friend and me were playing checkers."

They walked down a yellow-tiled, locker-lined corridor. They passed a wall clock that read twenty minutes past 10:00. They made a left turn. More students' lockers on either wall. A bulletin board. A poster reading:

COME CHEER THE TIGERS!
Saturday, Nov. 1, 2:00 P.M.
RAUCHER FIELD

To the right of that, another poster announcing:

SEBASTIAN THE GREAT!
HALLOWEEN MAGIC!
Auditorium. 4:00 P.M.

Beneath the lettering was a black-and-white photograph of a good-looking young man wearing a top hat and bow tie, grinning into the camera.

"Okay to take that poster?" Brown asked.

"Which one?" Buono said.

"The magician."

"Sure," Buono said, and shrugged.

Brown began pulling out the tacks.

"Come in handy, we find the head," he said to Hawes, and then folded the poster and put it in his inside jacket pocket.

Buono led them further down the hall, opened a door at the end of it. A sparsely furnished room. An upright locker, green in contrast to the reds, yellows, and oranges of the lockers in the halls. Long oak table, probably requisitioned from one of the administration offices. Four straight-backed chairs around it, checkerboard on one end of it. Coffeepot on a hot plate on one wall of the room, clock over it. Framed picture of Ronald Reagan on the wall opposite.

"This here's my friend, Sal Pasquali," Buono said.

Pasquali was in his late sixties, early seventies, wearing brown trousers, brown shoes and socks, a pale yellow sports shirt, and a brown sweater buttoned up the front. He looked like a candy store owner.

"These people here are detectives," Buono said, and looked at Pasquali, hoping he would understand what the look meant: Watch your onions about the chalk, and the paste, and the pencils, and the erasers, and the reams of paper.

Pasquali nodded sagely, like a Mafia don.

"Pleased to meetcha," he said.

"So," Buono said, "sit down. You want some coffee?"

"Thanks, no," Hawes said.

The detectives pulled out chairs and sat.

Buono could see Brown's gun in a shoulder holster under his jacket.

"We were just playing checkers here," Pasquali said.

"Who's winning?" Brown asked.

"Well, we don't play for money or nothing," Pasquali said.

Which meant that they did.

Brown suddenly wondered what these two old farts were hiding.

"I wanted to ask whether you saw anything that happened outside there this afternoon," Hawes said.

"Why?" Buono said at once. "Is something missing?"

"No, no. Missing? What do you mean?"

"Well, what do *you* mean?" Buono said, and glanced at Pasquali.

"I meant when the cars were being loaded."

"Oh."

"When Mr. Sebastiani was out there loading his tricks in the Citation."

"I didn't see him doing that," Buono said.

"You weren't out there after he finished the act, huh?"

"No. I didn't come on till four o'clock."

"Well, he'd have been out there around five-thirty."

"No, I didn't see him."

"Then you have no idea who might've dumped that stuff out of his car..."

"No idea at all."

"And driven off with it."

"No. Five-thirty, I was prolly down the north end of the building, starting with the classrooms there. I usually start cleaning the classrooms down the north end, it's like a routine, you know. Tradition."

"That's near the driveway, isn't it? The north end?"

"Yeah, the back of the building. But I didn't see anything out there. I mean, I *mighta* seen something if I was looking—there's windows in the classrooms, you know. But I wasn't looking for nothing. I was busy cleaning up the classrooms."

"You say you came on at four…"

"That's right. Four to midnight."

"Like us," Brown said, and smiled.

"Yeah?" Buono said. "Is that your shift? Whattya know? You hear this, Sal? They got shifts like us."

"What a coincidence," Pasquali said.

Brown still wondered what they were hiding.

"So you came on at four…" Hawes said.

"Yeah. Four to midnight. There's a man relieves me at midnight." He looked at the clock on the wall. "Be here in a few hours, well, less. But he's like just a watchman, you know."

"If you came on at four…"

"Yeah." A nod.

"Then you weren't here when the Sebastianis arrived, were you? They would've got here about a quarter after three. You weren't here then, is that right?"

"No. Sal was here."

Pasquali nodded.

"Sal works from eight to four," Buono said. "He's the *day* custodian."

"Shifts," Pasquali said. "Like you."

"He can't stay away from the place," Buono said. "Comes back to play checkers with me every night."

"I'm a widower," Pasquali explained, and shrugged.

"Did you see the cars when they arrived?" Brown asked him. "Tan Ford Econoline, blue Citation?"

"I seen one of them out there," Pasquali said. "But not when it came in."

"Which one did you see?"

"Little blue car."

"When was this? When you saw it?"

"Around...three-thirty, was it?"

"You asking me?" Buono said. "I wasn't here three-thirty."

"Three-thirty, it musta been," Pasquali said. "I remember I was heading out front, where the school buses come in. I usually go out there, talk to the drivers."

"They'd have been setting up the stage by then," Hawes said.

Brown nodded.

"And the van was already gone."

Brown nodded again.

"Did you see any people out there?" Hawes asked Pasquali. "Carrying things in? Unloading the cars?"

"All I saw was the one car."

"Blonde woman in her late twenties? Two men in their early thirties?"

"No," Pasquali said, and shook his head.

"Were the doors open?"

"What doors?"

"On the car."

"They looked closed to me."

"Anything lying in the driveway there?"

"Nothing I could see. What do you mean? Like what?"

"Tricks," Hawes said.

"Tricks?" Pasquali said, and looked at Buono.

"They done a magic show this afternoon," Buono said. "For the kids."

"Oh. No, I didn't see no tricks out there."

"You didn't happen to wander by that driveway later on, did you? Around five-thirty? When they were loading the—"

"Five-thirty I was home eating my dinner. I made a nice TV dinner for myself."

Hawes looked at Brown.

"Anything?" he asked.

Brown shook his head.

"Well, thanks a lot," Hawes said, and shoved back his chair.

"I'll let you out the building," Buono said.

The detectives followed him out of the office.

As soon as they were gone, Pasquali took out his handkerchief and mopped his brow.

At twenty minutes past 10:00, Larry's Bar was buzzing with activity.

Not a table empty. Not a stool unoccupied at the bar.

Eileen was sitting at one of the tables now, talking to a blonde hooker named Sheryl who was wearing a red skirt slit up one side, and a white silk blouse unbuttoned three buttons down. There was nothing under the blouse. Sheryl sat with her legs spread, her high heels hooked on the chair's top rung. Eileen could see track marks on her naked white thighs. She was telling Eileen how she'd come to this city from Baltimore, Maryland. Eileen was scanning the room, trying to figure out which one of these guys in here was her backup. Two waitresses, who could have passed for hookers themselves—short black skirts, high heels, overflowing white peasant blouses—were busily scooting back and forth between the tables and the bar, avoiding grabs at their asses.

"Got off the bus," the girl said, "first thing happens to me is this kindly old man asks can he help me with my valise. Had to be forty years old, am I right, a nice old man being friendly. Asks me have I got a place to stay, offers to get me a taxi to the Y, says 'I'll bet you're starving,' which I was, takes me to a hamburger joint, stuffs me with burgers and fries, tells me a nice young girl like me—I was only seventeen—had to be careful in the big, bad city, lots of people out there waiting to victimize me."

"Same old bullshit," Eileen said.

She figured there were only two men who could be Shanahan. Guy sitting there at one of the tables, talking up a hooker with frizzied brown hair, he had a hook nose that could've been a phony, black hair and blue eyes like Shanahan's, about his height and weight, wearing horn-rimmed eyeglasses. He could've been Shanahan.

"Well, sure, you know the story already," the girl said. "Mr. Nice turns out to be Big Daddy, takes me to his apartment, introduces me to two other girls living there, nice girls like me, he says, has me smoking pot that same night and shooting horse before the week is out. Turned me out two days later with a businessman from Ohio. Guy ast me to blow him, I didn't know what the fuck he meant. Man, that seems like ages ago."

"How old are you now?" Eileen asked.

"Twenty-two," Sheryl said. "I'm not with Lou no more…that was his name, Lou…I got me a new man, takes good care of me. Who you with?"

"Torpedo Holmes," Eileen said.

"Is he black, or what?"

"Black."

"Yeah, mine, too. Lou was white. I think the white ones are meaner, I really do. Lou used to beat the shit out of me. That first time, after the guy from Ohio, you know, where I didn't know

what to do, Lou beat me so I couldn't walk. Had a dozen of his
buddies come up the next morning, one after the other, twelve
of them, teach the little hayseed from Baltimore how to suck a
cock. Broke in my ass, too. That was when I *really* got turned out,
believe me. The guy from Ohio was child's play. In fact, everything after that night with Lou's buddies was child's play."

"Yeah, they can be rotten when they want to," Eileen said.

Guy sitting there talking to Annie was the other possibility,
though she doubted Shanahan would've made such obvious contact. Brown eyes, but those could be contacts if he was playing
this real fancy. Wearing a plaid jacket that made him look wider
than Shanahan. Sitting on a stool, so Eileen couldn't tell how tall
he was. But he was a possibility.

"This guy I got now…you know Ham Coleman?"

"I don't think so."

"Hamilton? Hamilton Coleman?"

"Yeah, maybe."

"Black as his name. Coal, you know. Coleman. Hung like a
stallion, likes to parade around the pad with only a towel around
him, dares the girls to snatch it off. Quick as a bullfighter. You
snatch off the towel, he gives you a little treat. My poison is still
hoss—well, you know, that's what Lou hooked me on. But some of
the girls—there's six of us with him—they dig the nose candy, and
he gets them whatever they need, good stuff too, I think he has
Colombian connections. It's like a game he plays with the towel,
snatch it off, suck his big dick, he lays the dope on you. I mean,
it's just a game, 'cause he keeps us supplied very nice, anyway. It's
kind of cute, though, the way he struts around in that towel. He's
really okay. Ham Coleman. You ever think of moving, you might
want to come over. We don't have any redheads. That your real
hair?"

"Yeah," Eileen said.

" 'Cause mine is straight from a bottle," Sheryl said, and laughed.

She still had a little-girl's laugh. Twenty-two years old, hooked on heroin, in the life since she was seventeen. Thought Ham Coleman with his towel was "kind of cute."

"What I'm really hoping for...well, this is just a *dream*, I know," she said, and rolled her eyes, "but I keep asking Ham about it all the time, who knows, it might really come true one day. I keep asking him to set us up like real call girls, you know, hundred-buck tricks, maybe two hundred, never mind dropping us here in the Zone where we're like common *whores,* you know what I mean? I mean, you and me, we're just common whores, ain't we? When you get right down to it?"

"Uh-huh. And what does he say?"

"Oh, he says we ain't got the class yet to be racehorses. I tell him class, shit. A blowjob's a blowjob. He says we still got a lot to learn, all six of us. He says maybe in time he'll set up a class operation like what I got in mind. So I tell him *when*? When we're all scaley-legged hookers, thirty, forty years old? Excuse me, I guess maybe you're in your thirties, I didn't mean no offense, Linda."

"Don't worry about it," Eileen said.

"Well, we all have our dreams, don't we?" Sheryl said, and sighed. "My dream when I first came to this city was I'd become an actress, you know? I was in a lot of plays in high school, in Baltimore, I figured I could make it big as an actress here. Well, that was just a dream. Like being a hundred-dollar call girl is probably just a dream, too. Still, you got to have dreams, am I right? Otherwise..."

"You girls gonna sit here talking to each other all night?"

The man standing by the table had padded up so quietly that he startled both of them. Blond guy, Eileen figured him at five-eleven, around 170 pounds, just like Shanahan. Wearing dark glasses, she couldn't see the color of his eyes. The blond hair could be a wig. Moved a bit like Shanahan, too, maybe he *was* Shanahan. If so, he'd just won the bet. One thing he wasn't was the killer. Not unless he'd lost three, four inches, thirty pounds, a pair of eyeglasses, and a tattoo near his right thumb.

He pulled out a chair.

"Martin Reilly," he said, and sat. "What's a nice Irish lad doing in a joint like this, right?"

Voice heavier than Shanahan's. Calm's Point accent. Turtle Bay section, most likely. Lots of Irish families still there.

"Hi, Morton," Sheryl said.

"Martin," he corrected at once.

"Ooops, sorry," Sheryl said. "I'm Sheryl, I know just how you feel. When people call me Shirley, it really burns my ass."

"You know what really burns my ass?" Reilly said.

"Sure. People calling you Morton."

"No," Reilly said. "A little fire about this high."

He held out his hand, palm down, to indicate a fire only high enough to burn a man's ass.

"That one has hair on it," Eileen said, looking bored.

"Like the palm of my hand," Reilly said, and grinned. "All those months at sea, ladies, a man marries his hand."

Still grinning. Rows of even white glistening teeth, the better to eat you with, my dear. If Shanahan had capped teeth like that, he'd be starring on *Hill Street Blues*.

"You just get in?" Sheryl asked.

"Docked tonight."

"From where?"

"Lebanon."

"Ain't there no girls there in Lebanon?" Sheryl said, and rolled her eyes.

"Not like you two," he said.

"Oooo, my," she said, and leaned over the table so he could look into the front of her blouse. "So what are you looking for?" she asked, getting straight to the point. "A handjob's fifteen," she said, quoting high, "a blowjob's twenty-five, and Miss Puss is forty."

"How about your friend here? What's your name, honey?" he asked, and put his hand on Eileen's thigh.

"Linda," she said.

She let his hand stay on her thigh.

"That means beautiful in Spanish."

"So they tell me."

"How much for both of you? Do I get a better price for both of you?"

"You're getting a bargain as it is," Sheryl said.

"Tell you what," Reilly said, and slipped his hand up under Eileen's skirt. "I'll give you…"

"Mister," Eileen said, and caught his hand at the wrist. "You ain't given us *nothing* yet, so don't grope the goods, okay?"

"I'm sampling it."

"You get what you see, you don't need samples. This ain't a grocery store honors coupons."

Reilly laughed. He folded his hands on the tabletop.

"Okay, let's talk numbers," he said.

"We're listening," Sheryl said, and glanced at Eileen.

"Fifty for the both of you," Reilly said. "Around the world."

"You talking fifty for *each* of us?" Sheryl said.

"I said *both* of you. Twenty-five each."

"No way," Sheryl said at once.

"Okay, make it *thirty* each. And you throw in a little entertainment."

"What kinda entertainment?" Sheryl asked.

"I wanna see you go down on the redhead here."

Sheryl looked at Eileen appraisingly.

"I hardly know her," she said.

"So? You'll get to know her."

Sheryl thought it over.

"Make it fifty apiece, we'll give you a good show," she said.

"That's too much," he said.

"Then fuck off," Sheryl said. "You're wasting our time here."

"I'll tell you what," Reilly said. "I'll make it forty apiece, how's that?"

"What are you?" Sheryl said. "A Lebanese rug merchant?"

Reilly laughed again.

"Forty-five," he said. "For each of you. And a ten-dollar bonus for whoever brings me off first."

"Count me out," Eileen said.

"What's the matter?" Reilly asked, looking offended. "That's a fair and honest deal."

"It really is, you know," Sheryl said.

"Sheryl can show you a good time all by herself," Eileen said, doing a fast tap dance. "I don't work doubles."

"Then what the fuck were we talking about here?" Reilly asked.

"You were doing all the talking," Eileen said. "I was only listening."

Reilly dismissed her at once.

"You got any other girlfriends in here?" he asked Sheryl.

"How about the frizzied brunette over there?" she said.

Reilly looked over to where the brunette was still in conversation with one of the other Shanahan possibilities.

"That's Gloria," Sheryl said. "I worked with her before."

"Is she a muff-diver?" Reilly said. "Or is she like your friend here?"

"She *loves* pussy," Sheryl said, lying. "You want me to talk to her?"

"Yeah, go talk to her."

"That's forty-five apiece," Sheryl said, cementing the deal, "and a ten-buck bonus." She was figuring they'd do a little show, then take turns blowing him, and share the extra ten for fifty each. Which wouldn't be bad for an hour's work. Maybe less than an hour if he'd been at sea as long as he'd said. "A hundred in all, right?"

"A hundred is what I said, ain't it?"

"It's just I have to tell Gloria," Sheryl said, and got up, long leg and thigh flashing in the slit skirt. "Don't go away, honey," she said, and walked over to the other table.

"You're in the wrong business," Reilly said to Eileen.

Maybe I am, Eileen thought.

There were four liquor stores on Culver Avenue between the last one hit on Twentieth, and the eastern edge of the precinct territory on Thirty-Fifth. After that, it was the neighboring precinct's problem, and welcome to it. They drove up Culver to the last store, and then doubled back to the one on Twenty-Third. The digital dashboard clock read 10:32 P.M.

The store was empty except for a man behind the counter who was slitting open a carton of Jack Daniels sour mash. He looked up when the bell over the door sounded, saw a burly bald-headed guy and another big guy with him, and immediately placed his hand on the stock of the shotgun under the counter.

"What'll it be, gents?" he asked.

Hand still on the shotgun stock, finger inside the trigger guard now.

Meyer flashed the potsy.

"Police," he said.

The hand under the counter relaxed.

"Detective Meyer," he said. "Detective Carella. 87th Squad."

"What's the problem?" the man said.

He was in his early fifties, not quite as bald as Meyer, but getting there. Brown eyes, slight build, wearing a gray cotton work jacket with the words ALAN'S WHISKIES stitched in red on the breast pocket.

"Who are we talking to, sir?" Meyer asked.

"I'm Alan Zuckerman."

"Is this your store, sir?"

"It is."

"Mr. Zuckerman," Carella said, "there've been three liquor-store holdups on Culver Avenue tonight. Starting on Ninth and working uptown. If there's a pattern—and there may not be—your store's next in line."

"I'm closing in half an hour," Zuckerman said, and turned to look at the clock on the wall behind the counter.

"They may come in before then," Meyer said.

"You don't know me, huh?" Zuckerman said.

"Should I know you?" Meyer said.

"Alan Zuckerman. I was in all the papers last year this time." He looked at Carella. "*You* don't know me, either, do you?"

"I'm sorry, sir, I don't."

"Some cops," Zuckerman said.

Meyer glanced at Carella.

"This very precinct, they don't know me."

"Why should we know you, sir?" Carella asked.

"Because last October I shot two people came in the store to rob me," Zuckerman said.

"Oh," Carella said.

"With *this*!" Zuckerman said, and yanked the shotgun from under the counter.

Both detectives backed away.

"*Bang*!" Zuckerman said, and Meyer flinched. "One of them falls on the floor screaming! *Bang,* the other barrel! And the second one goes down!"

"I seem to recall that now," Meyer said. "Mr. Zuckerman, you can put up the shotgun now, okay?"

"Made all the papers," Zuckerman said, the gun still in his hands, his finger inside the trigger guard. "Shotgun Zuckerman, they called me, the papers. They had the story on television, too. Nobody tried no tricks here since, I can tell you that. It's been a year already, a little more than a year."

"Well, these people tonight," Meyer said, "Mr. Zuckerman, could you please put up the gun?"

Zuckerman slid the gun under the counter again.

"Thank you," Meyer said. "These people tonight, there are four of them. All of them armed. So your shotgun there, if all four of them start shooting…"

"Shotgun Zuckerman can take care of them, don't worry."

"What we were thinking," Carella said, "is maybe we could lend you a hand."

"Sort of ride shotgun to your shotgun," Meyer said, nodding.

"Backups, sort of," Carella said.

"Only in case you need us."

"Otherwise we'll butt out."

Zuckerman looked at them.

"Listen," he said at last, "you want to waste your time, that's fine by me.

He yanked the phone from the receiver the moment it rang.

"Hello?" he said.

"Hi," Marie said.

"Where are you?"

"Metro West. I'm catching the ten forty-five home."

"How'd it go?"

"Tough night," she said. "Any trouble on your end?"

"Nope. They made identification, huh? I saw it on television."

"I was the one who made it. Where'd you leave the Citation?"

"Behind an A and P near the river."

" 'Cause I don't think they found it yet."

"Who's on the case?"

"A salt-and-pepper team. Brown and Hawes. Big redhead, big black guy. In case they come snooping."

"Why would they?"

"I'm saying in case. They're both dummies, but you oughta be warned. They got a bulletin out…they asked me for descriptions. They're gonna be watching all the airports. What flight are you on?"

"TWA's one twenty-nine. Leaves at twelve-oh-five tomorrow afternoon."

"What time do you get to Frisco?"

"Four forty-seven."

"I'll try you at the hotel around six-thirty. You'll be registered as Jack Gwynne, am I right?"

"All the dead ones," he said, and laughed. "Like Sebastian the Great."

"Give me the number of the Hong Kong flight again?"

"United eight-oh-five. Leaves Frisco at one-fifteen Sunday, gets there around eight the next morning."

"When will you call me?"

"Soon as I'm settled."

"You think that passport'll work?"

"It cost us four hundred bucks, it *better* work. Why? You running scared?"

"Nerves of steel," she said. "You shoulda seen me with the cops."

"No problem with the ID, was there?"

"None."

"You did mention the cock?"

"Oh, sure."

"Little birthmark and all?"

"Come on, we went over this a hundred times."

"*You* went over it a hundred times."

"And hated every minute of it."

"Sure."

"*You know* that, damn it."

"Sure."

"You going to start on me again?"

"I'm sorry."

"You oughta be. All we've been through."

"I said I was sorry."

"Okay."

There was a long silence on the line.

"So whattya gonna do till noon tomorrow?"

"Thought I'd go down for a drink, then come back and get some sleep."

"Be careful."

"Oh yeah."

"They know what you look like."

"Don't worry."

Another silence.

"Maybe you oughta call me later tonight, okay?"

"Sure."

"Be careful," she said again, and hung up.

"Torpedoman ain't gonna like this," Larry said.

"Who asked you?" Eileen said.

"For a working girl, all you done so far is sit and drink."

"Guess it just ain't my lucky night," Eileen said.

"Whattya talkin' about? I already seen you turn down a dozen guys."

"I'm particular."

"Then you shouldn't be in this dump," Larry said. "Particular ain't for the Canal Zone."

Eileen knew he was only pointing out the obvious: the name of the game was money, and a hooker working a bar wasn't a girl at the Spring Cotillion. You didn't tell a prospective John your card was filled, even if he looked like Godzilla. Larry was already suspicious, and that was dangerous. Get a few more guys giving her the fish eye, and she could easily blow the *real* reason she was here.

Sheryl and the frizzied brunette were still out with the blond sailor, but Eileen was ready to bet her shield they'd be back in business the moment they returned. There was no way any enterprising girl could avoid making a buck in here. The bar was in incessant motion, a whorehouse with a liquor license and a transient crowd. Any man who came in alone walked out not five minutes later with a girl on his arm. According to Shanahan, the girls—even some of them on the Canalside meat rack—used either a hot-bed hotel up the street or any one of fifty, sixty rooms for rent in the Zone. They usually paid five bucks for the room, got a kickback from the owner and also a share of the three bucks the John paid for soap and towels. That way, a twenty-dollar trick could net a girl the same twenty when all was said and done. Plus whatever tip a generous John might decide to lay on her for superior performance.

She glanced down the length of the bar to where Annie was sitting in earnest conversation with a little Hispanic guy wearing jeans, boots, and a black leather jacket studded with chrome. Looked like Annie was having the same problem. The only difference was that she could step outside every now and then, make it look like she was drumming up trade on the street. Eileen was glued to the bar. The bar was where the killer had picked up his three previous victims. She tried to catch Annie's eye. They had figured out beforehand that if they wanted to talk they'd do it in the ladies' room, not here in public. Eileen wanted to dope out a scam that would cool Larry's heat.

"Torpedoman's gonna whip your ass," he said.

"You wanna make a little side bet?" Eileen said. "You wanna bet I go home with six bills before the night's over?"

Annie finally looked over at her.

Eye contact.

Brief nod of her head.

Eileen got off the stool and started for the ladies' room. The
Hispanic guy sitting next to Annie got off his stool at the same
time. Good, Eileen thought, she's ditching him. But the Hispanic
guy walked straight toward her, meeting her halfway down the
bar.

"Hey, where you goin', Mama?" he said. Loud voice for a little
twerp, Spanish accent you could cut with a machete. Little brown
eyes, mustache under his nose, looked like an undernourished
biker in his leather jacket.

"Got to visit my grandma," Eileen said.

"You gran'ma can wait," he said.

Behind him, down the bar, Annie was watching them.

Another brief nod.

All right already, Eileen thought. As soon as I *shake* this guy.

The guy wasn't about to be shaken. He gripped Eileen's elbow
in his right hand, began steering her toward the stool she'd abandoned—"Come on, Mama, we ha' biss'niss to talk abou' "—same
loud voice, you could hear him clear across the river, fingers tight
on her elbow, plunked her down on the stool—"My name iss
Arturo, I been watchin' you, Mama"—and signaled to Larry.

"You want me to wet my pants?" Eileen asked.

"No, no, I sornly don' wann you to do that," he said.

Larry ambled over.

"See wha' my frien' here iss drinkin'," Arturo said.

She couldn't make a fuss about the ladies' room now, not with
Larry standing right here and already believing she was turning
down tricks left and right. Spot Annie trailing her in there, they'd
both be out of business.

"Larry knows what I'm drinking," she said.

"Rum-Coke for the lady," Larry said, "it's still prom night.
How about you, amigo?"

"Scotch on dee rahss," Arturo said. "Twiss."

Larry started pouring.

"So how much you get, Mama?" Arturo asked.

"What are you looking for?"

"This swee' li'l ting here," he said, and put his forefinger on her lips.

"That'll cost you twenty," she said.

Going price, in case Larry was listening. Which of course he was.

"You got someplace we can go, Mama?"

"Plenty of rooms for rent around here."

Everything kosher so far. But Larry was still here.

"How much do I pay for dee room?" Arturo asked.

"Five."

Larry raised his eyebrows. He knew the girls usually paid for the room themselves but he figured Linda here was hustling the little spic. Maybe she *would* go home with six bills tonight, who the hell knew?

"Muy bien, muchacha," Arturo said.

"Rum-Coke, scotch-rocks with a twist," Larry said, sliding the drinks closer to them. "Six bucks, a bargain."

Arturo put a ten-dollar bill on the counter. Larry started for the cash register at the far end. As soon as he was out of earshot, Arturo whispered, in perfect English, "I'm on the job, play along."

Eileen's eyes opened wide.

At the far end of the bar, Annie gave another brief nod. Larry rang open the register, put the ten in the drawer, took four bills out of it, slammed the drawer shut again, and then started back toward where they were sitting, sipping at their drinks now. Arturo had his hand on Eileen's knee, and he was peering down the front of her blouse. She was saying, " 'Cause like, you know, I'm a working girl, Artie, so I'd like to get started, if that's okay with you."

"Hey, no sweat, Mama," he said. "We can tay dee booze wid us."

"Not in *my* good glasses," Larry said, and immediately began transferring the drinks to plastic cups.

Eileen was already off the stool. She turned to Larry and said, "Glad you didn't take that bet?"

Larry shrugged.

He watched them as they picked up the cups and walked away from the bar. He was thinking he wouldn't mind a piece of that himself. As they started out the door, they almost collided with a man coming in at the same time.

"Oh, I beg your pardon," he said, and stepped aside to let them through.

Larry was sure he'd seen the guy before. He was at least six feet two inches tall, with wide shoulders and a broad chest, thick wrists, big hands. He was wearing jeans, sneakers, a little tan cap, and a yellow turtleneck sweater that matched the color of his hair. He looked like a heavyweight fighter in training.

"You're not *leaving*, are you?" he asked Eileen.

She breezed right past him, ignoring him.

But her heart was suddenly pounding.

Annie sat at the bar wearing a short tight black skirt, purple tube top cradling her cupcake breasts, high-heeled black patent leather shoes, face heavily pancaked, blood-red lipstick on her mouth, eyes lined in black, lids tinted to match the blouse, looking more like a hooker than any of the real ones in the place.

She thought, Terrific. Here he is.

All we need is this little trick of fate.

Eileen walking out while he walks in.

Eileen loaded to the gunnels, me wearing only a .38 in my handbag, terrific.

Eileen the decoy, me the backup, and in he walks.

Terrific.

If it's him.

He sure as hell looked like the blond guy Alvarez and
Shanahan had described. No eyeglasses, but the same height and
weight, the same bulk.

Standing just inside the doorway now, looking over the place,
cool, confident in his size, ready to take on any guy in the place,
mop up the floor with him, this cat had nothing to worry about,
oh no, handsome as the devil, oh so cool, scanning the room,
checking out the girls, then walking up toward the bar, passing
the cash register where she sat…

"Hi," she said. "Wanna join me?"

"Danny Ortiz," Arturo said on the street outside. "Detective/sec-
ond, Undercover Narcotics. I got a call from Lou…"

Lou, Eileen thought. Not Lou the friendly white man who'd
turned out Sheryl, if that was her real name. In novels, everybody
had different names so you could tell them apart. In real life, Lou
could be a pimp and a detective at the same time. Lou Alvarez of
the Seven-Two.

"…said I ought to check out Larry's Bar, see his decoy needed
some help. Described you and Rawles, sat with her, talked her
up, she told me the Johns were hitting on you like locusts. Am I
screwing anything up?"

Lou Alvarez, calling his buddy Danny Ortiz in Narcotics,
asking him to run on over here, hit on the decoy, take her out of
the joint to preserve her credibility.

"You saved my life," Eileen said.

Bit of an exaggeration, but at least he'd saved her cover.

"So you wanna neck or anything?" Ortiz said. "Pass the
time?"

"That's the best offer I've had all night," she said. "But I gotta get back in there."

Ortiz looked at her.

"Our man just walked in," she said.

His size was intimidating. He filled the stool, filled the bar, seemed to fill the entire room. Sitting next to him, Annie was scared. If this was the guy...

"So what's your name?" she asked.

"What's yours?"

"Jenny," she said.

"I'll bet."

Deep voice rumbling up out of his barrel chest.

"Well," she said, "my straight handle is Antoinette Le Fevrier, but who'll believe that on a hooker?"

"Oh, is that what you are?" he asked.

Voice almost toneless. Bored attitude. Looking in the mirror, checking out the other girls in the place even as he talked to her.

"No, I'm a famous brain surgeon," Annie said, and smiled.

He did not smile back. Turned to look at her. Eyes the color of steel. A chill ran up her spine. Where the hell was Shanahan?

"You still didn't tell me your name," she said.

"Howie," he said.

Sounded square enough to be true.

"Howie what?"

"Howie's enough," he said, and folded his hands on the tabletop. No tattoo on either one of them. Was he, or wasn't he? "So what you do is make love to strangers, huh?" he said. "For money."

She didn't want this guy to ask her outside. Not with only the .38 in her bag and Shanahan nowhere in sight.

"That's my job. You interested?"

"You're not my type," he said.

"Oh? And what's your type?" she asked. Keep him talking. Keep him interested till Eileen walked back in. And if Eileen *didn't* walk in soon, then talk him into taking *her* outside to make his move. If Shanahan was anywhere around, he'd be tracking both of them.

"I like them younger," he said. "And fresher."

"Well, what you see is what you get," she said.

"You seem too far gone."

"Uh-huh," she said, "practically ancient." One of the dead girls had been sixteen. The others were in their twenties. Keep him here, she thought. Don't let him wander off to any of the younger girls in here, or they'll drift away together and he'll score another one tonight.

"I mean, what can I tell you?" she said. "I'm not a teenager, but I'm pretty good for an old lady."

He turned to look at her again.

No smile.

Christ, he was chilling.

"Really?" he said.

"Really."

Come-on look in her eyes. She licked her lips. But she had only the .38 in her bag. No backup artillery. And Shanahan God knew where. Ortiz heading back home soon as he cleared Eileen, wham, bam, thank you, ma'am, or so it would appear to Larry.

"Ten for a handjob," she said, "how about it? Twenty for a blowjob, thirty if you want the pearly gates."

"My, my," he said. "You really are a seasoned pro, aren't you?"

"Exactly what I am," she said. "How about it?"

"No, you're too far gone," he said.

Eyes on the mirror again. The blonde who'd been talking with Eileen earlier was back now, together with her frizzied brunette friend. Both of them young and looking for more action. His eyes checked them out. Stick with me, pal, she thought. Here's where the action is.

"Are you a cop?" he asked without even looking at her.

Mind-reader, she thought.

"Sure," she said. "Are you a cop, too?"

"I used to be," he said.

Oh, shit, she thought. A renegade. Or a malcontent.

"I can always tell a cop," he said.

"You wanna see my badge?" she said.

Deliberately using the word badge. A cop called it a shield.

"Are you with Vice?" he asked.

"Oh, man, *am* I," she said. "Clear down to my tonsils."

"I used to be with Vice," he said.

"So *I'm* the one who caught myself a cop, huh?" she said, and smiled. "Well, Howie, that makes no difference to me at all, the past is the past, all water under the bridge. What do you say we take a little stroll up the street, I'll show you a real good—"

"Get lost," he said.

"Let's get lost together, Howie," she said, and put her hand on his thigh.

"You understand English?" he said.

"French, too," she said. "Come on, Howie, give a working girl a—"

"Get *lost!*" he said.

A command this time.

Eyes blazing, big hands clenched on the bar top.

"Sure," she said. "Relax."

She got off the stool.

"Relax, okay?" she said, and walked down to the other end of the bar. Inexplicably, her palms were wet.

Guy sitting next to him at the bar was running a tab, $20 bill tucked under the little bowl of salted peanuts. Big flashy Texan sporting a diamond pinky ring, a shirt as loud as he himself was, and a black string tie held with one of those turquoise-and-silver Indian clasps. He was drinking martinis, and talking about soybeans. Said soybeans were the nation's future. No cholesterol in soybeans.

"So what do *you* do?" he asked.

"I'm in insurance."

Which wasn't too far from the truth. Soon as Marie made the insurance claim…

"Lots of money in insurance," the Texan said.

"For sure."

At double indemnity, the policy came to 200 grand. More money than he could make in eight years' time.

"By the way, my name's Abner Phipps," the Texan said, and extended a meaty hand.

He took the hand. "Theo Hardeen," he said.

"Nice to meet you, Theo. You gonna be in town long?"

"Leaving tomorrow."

"I'm stuck here all through next week," Phipps said. "I hate this city, I truly do. There're people who say it's a nice place to visit, but I can't even see it for that. Worth your life just walkin' the streets here. You see that thing on television tonight?"

"What thing is that?"

The black bartender was listening silently, standing some six feet away from them, polishing glasses. The clock on the wall read ten to 11:00. Shows'd be breaking soon, he wanted to be ready for the crowd.

"Somebody chopping up a body, leaving pieces of it all over town," Phipps said, and shook his head. "Bad enough you *kill* somebody, you got to chop him up in pieces afterward? Why you suppose he did that, Theo?"

"Well, I'll tell you, Abner, there're all kinds of nuts in this world."

"I mean, there're two rivers in this city, Theo. Why didn't he just throw the whole damn *body* in one of them?"

That's where the head is, he thought. And the hands.

"Still," Phipps said, "if you got a body to get rid of, I guess it's easier to dump in sections. I mean, somebody sees you hauling a corpse around, that might raise suspicion, even in *this* city. An arm, a head, whatever, you can just drop in a garbage can or down the sewer, nobody'll pay any attention to you, am I right, Theo?"

"I guess maybe that's why he did it."

"Well, who can figure the criminal mind?" Phipps said.

"Not me, that's for sure. I have a hard enough time selling insurance."

"Oh, I'll bet," Phipps said. "You know why? Nobody likes to think he's gonna kick off one day. You sit there tellin' him how his wife's gonna be sittin' pretty once he's dead, he don't want to hear that. He wants to think he's gonna live forever. I don't care *how* responsible a man he is, it makes him uncomfortable talkin' about death benefits."

"You hit it right on the head, Abner. I talk myself blue in the face, and half the time they're not even listening. Explain, explain, explain, they don't know what the hell I'm talking about."

"People just don't listen anymore," Phipps said.

"Or they don't listen carefully enough. They hear only what they want to hear."

"That's for sure, Theo."

"I'll give you an example," he said, and then immediately thought, Come on, he's too easy. On the other hand, it might teach him a valuable lesson. Chatting up a stranger in a bar, no real sense of how many con artists were loose and on the prowl in this city. Teach him something he could take back home to Horse's Neck, Texas.

He reached into his pocket, took out a dime and a nickel.

"What have I got here?" he asked.

"Fifteen cents," Phipps said.

"Okay, open your hand."

Phipps opened his hand.

"Now I'm putting this dime and this nickel on the palm of your hand."

"Yep, I see that, Theo."

"And I'm not touching them anymore, they're in your hand now, am I right?"

"Right there on the palm of my hand, Theo."

"Now close your hand on them."

Phipps closed his hand. The bartender was watching now.

"You've got that fifteen cents in your fist now, am I right?"

"Still there," Phipps said.

"A dime and a nickel."

"A dime and a nickel, right."

"And I haven't touched them since you closed your hand on them, right?"

"You haven't touched them, right."

"Okay, I'll bet you when you open your hand, one of them won't be a dime."

"Come on, Theo, you're lookin' to lose money."

"Man's lookin' to lose money for sure," the bartender said.

"I'll bet you the twenty dollars under that peanut bowl, okay?"

"You got a bet," Phipps said.

"Okay, open your hand."

Phipps opened his hand. Fifteen cents still on his palm. Same dime, same nickel. The bartender shook his head.

"You lose," Phipps said.

"No, I win. What I said—"

"The bet was that one of these coins wouldn't be a dime no more."

"No, you weren't listening. The bet was that one of them wouldn't be a dime."

"That's just what—"

"And one of them isn't. One of them's a nickel."

He slid the twenty-dollar bill from under the peanut bowl, and tucked it into his jacket pocket. "You can keep the fifteen cents," he said, and smiled and walked out of the bar.

The bartender said, "That's a good trick to know, man."

Phipps was still looking at the fifteen cents on the palm of his hand.

Genero was a celebrity.

And he was learning that a celebrity is expected to answer a lot of questions. Especially if he shot four teenagers. There were two people waiting to ask questions now. One was a roving investigative reporter from Channel 6. The other was a Duty Captain named Vince Annunziato, who was filling in for the Eight-Seven's Captain Frick. The reporter was interested only in a sensational news story. Annunziato was interested only in protecting the Department. He stood by silently and gravely while the reporter set up the interview; one sure way to get the media dumping on cops was to act like you had something to hide.

"This is Mick Stapleton," the reporter said, "at the scene of a shooting on North Eleventh Street, here in Isola. I'm talking to Detective/Third Grade Richard Genero, who not forty-five minutes ago shot four teenagers who allegedly started a fire in the apartment building behind me."

Annunziato caught the "allegedly." Protecting his ass in case this thing blew up to something like the Goetz shootings in New York. Guy with a hand-held camera aimed at Stapleton, another guy working some kind of sound equipment, third guy handling lights, you'd think they were shooting a Spielberg movie instead of a two-minute television spot. Crowds behind the police barriers. Ambulances already here and gone, carting away the four teenagers. Annunziato was happy they weren't black.

"Detective Genero, can you tell us what happened here?" Stapleton asked.

Genero blinked into the lights, looked at the red light on the front of the camera.

"I was making a routine tour of the sector," he said. "This is Halloween night and the lieutenant put on extra men to handle any problems that might arise in the precinct."

So far, so good, Annunziato thought. Care and caution on the part of the commanding officer, concern for the citizenry.

"So you were driving past the building here…"

"Yes, and I saw the perpetrators running into the premises with objects in their hands."

"What kind of objects?" Stapleton asked.

Careful, Annunziato thought.

"What turned out to be firebombs," Genero said.

"But you didn't know that at the time, did you?"

"All I knew was a roving band running into a building."

"And this seemed suspicious to you?"

"Yes, sir."

"Suspicious enough for you to draw your gun and…?"

"I did not unholster my revolver until fire broke out in the premises."

Good, Annunziato thought. Felony in progress, reason to yank the piece.

"But when you first saw these youngsters, you didn't know they were carrying firebombs, did you?"

"I found out when the fires went off inside there, and they came running out."

"What did you do then?"

"I drew my service revolver, announced that I was a policeman and warned them to stop."

"And did they stop?"

"No, sir, they threw one of the firebombs at me."

"Is that when you shot at them?"

"Yes, sir. When they ignored my warnings and came at me."

Good, Annunziato thought. Proper procedure all the way down the line. Firearm used as a defensive weapon, not a tool of apprehension.

"When you say they came at you…"

"They attacked me. Knocked me over and kicked me."

"Were they armed?"

Careful, Annunziato thought.

"I did not see any weapons except the firebombs. But they had just committed a felony, and they were attacking me."

"So you shot them."

"As a last resort."

Perfect, Annunziato thought.

"Thank you, Detective Genero. For Channel Six News, this is Mick Stapleton on Eleventh Street."

With the edge of his hand, Stapleton made a throat-slitting gesture to his cameraman, and a brief "Thanks, that was swell" to Genero, and then walked quickly to where the mobile van was waiting at the curb.

Annunziato came over to where Genero was standing, looking surprised that it was over so fast.

"Captain Annunziato," he said. "I've got the duty."

"Yes, sir," Genero said.

"You handled that okay," Annunziato said.

"Thank you, sir."

"Handled *yourself* okay with them four punks, too."

"Thank you, sir."

"But you better call home now, tell 'em we're taking you off the street."

"Sir?"

"Few questions we'll have to ask you downtown. Make sure we get all the facts before the bleeding hearts come out of the woodwork."

"Yes, sir," Genero said.

He was thinking the goddamn shift would be relieved at a quarter to twelve, but he'd be downtown answering questions all night.

Train speeding through the night now, leaving behind the mills and factories just over the river, coming into rolling green land where you could see the lights of houses twinkling like it was Christmas instead of Halloween.

By Christmas they'd be sitting fat and pretty in India someplace.

Person could live on 10¢ a day in India—well, that was an exaggeration. But you could rent yourself a luxurious villa, staff it with all the servants you needed, live like royalty on just the interest the $200,000 would bring. New names, new lives for both of them. Never mind trying to live on the peanuts Frank had earned each year.

She sighed heavily.

She'd have to call his mother as soon as she got home, and then his sister, and then she guessed some of his friends in the business. Had to get in touch with that detective again, find out when she could claim the body, arrange for some kind of funeral, have to keep the casket closed, of course, she wondered how soon that would be. Today was Friday, she didn't know whether they did autopsies on the weekend, probably wouldn't get around to it till Monday morning. Maybe she could have the body by Tuesday, but she'd better call an undertaker first thing in the morning, make sure they could handle it. Figure a day in the funeral home—well, two days, she guessed—bury him on Thursday morning. She'd have to find a cemetery that had available plots, whatever you called them, maybe the undertaker would know about that. Had to have a stone cut, too, HERE LIES FRANK SEBASTIANI, REST IN PEACE—but that could wait, there was no hurry about a stone.

She'd call the insurance company on Friday morning.

Tell them her husband had been murdered.

Make her claim.

She didn't expect any problems. Sensational case like this one? Already on television and in one of the early morning papers she'd bought at the terminal. MAGICIAN MURDERED, the headline read. Bigger headline than he'd ever had in his life. Had to get himself killed to get it.

$200,000, she thought.

Invest it at 10 percent, that'd bring them $20,000 a year, more than enough to live on like a king and queen. A maharajah and maharanee was more like it. Go to the beach every day, have someone doing the cleaning and the cooking, have a man polishing the car and doing the marketing, buy herself a dozen saris, learn how to wrap them, maybe get herself a little diamond for her nose. Even at 8 percent, the money would bring in $16,000 a year. More than enough.

And all they'd had to do for it was kill him.

The train rumbled through the night, lulling her to sleep.

He approached Eileen almost the moment she sat down at one of the tables.

"Hi," he said. "Remember me?"

No eyeglasses, no tattoo, but otherwise their man down to his socks. The eyeglasses he'd worn on his earlier outings could have been windowpane. The tattoo could have been a decal. Her heart was beating wildly. She didn't realize until this moment just how frightened she really was. You're a *cop*, she told herself. *Am* I? she wondered.

"I'm sorry," she said, "have we met?"

"Mind if I sit down?"

"Please do."

The prim and proper hooker.

But crossed her legs anyway, to show him thigh clear to Cincinnati.

"I'm Linda," she said. "Are you looking for a good time?"

"That depends," he said.

"On what?"

"On what you consider a good time."

"That's entirely up to you."

"I noticed you when I was coming in," he said. "You were leaving with a little Puerto Rican."

"You're very observant," she said.

"You're a beautiful woman, how could I miss you?"

"What's your name?" she asked.

"Howie."

"Howie what?"

"Howie gonna keep 'em down on the farm."

He had them in stitches. Shanahan's words. Kept telling them jokes. A stand-up comic with a knife.

"So what're you interested in, Howie?"

"Let's talk," he said.

"Candy store's open," she said. "You want to know how much the goodies cost?"

"Not right now."

"Just say when, Howie."

He folded his hands on the tabletop. Looked into her eyes.

"How long have you been hooking, Linda?"

"First time tonight," she said. "In fact, I'm a virgin."

Not a smile. Not even the *hint* of a smile. Some stand-up comic. Just sat there looking into her eyes, big hands folded on the table.

"How old are you?"

"You should never ask a woman her age, Howie."

"Early thirties, in there?"

"Who knows?" she said, and rolled her eyes.

"What's your real name?"

"What's yours?"

"I told you. Howie."

"But you didn't tell me Howie what."

"Howie Cantrell," he said.

"Eileen Burke," she said.

The name would mean nothing to him. If he was their man, he'd learn soon enough who Eileen Burke was. If he was looking for action, her name wouldn't mean beans to him.

"Why are you using Linda?" he asked.

"I hate the name Eileen," she said. Which wasn't true. She'd always thought the name Eileen was perfect for the person she was. "Linda sounds more glamorous."

"You're glamorous enough," he said, "you don't need a phony name. May I call you Eileen?"

"You can call me Lassie if you like."

Still no smile. Totally devoid of a sense of humor. So where was the comedian? Flat, steel-gray eyes reflecting nothing. But were they the eyes of a triple murderer?

"So where're you from, Howie?"

"I'll ask the questions," he said.

"Now you sound like a cop."

"I used to be one."

Bullshit, she thought.

"Oh?" she said. "Where?"

"Philadelphia," he said. "Do you see that girl sitting at the bar?"

"Which one?" Eileen asked.

"In the black skirt. With the short dark hair."

He was indicating Annie.

"What about her?"

"I think she's a cop," he said.

Eileen burst out laughing.

"Jenny?" she said. "You've got to be kidding."

"You know her?"

"She's been hooking since she was thirteen. Jenny a cop? Wait'll I tell her!"

"I already told her."

"Mister, let me tell *you* something about hookers and cops, okay?"

"I know all about hookers and cops."

"Right, you're a cop yourself."

"*Used* to be one," he said. "I can always tell a cop."

"Have it your way," she said. "Jenny's a cop, you're a cop, I'm a cop, when you're in love the whole world's a cop."

"You don't believe I used to be a cop, do you?"

"Howie, I'll believe anything you tell me. You tell me you used to be a Presbyterian minister, I'll believe you. An astronaut, a spy, a…"

"I was with the Vice Squad in Philly."

"So what happened? Didn't you like the work?"

"It was good work."

"So how come you ain't doing it no more?"

"They fired me."

"Why?"

"Who knows?" he said, and shrugged.

"Can't stay away from the job, though, huh?"

"What does that mean?"

"Well, here you are, Howie."

"Just thought I'd drop by."

"You been here before?"

First leading question she'd asked him.

"Couple of times."

"Guess you like it, huh?"

"It's okay."

"Come on, Howie, tell me the truth." Teasing him now. "You really dig the girls here, don't you?"

"They're okay. Some of them."

"Which ones?"

"Some of them. Lots of these girls, you know, they're in this against their will, you know."

"Oh, sure."

"I mean, they were forced into it, you know."

"You sure you were a Vice cop, Howie?"

"Yes."

"I mean, you sound almost *human*."

"Well, it's true, you know. A lot of these girls would get out of it if they knew how."

"Tell me the secret. How do I get out of it, Howie?"

"There are ways."

A big, wiry, gray-haired guy walked over from the bar. Had to be in his mid-fifties, grizzled look, sailor's swagger. Wearing jeans and white sneakers, blue T-shirt, gold crucifix hanging on a chain outside the shirt, metal-buttoned denim jacket open over it. Right arm in a plaster cast and a sling. Shaggy gray eyebrows, knife scar angling downward through the right brow and partially closing the right eye. Brown eyes. Thick nose broken more than once. Blue watch cap tilted onto the back of his head. Shock of gray hair hanging on his forehead. He pulled out a chair, sat, and said, "Buzz off, Preacher."

Howie looked at him.

"Buzz off, I wanna talk to the lady."

"Hey mister," Eileen said, "we're—"

"You hear me, Preacher? Move!"

Howie shoved back his chair. He glared angrily at the guy with the broken arm, and then walked across the bar and out into the street. Annie was already up and after him.

"Thanks a lot," Eileen said. "You just cost me—"

"Shanahan," he said.

She looked at him.

"Put your hand on my knee, talk nice."

The midgets came in at a minute before 11:00.

Shotgun Zuckerman was ready to close the store.

They came in yelling "Trick or treat!"

Alice opened fire at once.

("It was us taking all the risk," she said at the Q & A later. "Never mind what Quentin told us. If anybody pegged us for little people, we were finished. It was better to kill them. Easier, too.")

Zuckerman didn't even have a chance to reach for the shotgun. He went down dead in the first volley.

Meyer and Carella broke out of the stockroom the moment they heard the bell over the door sound. By the time they came through the curtain shielding the front of the store from the back, Zuckerman was already dead.

In the station wagon outside, the blonde began honking the horn.

"Police!" Meyer shouted, and Alice opened up with a second volley.

This wasn't a cops-and-robbers movie, this was real life.

Neither of the detectives got off a shot.

Meyer went down with a bullet through his arm and another through his shoulder.

Carella went down with a bullet in his chest.

No tricks. Real blood. Real pain.

Three of the midgets ran out of the store without even glancing at the cash register. The only reason Alice ran out after them, without first killing the two cops on the floor, was that she thought there might be more cops in the place.

This came out during the Q & A at ten minutes past 2:00 on the morning of All Hallows' Day.

The more Parker presented himself as a *fake* cop, the more he began feeling like a *real* cop. Everybody at the party kept telling him he could pass for a detective anywhere in the city. Everybody told him his shield and his gun, a .38 Smith & Wesson Detective Special, looked very authentic. One of the women—a sassy brunette dressed as a Las Vegas cigarette girl, in a flared black skirt and a flimsy top, high-heeled black shoes, and seamed silk stockings—wanted to hold the gun but he told her cops didn't allow straights to handle dangerous weapons. He had deliberately used police jargon for "honest citizens." In this city, a straight was anyone victimized by a thief. In some cities, victims were called "civilians." In any city, a thief was anyone who wasn't a cop, a straight, or a civilian. To the cops in this city, most thieves were "cheap" thieves.

A homosexual wearing a blond wig, a long purple gown, and amethyst earrings to match, objected to the use of the word "straight" to describe an honest citizen. The homosexual, who said he was dressed as Marilyn Monroe, told Parker that all the *gays* he knew were also honest citizens. Parker apologized for his use of police terminology. "But, you see," he said, "I ain't a *real* cop." And yet he felt like one. For the first time in as long as he could remember, he felt like a bona fide detective on the world's finest police force.

It was peculiar.

Even more peculiar was the fact that he was having such a good time.

Peaches Muldoon had a lot to do with that.

She was the life of the party, and some of her exuberance and vitality rubbed off on Parker. She told everyone stories about what it was like growing up as a victim on a sharecropper's farm in Tennessee. She told them incest was a way of life on the farm. Told them her first sexual experience was with her father. Told them her *brother's* first sexual experience—other than with the sheep who was his steady girlfriend—had been with his sister Peaches Muldoon one rainy afternoon when they were alone together in the house. She told everyone that she'd enjoyed her brother more than she had her father. Everyone laughed. They all thought she was making up victim stories. Only Parker knew that the stories were true; she'd told him ten years earlier that her priest-killing son was the bastard child of her relationship with her brother.

The stories Peaches told encouraged Parker to tell some stories of his own. Everyone thought he was making them up, the way Peaches had made up her stories about the *Tobacco Road* dirt farm. He told them the story about the woman who'd cut off her husband's penis with a straight razor. He said, "I substituted the word penis for cock, because I didn't want to offend anybody here who might be a vigilante for the Meese Commission." Everyone laughed at the story and also at his comment about the Meese Commission. Somebody wondered out loud if the attorney general considered it pornographic that the unauthorized sale of arms to Iran had provided unauthorized funds for Nicaraguan rebels.

This was straying into intellectual territory beyond Parker's scope.

He laughed, anyway.

Pornography was something he dealt with on a daily basis, and he believed straights ought to keep their noses out of it, period. Complicated and illegal arms deals were something else, and he never wondered about them except as they might effect his line of work. When you dealt with cheap thieves day and night, you already knew that they weren't only in the streets but also in the highest reaches of government. He didn't say this to anyone here at the party because he was having too good a time, and he didn't want to get too serious about cause and effect. He didn't even think of it consciously as cause and effect. But he knew, for example, that when a star athlete was exposed as a coke addict, the kids playing pickup ball in the school yard thought, "Hey, I gotta try me some of that shit." He also knew that when somebody high up in government broke the law, then your punk dealing grams of crack in the street could justify his actions by saying, "See? *Everybody* breaks the law." Cause and effect. It only made Parker's job harder. Which was maybe why he didn't work too hard at the job anymore. Although tonight, *playing* at the job, he felt as if he was working harder at it than he had in years.

It was really very peculiar.

He told everybody that one day he was going to write a book about his experiences.

"Ah-ha!" somebody said, "you're a *writer*!"

"No, no, I'm a cop," he protested.

"So how come you want to be a writer?" someone else said.

" 'Cause I ain't got the guts to be a burglar," Parker said, and everyone laughed again.

He'd never realized he was so witty.

At a little after 11:00, Peaches suggested that they move on to another party.

Which is how Parker got to meet the wheelman and one of the midgets on the liquor-store holdups.

There were a lot of things bothering Brown about the Sebastiani case.

The three most important things were the head and the hands. He kept wondering why they hadn't turned up yet. He kept wondering where Jimmy Brayne had dropped them.

He also wondered where Brayne was right now.

The blues from the Two-Three, armed with the BOLO that had gone out all over the city, had located the blue Citation in the parking lot of an A & P not far from the River Dix. The techs had crawled over the car like ants, lifting latent prints, collecting stain samples, vacuuming for hairs and fibers. Anything they'd got had already been bagged and sent to the lab for comparison with whatever had been recovered from the Econoline van. Brown had no illusions about the lab getting back to them before sometime Monday. Meanwhile, both cars had been dumped—which left Brayne without wheels. His last location had been in the 23rd, where he'd dropped the Citation, way over on the south side of the city. Was he now holed up somewhere in that precinct? Had he cabbed east, west, or north to a hotel someplace else? Or was he already on an airplane, bus, or train heading for parts unknown?

All of this bothered Brown.

He also wondered why Brayne had killed his mentor and employer.

"You think they're making it?" he asked Hawes.

"Who?"

"Brayne and the woman."

"Marie?"

The possibility had never occurred to Hawes. She had seemed so honestly grieved by her husband's disappearance and death. But now that Brown had mentioned it—

"I mean, what I'm looking for is some motive here," Brown said.

"The guy could've just gone berserk, you know. Threw those tricks all over the driveway, ran off in the Citation…"

"Yeah, I'm curious about that, too," Brown said. "Let's try to dope out a timetable, okay? They come into the city together, Brayne in the van, Marie and her husband in the Citation…"

"Got to the school around a quarter past three."

"Unloaded the car and the van…"

"Right."

"And then Brayne went off God knows where, said he'd be back at five, five-thirty to pick up the big stuff."

"Uh-huh."

"Okay, they finish the act around five-fifteen. Sebastiani changes into his street clothes, goes out back to load the car while Marie's getting out of her costume. She comes out later, finds the stuff all over the driveway and the Citation gone."

"Right."

"So we got to figure Brayne dumped the van on Rachel Street sometime between three-thirty and five-fifteen, grabbed a taxi back to the school, and cold-cocked Sebastiani while he was loading the car."

"That's what it looks like," Hawes said.

"Then he chops up the body—where'd he do that, Cotton? Blood stains in the Citation's trunk, you know, but nowhere else in the car."

"Coulda done it anywhere in the city. Found himself a deserted street, an abandoned building…"

"Yeah, you could do that in this city. So he chops up the corpse, loads the pieces in the trunk, and starts dropping them all around town. When he gets rid of the last one, he leaves the car behind that A and P and takes off."

"Yeah."

"So where's the motive?"

"I don't know."

"She's an attractive woman," Brown said.

Hawes had noticed that.

"If she was playing house with Brayne in that apartment over the garage…"

"Well, you've got no reason to believe that, Artie."

"I'm snowballing it, Cotton. Let's say they had a thing going. Brayne and the woman."

"Okay."

"And let's say hubby tipped to it."

"You're thinking movies or television."

"I'm thinking real life, too. Hubby tells Brayne to lay off, Brayne's still hungry for her. He chops up hubby, and him and the woman ride off into the sunset."

"Except Brayne's the only one who rode off," Hawes said. "The woman's—"

"You think she's home yet?" Brown asked, and looked up at the clock.

Ten minutes past 11:00.

"Half hour or so to Collinsworth," Hawes said. "She was catching the ten forty-five."

"Whyn't we take a ride out there?" Brown said.

"What for?"

"Toss that apartment over the garage, see we can't find something."

"Like what?"

"Like maybe where Brayne's heading. Or better yet, something that links him to the woman."

"We'll need a warrant to toss that garage."

"We haven't even got jurisdiction across the river," Brown said. "Let's play it by ear, okay? If the lady's clean, she won't ask for a warrant."

"You want to call her first?"

"What for?" Brown said. "I love surprises."

Kling waved so long to them as they headed out of the squadroom. He looked up at the clock. The graveyard shift should be here in half an hour or so—O'Brien, Delgado, Fujiwara, and Willis. Fill them in on what had gone down on the four-to-midnight, grab one of the sedans, and head for Calm's Point. Make himself invisible in the Zone, just another John looking for a little Friday-night sport. But keep an eye out for Eileen.

He thought she was dead wrong about this one.

His being there in the Zone could only help an undercover situation that had been hastily planned and recklessly undermanned.

This time, *he* was the one who was dead wrong.

They sat at the table talking in whispers, just another hooker and a potential trick. Negotiating the deal, Larry figured. Never seen the guy with the broken arm in here before, wondered who'd be on top in the sack, might get a little clumsy with that arm in a sling. Wondered about that and nothing else. The place was still busy, there was booze to be poured.

"Howie Cantrell is his real name," Shanahan whispered. "Used to be with Vice in Philly, that's all straight goods. Went off his rocker six years ago, first started beating up hookers in the street, then began preaching salvation to them. The Philly PD didn't so much mind the beatings. Worse things than beatings go down in Vice. But they didn't like the idea of a plainclothes minister on the force. They sent him up for psychiatric, and the shrinks decided he was under considerable stress as a result of his proximity to the ladies of the night. Retired him with full pension, he drifted first to Boston, then here, started his missionary work all over again in the Zone. Everybody calls him the Preacher. He looks for the young ones, spouts Jesus to them, tries to talk them out of the life. Takes one of them to bed every now and then, for old times' sake. But he's harmless. Hasn't raised a hand to anybody since Philly let him go."

"I thought he was our man," Eileen said.

"We did, too, at first. Dragged him in right after the first murder, questioned him up and down, but he was clean as a whistle. Talked to him again after the second one, and again after the third. Alibi's a mile long. We shoulda warned you about him. Be easy to make the mistake you made. How's it going otherwise?"

"I almost lost my virginity, but Alvarez bailed me out."

"Who'd he send?"

"Guy named Ortiz. Narcotics."

"Good man. Looks eighteen, don't he? He's almost thirty."

"You coulda told me I'd have help."

"We're just full of tricks," Shanahan said, and smiled.

"You gonna plant yourself in here?" Eileen asked.

"Nope. I'll be outside. Watching, waiting."

"Who grizzled up your hair?" she asked.

"The Chameleon," he said, and grinned.

"I hope you can *see* through that eye."

"I can see just fine."

"And I hope our man doesn't want to arm wrestle," she said, glancing at the cast.

Across the room, Annie was coming back into the bar. She walked to where Larry was standing, put four dollars on the bar top and said, "Your end, pal."

"Why, thank you, honey," he said, "much obliged," and tucked the bills into his shirt pocket, figuring the four represented twenty percent of whatever she'd got for her last trick. I *do* love an honest hooker, he thought, and immediately wondered if she'd short-changed him.

Annie wandered over to where Eileen and Shanahan were sitting.

"Your blond friend went home," she said. "Caught a bus on the corner."

"That's okay," Eileen said, "I'm still waiting for Mr. Right."

Annie nodded, and then walked over to a table on the other side of the room. She wasn't alone for more than a minute when a big black guy sat down next to her.

"She needs help," Eileen whispered.

"Bring her outside," Shanahan said, and then rose immediately and said in a voice loud enough for everyone in the bar to hear, "I'll see you around the corner, honey."

Eileen went over to Annie and the black man.

"I got a one-armed bandit waiting in a car around the corner," she said. "He's looking for a hands-on trio, me driving, him in the middle, both of us dancing his meat around the block. You interested in a dime for ten minutes' work?"

"Dimes add up," Annie said, and immediately got to her feet.

"Hurry on back, hear?" the black man said.

"I did not appreciate all the shooting," Quentin Forbes said, looking petulant. He was still wearing the dress, pantyhose, and low-heeled walking shoes he'd worn while driving the station wagon, but the long blond wig was hooked over the arm of a ladder-backed wooden chair. "There was no need for such violence, Alice. I warned you repeatedly…"

"It was only insurance," she said, and shrugged.

"The costumes were all the insurance we—"

"The costumes were bullshit," Alice said.

She was a beautiful little blonde woman in her late thirties, blue eyes and a Cupid's-bow mouth, perfect legs and breasts, four feet two inches tall and weighing a curvaceous seventy-one pounds. In the circus, she was billed as Tiny Alice. This went over big with homosexual men. She had changed out of the clown costume they'd worn on the last two holdups, and was now wearing a dark green dress and high-heeled pumps. To Forbes, she looked wildly sexual.

"Did you want the cops to think three *separate* gangs of kids were holding up those stores?" she asked.

"I wanted to confuse the cops, was all," Forbes said. "If you want to know what *I* think, Alice, I think your shooting spree was what brought them down on us, is what I think."

"We should have finished them off," she said. "If you hadn't started honking the horn…"

"I honked the horn to warn you. The moment I saw them coming from the back room…"

"We should have finished them off," she said again, and took a tube of lipstick from her handbag and went to the mirror on the wall.

"The point of the costumes," Forbes insisted, "was to—"

"The point was you wanted to put on a dress," Alice said. "I think you enjoy being in drag."

"I do indeed," Forbes said. "First time I've been in a woman's pants in more than a month."

"Braggart," Corky said.

She was slightly taller than Alice, a bad failing for a midget, but she was prettier in a delicate, small-boned, almost Oriental way. She, too, had changed into street clothes, a black skirt and a white silk blouse, a pink cardigan sweater, high-heeled patent leather pumps. She looked like a tiny, young Debbie Reynolds.

The two men who'd been in on the holdups were sitting at the table, still wearing their clown suits, counting the money.

"That's five thousand here," one of them said.

High Munchkin voice, wearing glasses, brown eyes intent behind them. His name was Willie. In the circus, he was billed as Wee Willie Winkie. Next month, he'd be down in Venice, Florida, rehearsing for the season. Tonight he was helping to stack and count the money from four stickups—well, *three* actually, since they hadn't got anything but cops on the last one. The stickups had been Forbes's idea, but Corky was the one who talked Willie into going along, said it'd be a good way to pick up some quick off-season change. Corky was his wife, and Alice was her best friend. This made Willie nervous. Alice was the only one who'd shot anyone tonight. The others had all fired their pistols well over the heads of the store owners, the way Forbes had told them to.

"What we should do," Willie said to the other man at the table, "we should both of us count each stack."

His hands were sweating. He was still very nervous about this whole thing. He was sure the police would come breaking in here any minute. All because of Alice. He had never heard of a midget doing time in prison. Or getting the electric chair. He did not want to be the first one in history.

"Can I trust you little crooks to give me a true count?" Forbes asked.

"You can help count it, you want to," the other man at the table said.

He was older than the other midgets, shorter and more delicate than even the women. His name was Oliver. In the circus, he was billed as Oliver Twist. He never understood why. He had red hair and blue eyes, and he was single, which was just the way he wanted it. Oliver was a great ladies' man. Full-sized women loved to pick him up and carry him to bed. Full-sized women considered him too darling for words, and they were never threatened by his tiny erect pecker. Full-sized women were always amazed that they could swallow him to the hilt without gagging. In some ways, being a midget had its benefits.

"Here's another five," Willie said, and slid the stack to Oliver, who began riffling the bills like a casino dealer.

"My rough estimate," Forbes said, "is we took in something like forty thousand."

"I think that's high," Alice said.

Standing at the mirror, putting on her lipstick. Lips puckered to accept the bright red paint, pretty as a little doll. Forbes had tried making her last year when they were playing the Garden in New York. She'd turned him down cold, said he would break her in half, although he knew she was sleeping with half the Flying Dutchmen. Corky watched her intently, as if hoping to pick up some makeup tricks.

"Twelve, thirteen thousand each store," Forbes said, "that's what I figure. Thirty-five, forty thousand dollars."

"There wasn't any thirteen in that store with the lady owner," Oliver said.

He was the one who'd cleaned out the register after Alice shot that lady in the third store. They weren't supposed to talk in the stores, but he'd yelled, "Hold it *open*, Alice!" because Alice's hands were trembling, and the bag was shaking as if there was a snake in it trying to get out.

"Mark my words, forty," Forbes said.

"Here's another five," Willie said.

"Fifteen already," Forbes said. "Mark my words."

Turned out, when all was said and done, that there was only $32,000.

"What'd I tell you?" Alice said.

"Somebody must be skimming," Forbes said, and winked at her.

"What does that come to?" Corky asked. "Five into thirty-two?"

"Something like sixty grand apiece," Oliver said.

"You *wish*," Alice said.

"Six, I mean."

Willie was already doing the long division on a scrap of paper.

"Six-four," he said.

"Which ain't bad for a night's work," Forbes said.

"We should've finished those cops," Alice said idly, blotting her lipstick with a piece of Kleenex. Willie shivered. He looked at his wife. Corky was staring at Alice's mouth, a look of idolatrous adoration on her face. Willie shivered again.

"What I'm gonna do right now," Forbes said, "is get out of this dress, and put on my own clothes, and then I'm gonna go partying. Alice? You wanna come along?"

She looked him up and down as if seeing him for the first time.

Then she shrugged and said, "Sure. Why not?"

She called her mother-in-law the moment she was in the house.

The place felt empty without him.

"Mom," she said. "This is Marie."

Crackling on the line to Atlanta.

"Honey," her mother-in-law said, "this is a *terrible* connection, can you get the operator to ring it again?"

Terrific, she thought. I'm calling to tell her Frank is dead, and she can't hear me.

"I'll try again," she said, and hung up, and then dialed the operator and asked her to place the call. Her mother-in-law picked up on the second ring.

"How's that?" Marie asked her.

"Oh, much better. I was just about to call *you*, this must be psychic." Susan Sebastiani believed in psychic phenomena. Whenever she held a séance in her house, she claimed to converse with Frank's father, who'd been dead and gone for twenty years. Frank's father had been a magician, like his son. "What it is," she said, "I had this terrible premonition that something was wrong. I said to myself, 'Susan, you'd better call the kids.' Are you okay? Is everything all right?"

"Well…no," Marie said.

"What's the matter?" Susan said.

"Mom…"

How to tell her?

"Mom…this is very bad news."

"What is it?"

"Mom…Frank…"

"Oh, my God, something's happened to him," Susan said at once. "I knew it."

Silence on the line.

"Marie?"

"Yes, Mom."

"What happened? Tell me."

"Mom…he's…Mom, he's dead."

"What? Oh, my God, my God, oh, dear God," she said, and began weeping.

Marie waited.

"Mom?"

"Yes, I'm here."

"I'm sorry, Mom. I wish I wasn't the one who had to tell you."

"Where are you?"

"Home."

"I'll come up as soon as I can. I'll call the airlines, find out when there's...what happened? Was it an automobile accident?"

"No, Mom. He was murdered."

"What?"

"Someone..."

"What? *Who?* What are you talking about? Murdered?"

"We don't know yet, Mom. Someone..."

She couldn't bring herself to tell his mother that someone had chopped up his body. That could wait.

"Someone killed him," she said. "After a show we did this afternoon. At a high school up here."

"Who?"

"We don't know yet. The police think it might have been Jimmy."

"Jimmy? Jimmy Brayne? Who Frank was teaching?"

"Yes, Mom."

"I can't believe it. Jimmy?"

"That's what they think."

"Well, where is he? Have they questioned him?"

"They're still looking for him, Mom."

"Oh, God, this is terrible," Susan said, and began weeping again. "Why would he do such a thing? Frank treated him like a brother."

"We both did," Marie said.

"Have you called Dolores yet?"

"No, you're the first one I—"

"She'll have a heart attack," Susan said. "You'd better let me tell her."

"I can't ask you to do that, Mom."

"She's my daughter, I'll do it," Susan said.

Still weeping.

"I'll tell her to come there right away, you'll need help."

"Thank you, Mom."

"What is it from her house? An hour?"

"Tops."

"I'll tell her to get right there. Are you okay?"

"No, Mom," she said, and her voice broke. "I feel terrible."

"I know, I know, sweetie, but be brave. I'll come up as soon as I can. Meanwhile, Dolores will be there. Oh, my God, so many people I'll have to call, relatives, friends…when is the funeral going to be? They'll want to know."

"Well…they'll be doing an autopsy first."

"What do you mean? Chopping him up?"

Silence on the line.

"You didn't give them permission to do that, did you?"

Opportunity right there to tell her he was *already* chopped up. She let the opportunity pass.

"They have to do an autopsy in a murder case," she said.

"Why?"

"I don't know why, it's the law."

"Some law," Susan said.

Both women fell silent.

Susan sighed heavily.

"All right," she said, "let me call Dolores, let me get to work. She'll be there in a little while, will you be okay till then?"

"I'll be fine."

Another silence.

"I know how much you loved him," Susan said.

"I did, Mom."

"I know, I know."

Another sigh.

"All right, honey, I'll talk to you later. I'll try to get a plane tonight if I can. You're not alone, Marie. Dolores will be right there, and I'll be up as soon as I can."

"Thank you, Mom."

"All right now," Susan said, "I have to go now. Call me if you need me."

"Yes, Mom."

"Good night now, honey."

"Good night, Mom."

There was a small click on the line. Marie put the receiver back on the cradle. She looked up at the clock on the kitchen wall. Only forty minutes left to what had been the longest day of her life.

The clock ticked noisily into the stillness of the empty house.

The clock on the hospital wall read twenty-five minutes past 11:00.

Lieutenant Peter Byrnes had not yet called the wives. He would have to call the wives. Speak to Teddy and Sarah, tell them what had happened. He was standing in the corridor with Deputy Police Commissioner Howard Brill, who'd come uptown when he'd heard that two detectives had been shot in a liquor-store stakeout. Brill was a black man in his early fifties; Byrnes had known him when they were both walking beats in Riverhead. About the same size as Byrnes, same compact head and intelligent eyes; the men could have been cast from the identical bullet mold, except that one was black and the other was white. Brill was upset; Byrnes could understand why.

"The media's gonna have a ball," Brill said. "Did you see this?"

He showed Byrnes the front page of one of the morning tabloids. The headline looked as if it had been written for a sensational rag that sold at the local supermarket. But instead of MARTIAN IMPREGNATES CAMEL or HITLER REINCARNATED AS IOWA HOUSEWIFE, this one read:

MIDGETS 2—COPS 0 POLICE CAUGHT SHORT

"Very funny," Byrnes said. "I got one cop in intensive care, and another one in surgery, and they're making jokes."

"How are they?" Brill asked.

"Meyer's okay. Carella…" He shook his head. "The bullet's still inside him. They're digging for it now."

"What caliber?"

".22. That's according to the slugs we recovered in the store. Meyer took two hits, but the bullets passed through."

"He was lucky," Brill said. "They're worse than a goddamn .45, those low-caliber guns. Hit a man where there's real meat, the bullet hasn't got the force to exit. Ricochets around inside there like it's bouncing off furniture."

"Yeah," Byrnes said, and nodded bleakly.

"Lot of shooting tonight," Brill said. "You'd think it was the Fourth of July, 'stead of Halloween. Your man clean on that other one?"

"I hope so," Byrnes said.

"Four teenagers, Pete, the media *loves* kids getting shot. What's the report on their condition?"

"I haven't checked it. I ran over here the minute…"

"Sure, I understand."

Byrnes guessed he should have checked on those kids before he'd come over here—not that he really cared *how* they were, except as their condition reflected on his squad. On his block, if you were looking for trouble with a cop, you should be happy you found it. But if Genero had pulled his gun without prudent care and reasonable cause, and if one of those punks died, or worse yet ended up a vegetable...

"How smart is he?" Brill asked.

"Not very."

" 'Cause they'll be coming at him, you know."

"I realize that."

"Where is he now?"

"Still downtown. I think. I really don't know, Howie. I'm sorry, but when I heard about Meyer and Carella..."

"Sure, I understand," Brill said again.

He was wondering which of the incidents would cause the Department the biggest headache. A dumb cop shooting four kids, or two dumb cops getting shot by midgets.

"Midgets," he said aloud.

"Yeah," Byrnes said.

Tricky, he thought.

I know that.

Coming back to the same bar a fourth time.

But that's part of the fun.

Look the same, act the same, makes it more exciting that way. Big blond guy is who they're looking for, so Heeeeeere's *Johnny*, folks! No description in the newspapers yet, but that's the cops playing it tricky, too.

Tricks all around, he thought.

Suits me fine.

By now they're thinking psycho.

Some guy who once had a traumatic experience with a hooker. Hates all hookers, is systematically eliminating them.

They ought to boot up their computer, check with Kansas City. In Kansas City, it was only two of them. Well, when you're just starting, you start small, right? In Chicago, it was three. Good night, folks! Do my little song and dance in each city, listen to the newspaper and television applause, take my bow, and shuffle off to Buffalo. Slit their throats, carve up their pussies, the cops *have* to be thinking psycho. I'll do four of them here, he thought, and then move on. Two, three, four, a nice gradual escalation.

Let the cops think psycho.

A psycho acts compulsively, hears voices inside his head, thinks someone's commanding him to do what he's doing. Me, I never hear voices except when I'm listening to my Sony Walkman. Comedians. Walk along with the earphones on, listen to their jokes. Woody Allen, Bob Newhart, Bill Cosby, Henny Youngman…

Take my wife. Please.

For our anniversary, my wife said she wanted to go someplace she'd never been. I said, How about the kitchen?

My wife wanted a mink coat, and I wanted a new car. We compromised. I bought her a mink coat and we keep it in the garage.

Walk along, listen to the comics, laugh out loud, people probably think I'm nuts. Who cares? There isn't anyone *commanding* me to kill these girls—

Ooops, excuse me, I beg your parmigiana. Mustn't get the feminists on my back, they'd be worse to deal with than cops. Next city, maybe I'll do five. Get five of them and then move on. Two, three, four, five, nice arithmetical progression. Keep moving, keep having fun, just the way Mother wanted it. What's the sense of life if you can't enjoy it? Live a little, laugh a little, that's the thing. These women—got it right that time, Ms. Steinem—are *fun* to do.

Try to dope *that* one out, officers.

Keep on looking for a psycho, go ahead.

When all you're dealing with is somebody as sane as Sunday.

Larry's Bar.

Welcome home, he thought, and opened the door.

"What'll it be?" Larry asked him.

"This guy comes into a bar, has a little monkey on his shoulder."

"Huh?" Larry said.

"This is a joke," he said. "The bartender asks him 'What'll it be?' The guys says, 'Scotch on the rocks,' and the monkey says, 'Same for me.' The bartender looks at both of them and says, 'What are you, a ventriloquist?' The monkey says, 'Were my lips moving?' "

"That's a joke, huh?" Larry said.

"Gin and tonic," he said, and shrugged.

"How about your monkey?"

"My monkey's driving," he said.

Larry blinked.

"That's another joke."

"Oh," Larry said, and looked at him. "You been in here before?"

"Nope. First time."

" 'Cause you look familiar."

"People tell me I look like Robert Redford."

"Now *that's* a joke," Larry said, and put the drink in front of him. "Gin and tonic, three bucks, a bargain."

He paid for the drink, sat sipping it, eyes on the mirror.

"Nice crop tonight, huh?" Larry said.

"Maybe."

"What are you looking for? We had a Chinese girl in here ten minutes ago. You dig Orientals?"

"This samurai comes home from the wars," he said.

"Is this another joke?"

"His servant meets him at the gate, tells him his wife's been making it with a black man. The samurai runs upstairs, breaks down the bedroom door, yanks out his sword, yells, 'Whassa this I hear, you make it with a brack man?' His wife says, 'Where you hear such honkie jive?' "

"I don't get it," Larry said.

"I guess you had to be there."

"Where?"

"Forget it."

"We got some nice black girls in here tonight, if that's what you're lookin' for."

Larry was thinking about his 20 percent commission. Drum up a little trade here.

"This old man goes into a whorehouse…"

"This ain't a whorehouse," Larry said defensively.

"This is another joke. Old guy, ninety-five years old. He tells the madam he's looking for a blowjob. The guy's so frail he can hardly stand up. The madam says, 'Come on, mister, you've had it.' He says, 'I have? How much do I owe you?' "

"Now *that's* funny," Larry said.

"I know a hundred jokes about old people."

"*That* funny, it wasn't."

"This old guy is sitting on a park bench, crying his heart out. Another guy sits next to him, says—"

"Hi."

He turned.

A good-looking blonde girl was sitting on the stool next to his.

"My name's Sheryl," she said. "Wanna party?"

The minute he saw her, he knew she was going to be more fun than any of the others. Something in her eyes. Something in her smile. Something in the way she plumped her cute little bottom down on the bar stool, and crossed her legs, and propped one elbow on the bar, and her chin on her hand, and looked him mischievously in the eye—a fun girl, he could tell that at once.

"Well, well, well, hello, Sheryl," he said.

"Well, well, well, hello to you," she said.

"Barkeep," he said, "see what the lady'll have."

"Barkeep, I love that," Sheryl said.

A fun girl. He knew it.

"So what'll it be?" he asked.

"What are *you* drinking?"

"Gin and tonic."

"I'll have the same," she said.

"A gin and tonic for the lady," he said to Larry, and then immediately, "This guy walks into a bar…"

"You already told this one," Larry said.

"This is another one. Guy walks into a bar, says, 'See that cat over there?' Everybody looks at the cat. Big tomcat with an enormous tail. The guys says, 'I'll bet any man in the house my penis is longer than that cat's tail.' Everybody wants to bet him. Hundred-dollar bills come out all over the place. The guy says to the bartender—"

"Gin and tonic," Larry said, "three bucks, a bargain."

"You should learn not to interrupt a story," he said.

"Tell 'im," Sheryl said.

"The guy says to the bartender, 'Okay, measure us.' So the bartender takes out a tape measure, goes over to the cat, measures the cat's tail, and says, 'Fourteen inches.' The guy nods and says, 'Okay, now measure my penis.' The bartender measures the penis. 'Eight inches,' he says. 'You lose.' The guy looks at him. 'Excuse me,' he says, 'but exactly *how* did you measure that cat's tail?' The bartender says, 'I put one end of the tape against his asshole and the other end…' and the guy says, 'Would you mind showing me the same consideration?' "

Sheryl burst out laughing.

Larry said, "I don't get it. You owe me three bucks."

He paid for the drink. Sheryl was still laughing.

A fun girl.

"What's your name?" she asked.

"Robert Redford," he said, which wasn't too far from the truth in that his first name really was Robert.

"I believe you," she said, and winked at Larry. "What do people call you? Rob? Bob? Bobby?"

"Bobby," he said, which was absolutely the truth.

"And how does *your* tail measure up against that cat's, Bobby?"

"Want to find out?" he said.

"Oooo, yes," Sheryl said, and rolled her eyes.

"Think that might be fun, huh?" he said.

"I think it'd be *loads* of fun," she said. "I'll tell you what I get, Bobby. A handjob's—"

"Not yet," he said.

"Well, you see, Bobby, I'm a working girl. So whereas there's nothing I'd enjoy more than sitting here all night with you…"

He put a $20 bill on the bar top.

"Let's say we're running a tab," he said.

"You mean you and me? Or you and Larry?"

"You and me. The twenty's yours. It buys twenty minutes, a dollar a minute. We'll talk about renewing the option when the meter runs out. How's that sound, Sheryl?"

"No problem," she said, and scooped up the bill.

"Four bucks of that is mine," Larry said, and held out his hand. Sheryl made a face, but she gave him the $20, and watched him as he walked down to the cash register to make change.

"So where you from, Bobby?" she asked.

"Most recently? Chicago. Before that, Kansas City."

Playing it recklessly. Those were the two cities exactly. But that's what made this so exciting. Playing the game for the ultimate risk.

Larry was back with her change. "Here's your sixteen," he said, handing her three $5s and a $1.

"You take out a fourteen-inch whanger in here," she said, "Larry'll want twenty percent of it."

"I never yet seen nobody with a fourteen-incher," Larry said.

"You been looking?" she asked, and winked at Bobby and put the bills into her handbag. "What Larry does, he checks out the men's room for fourteen-inchers."

"This soldier is in the men's room taking a shower," Bobby said. "All the other guys in his company—"

"Is this another one?" Larry said.

"I thought I told you not to interrupt my stories," Bobby said.

"Stories like yours—"

"Be quiet," he said.

He spoke the words very softly.

Larry looked at him.

"Do you understand?" he said. "When I'm telling a story, be quiet."

Larry looked into his eyes.

Then he shrugged and walked to the other end of the bar.

"Serves him right," Sheryl said. "Let me hear the story, Bobby."

"This soldier is taking a shower. All the other guys in his company are crowded around the stall, looking in at him, craning for a look at him. That's because the guy has a penis that's only an inch long. Finally, the guy can't take it anymore. He turns to them and yells, 'What's the matter? You never seen anybody with a hard-on before?'"

Sheryl burst out laughing again.

From the other end of the bar, Larry grimaced sourly, and said, "Very funny."

"So which one are you, Bobby?" Sheryl asked. "The fourteen-incher or the inch-long wonder?"

"I thought we weren't going to hurry," he said.

"Listen, it's your money," Sheryl said. "Take all the time you need."

"I mean, I thought we were having fun here," he said.

"We are," she said.

"I mean, isn't this fun?"

"I love your stories, Bobby," she said.

"You're a fun girl," he said. "I can tell that."

"That's what I've been told, Bobby."

"I mean, I'll bet you like to do new and exciting things, don't you?"

"Oh, sure," she said. "I even did it with a police dog once."

"That's not what I meant. I meant *new* things. Exciting things."

"Well, to me that was new. Six guys watching while I did it with a police dog? That was new."

"It may have been new, but I'll bet it wasn't exciting," Bobby said.

"Well, I have to admit, when the dog went down on me that was sort of exciting. He had like this very raspy tongue, you know? Like sandpaper. I guess you could say that was sort of exciting. I mean, once you got past the idea of him being a *dog*, which was disgusting, of course."

"Sheryl," he said, "I think you're terrific, I really do. We're going to have a lot of fun together, you'll see."

"Oh, I'm sure."

"We're going to do some new and very exciting things."

"I can hardly wait," she said.

"Lots of laughs," he said.

"I already find you very funny," she said.

"This midget goes into a men's room," he said. "And there's a guy standing there at one of the…"

This second party was even better than the first one had been.

Parker was having the time of his life.

At the first party, he'd got drunk enough to believe he was really a writer passing himself off as a cop who only wanted to be a writer. At this party, he didn't tell anyone he was a cop because no one was in costume here, it wasn't that kind of a party. But even without the masquerade, he was having a marvelous time. Maybe because there were all sorts of interesting people here, most of

them women. Or maybe because these interesting women all
found *him* interesting.

This was very amazing to him.

He thought he was just being his usual shitty self.

It turned out that the woman whose apartment they were
in was celebrating her sixty-third birthday tonight, which was
why there was a party in the first place, never mind Halloween.
Her name was Sandra, and she was the one Peaches had been
expecting a call from earlier tonight, which was the only reason
she'd answered the phone after that heavy-breathing creep got off
the line. Sandra was her next-to-best friend; her best friend was
the woman who'd thrown the costume party. Still, Peaches liked
Sandra a lot, especially because she never expected a present on
her birthday. She was a bit surprised, therefore, and somewhat
annoyed, when Parker flatly and rudely expressed the opinion
that no one over the age of sixty should be asked to blow out all
the candles on a birthday cake in a single breath. And she was
even more surprised when Sandra burst out laughing and said,
"Oh, baby, how true! Who the hell needs such a humiliating stress
test?"

Everyone laughed. Even Peaches.

Sandra then blew out all the candles in a single breath, and
pinched Parker on the behind and asked him if he'd like the candles on *his* cake blown. "Out," she added.

Everyone laughed. Except Peaches.

A little later on, encouraged by the attention a lot of these very
interesting women were paying to ideas he'd never even known
he'd had, Parker ventured a bit closer to home and suggested to a
lady trial lawyer that *anyone* committing a murder was at least a
little bit crazy and that therefore the "legal insanity" defense was
meaningless. The lady lawyer said, "That's very interesting, Andy.
I had a case last week where…"

It was astonishing.

Parker said to a woman wearing horn-rimmed eyeglasses and no bra that he found pornographic movies more honest than any of the nighttime soaps on television, and the woman turned out to be a film critic who encouraged him to expand upon the idea.

Parker told a woman writer—a *real* writer—that he never spent more than five pages with any book if he wasn't hooked by then, and the woman expounded upon the importance of a book's opening and closing paragraphs, to which Parker said, "Sure, it's like foreplay and after-play," and the woman writer put her hand on his arm and laughed robustly, which Peaches did not find at all amusing.

Peaches, in fact, was becoming more and more irritated by the fact that Sandra had invited her to a party where the women outnumbered the men by an approximate two-to-one and where Parker was suddenly the center of all this female attention. She had liked it better when they were a couple pretending to be a cop and a victim. They were *sharing* something then. Now Parker seemed to be stepping out on his own, the small-time flamenco dancer who'd been offered a movie contract provided he ditched his fat lady partner. This miffed Peaches because for Christ's sake she was the one who'd introduced him to show biz in the first place!

When the female midget walked in at twenty-five minutes to 12:00, Peaches immediately checked out the man with her. Burly guy going a bit bald, but with a pleasant craggy face, and a seemingly gentle manner. Five-ten or -eleven, she guessed, merry blue eyes, nice speaking voice now that she heard him wishing Sandra a happy birthday. Sandra took their coats and wandered off, muttering something about mingling. Peaches moved in fast before the other sharks smelled blood on the water. She introduced herself to the man and the midget—

"Hi, I'm Peaches Muldoon."

"Quentin Forbes. Alice—"

—and then took the man's arm before he could finish the midget's name, and said, "Come on, I'll get you a drink," and sailed off with him, leaving the midget standing there by the door looking forlornly and shyly into the room.

Parker had never seen a more beautiful woman in his life.

He went over to her at once.

"Small world," he said.

And to his enormous surprise—the night was full of surprises—she burst out laughing, and said, "I feel like a fire hydrant waiting for an engine company. Where's the bar?"

Hal Willis came into the squadroom at twenty minutes to midnight. The teams usually relieved at a quarter to the hour, and so he was early—which was a surprise. Nowadays, ever since he'd taken up with Marilyn Hollis, he was invariably late. And rumpled-looking. He was rumpled-looking tonight, too, giving the impression of a man who'd leaped out of bed and into his trousers not five minutes earlier.

"Getting a bit brisk out there," he said.

He was wearing a short car coat over slacks and a sports jacket, no tie, the top button of his shirt unbuttoned. At five feet eight inches tall, he was the shortest man on the squad—even shorter than Fujiwara, who was of Japanese descent—but Willis knew judo and karate, and he'd fooled many a cheap thief who'd figured him for a pushover. He took off the coat and hung it on the coatrack, glanced idly at the bulletin board, and then looked at the duty chart to see who'd be sharing the shift with him. He moved like a man underwater nowadays. Kling attributed his eternal weariness to Marilyn Hollis. Eileen said Marilyn Hollis was poison. Maybe she was right. Kling looked up at the clock.

"Let me fill you in," he said.

He told Willis about the four teenagers Genero had shot.

"Genero?" Willis said, amazed.

He told Willis about the four midgets who'd held up a series of liquor stores.

"Midgets?" Willis said, amazed.

He told Willis that Carella and Meyer had taken three bullets between them and were both at Buenavista Hospital.

"You going over there?" Willis asked.

"Maybe later. I have to run out to Calm's Point."

He looked up at the clock again.

"Brown and Hawes caught a homicide," he said, "all the paperwork is on Brown's desk. There's a picture of the victim, too, a magician. They found him in four separate pieces."

"Four pieces?" Willis said, amazed.

"There's a number you can reach them at in Collinsworth, case anything breaks. They got an all-points out on a guy named Jimmy Brayne."

"Good evening, gentlemen," O'Brien said from the slatted rail divider, and then pushed his way through the gate into the squadroom. "Winter's on the way." He was indeed dressed for winter, wearing a heavy overcoat and a muffler, which he took off now and carried to the coatrack. Willis wasn't happy to be partnered with O'Brien. O'Brien was a hard-luck cop. You went on a call with O'Brien, somebody was bound to get shot. This wasn't O'Brien's fault. Some cops simply attracted the lunatics with guns. On Christmas Day, not too long ago—well, not too long ago by *precinct* time, where sometimes an hour seemed an eternity—O'Brien and Meyer had stopped to check out a man changing a flat tire on a moving van. A moving van? Working on Christmas Day? The man turned out to be a burglar named Michael Addison, who'd just cleaned out half a dozen houses in

Smoke Rise. Addison shot Meyer twice in the leg. Brown later dubbed the burglar Addison and Steal. This was pretty funny, but the bullets in Meyer's leg weren't. Willis—and everyone else on the squad—was convinced Meyer had got himself shot only because he'd been partnered with O'Brien. Still, he'd been shot again tonight, hadn't he? And he'd been working with Carella. Maybe in this line of work, there were bullets waiting out there with your name on them. In any event, Willis wished O'Brien was home in bed, instead of here in the squadroom with him.

"Steve and Meyer took a couple, did you hear?" he said.

"What are you talking about?"

"Some midgets shot them," Kling said.

"Come on, midgets," O'Brien said.

Kling looked up at the clock again.

"I'll be checking out a car," he said to no one.

"You want a cup of coffee?" O'Brien asked Willis.

It was only fifteen minutes before the beginning of All Hallows' Day.

In the Roman Catholic and Anglican churches, the first day of November is a feast day upon which the church glorifies God for all his saints, known or unknown. The word "hallow" derives from the Middle English *halowen,* further derived from the Old English *hālgian,* and it means "to make or set apart as holy; to sanctify; to consecrate." All Hallows' Day and Hallowmass are now archaic names for this feast; today—except in novels—it is called All Saints' Day. But it has always been celebrated on the first day of November, which in Celtic times was coincidentally the first day of winter, a time of pagan witches and ghosts, mummery and masquerade. Wholly Christian in origin, however, are the vigil and fasting that occur on the day before.

On the eve of All Hallows' Day, a Christian and a Jew kept vigil in a corridor of the Ernest Atlas Pavilion on the fourth floor of Buenavista Hospital.

The Christian was Teddy Carella.

The Jew was Sarah Meyer.

The clock on the corridor wall read 11:47 P.M.

Sarah Meyer had brown hair and blue eyes and lips her husband had always considered sensual.

Teddy Carella had black hair and brown eyes, and lips that could not speak, for she had been born deaf and mute.

Sarah had not seen the inside of a synagogue for more years than she cared to count.

Teddy scarcely knew the whereabouts of her neighborhood church.

But both women were silently praying, and they were both praying for the same man.

Sarah knew that her husband was out of danger.

It was Steve Carella who was still in surgery.

On impulse, she took Teddy's hand and squeezed it.

Neither of the women said a word to the other.

Neither of the women said a word to the other.

They spotted him the moment they came back into the bar. Annie knew he was their man. So did Eileen. They headed immediately for the ladies' room.

A black hooker wearing a blond wig was standing at the sink, looking into the mirror over it, touching up her lipstick. She was a woman in her early forties, Eileen guessed, wearing a black dress and a short, fake fur jacket, going a bit thick in the middle and around the ankles. Eileen was certain she had just come in off the meat rack on the street outside.

"Getting chilly out there, ain't it?" the woman said.

"Yeah," Annie said.

"I'd park in here a while, but Larry gets twenty percent."

"I know."

"My man take a fit I give away twenty percent of the store."

There was a knife scar across the bridge of her nose.

She must have been pretty once, Eileen thought.

"One last pee," she said, and went into one of the stalls.

Annie lighted a cigarette. They chatted idly about how cold it was. The black hooker chimed in from behind the closed door of the stall, reporting on the really cold weather in Buffalo, New York, where she used to work years ago. They waited for her to flush the toilet. They waited while she washed her hands at the sink.

"Have a nice night," she said, and was gone.

"He's our man, isn't he?" Eileen said at once.

"Looks like him."

"Hitting on the wrong hooker."

"You'd better move in," Annie said.

"Sheryl won't like it."

"She'll like a slab even less."

"Will Shanahan know he's here?" Eileen asked.

"He'll know, don't worry."

Eileen nodded.

"You ready for this?" Annie asked. "I'm ready."

"You sure?"

"I'm sure."

Annie searched her face. "Because if you—"

"I'm ready," Eileen said.

Annie kept searching her face. Then she said, "Let's go then," and tossed her cigarette into one of the toilet bowls.

The cigarette expired with a short tired hiss.

He was telling another joke when Eileen took the stool on his right.

Blond. Six-two, six-three. 210 easy. Eyeglasses. A tattoo near his right thumb, a blue heart lined in red, nothing in it.

"...so he says to the old man, 'What's the matter? Why are you crying?' The old man just keeps sitting there on the park bench, crying his eyes out. Finally he says, 'A year ago, I married this beautiful twenty-six-year-old girl. I've never been happier in my life. Before breakfast each morning, she wakes me up and blows me, and then she serves me bacon and eggs and toasted English muffins and piping hot coffee, and I go back to bed and rest till lunchtime. Then she blows me again before lunch, and she serves me a hot, delicious lunch, and I go back to bed again and rest till dinnertime. And she blows me again before dinner and serves me another terrific meal, and I fall asleep until morning when she wakes me up again with another blowjob. She's the most wonderful woman I've ever met in my life.' The guy looks at him. 'Then why are you crying?' he asks. And the old man says, 'I forgot where I *live!*'"

Sheryl burst out laughing.

Eileen was thinking about the dead hookers he'd had in stitches.

"This guy's marvelous," Sheryl said, still laughing, leaning over to talk across him. "Linda, say hello to Bobby, he's marvelous."

"Hello, Bobby," Eileen said.

Terrific name for a slasher, she thought.

"Well, well, well, hello, Linda," he said, turning to her.

"Me and Bobby's running a tab," Sheryl said. "Which by the way, time's almost up."

"That right?" Eileen said.

"Just having a little fun here," Bobby said.

"The real fun comes later, honey," Sheryl said. "This is just the warm-up."

"I hear redheads are a lot of fun," Bobby said. "Is that true?"

"I haven't had any complaints," Eileen said.

She was wondering how she could get rid of Sheryl. If they were running a bar tab...

"But they burn in the sun," Bobby said.

"Yeah, I have to watch that."

"Just don't go out except at night, that's all," Sheryl said. "Listen, Bobby, I hate to be pushy, but your time's running out. You said twenty bucks for twenty minutes, remember?"

"Uh-huh."

"So take a look at the clock. You got about a minute left."

"I see that."

"So what do you say? We're having fun here, am I right?"

"Lots of fun."

"So how about another twenty, take us into Saturday?"

"Sounds like a good idea," he said, but he made no move for his wallet. Sheryl figured she was losing him.

"Matter of fact," she said, "whyn't you put Linda on the tab, too?"

"Thanks, no, I've been drinking too much tonight," Eileen said.

"This ain't a booze tab," Sheryl said. "This is accounts receivable. What do you say, Bobby? Lay a couple of twenties on the bar there, you buy both of us till a quarter past. Double your pleasure, double your fun. And later on, you still interested, we do a triad."

"What's a triad?" he asked.

"I read it in a book. It's like a two-on-one. A triad."

"I'm not sure I could handle two of you," he said.

But Eileen could see the sudden spark of ambition in his eyes. Blue to match the blue in the tattooed heart near his thumb. Seriously considering the possibility now. Take them *both* outside, slash them both, maybe go for a third one later on, do the hat trick tonight.

She didn't want a civilian getting in the way.

She had to get rid of Sheryl.

"I don't work doubles," she said.

A risk.

"How come?" Bobby asked.

"Why should I share this?" she said, and put her left hand on his thigh. He thought she was going for the meat. She was frisking him for the knife. Found it, too. Outlined in his right-hand pants pocket, felt like a six-incher at least. Maybe eight.

A shiver ran up her spine.

Sheryl was getting nervous. Her eyes flicked up to the clock again. The twenty minutes were gone, and she didn't see another twenty bucks coming out of his wallet. She was afraid she'd already lost him. So she tried again, appealing not to *him* now, but to the redheaded hooker sitting on his right, a sorority sister, so to speak, someone who knew how tough it was to earn a buck in a dog-eat-dog world.

"Change your mind, Linda," she said.

There was something almost plaintive in her voice.

"Come on, okay? It'll be fun."

"I think Linda might be more fun alone," Bobby said.

Eileen's hand was still on his thigh. Off the knife now, like finding the knife was an accident. Fingers spread toward his crotch.

Sheryl looked up at the clock again.

"Tell you what," she said. "I'll make it only ten bucks for the next twenty minutes, how's that? We'll sit here, I'll let you tell me some more of your jokes, be a lot of fun, what do you say?"

A last desperate try.

"I say it's up to Linda here. What do you say, Linda?"

"I told you. I don't do doubles."

Flat out. Get rid of her.

"You heard her," he said.

"Hey, come on, what kinda—"

"So long, Sheryl," he said.

She got off the stool at once.

"You're some cunt, you know that?" she said to Eileen, and turned away angrily and walked toward a table where three men were sitting drinking beer. "Who wants me?" she said angrily, and pulled out a chair and sat.

"I hate it when the fun goes out of it," Bobby said.

"We'll have lots of fun, don't worry," Eileen whispered, and tightened her hand on his thigh. "You want to get out of here this minute? I get ten bucks for a handjob…"

"No, no, let's talk a while, okay?" He reached into his right hip pocket, pulled out his wallet. Big killer, she thought, keeps his wallet in the sucker pocket. "Same deal as with Sheryl, okay? A buck a minute, here's a twenty"—reaching into the wallet, pulling out a bill, looking up at the clock—"we'll see how it goes, okay?"

"What is this?" Eileen asked. "An audition?"

"Well, I'd like to get to know you a little before I…"

He cut himself short.

"Before you what?" she said.

"You know," he said, and smiled, and lowered his voice. "Do it to you."

"What would you like to do to me, Bobby?"

"New and exciting things," he said.

She looked into his eyes.

Another shiver ran up her back.

"You cold?" he asked.

"A little. The weather's changing all of a sudden."

"Here," he said. "Take my jacket."

He shrugged out of the jacket. Tweed. He was wearing a blue flannel shirt under it, open at the throat. Blue to match his eyes and the tattooed heart near his thumb. He draped the jacket over her shoulders. There was the smell of death on the jacket, as palpable as the odor of smoke hanging on the air. She shivered again.

"So what do you say?" he asked her. "A buck a minute, does that sound all right?"

"Sure," she said.

"Well, good," he said, and handed her the $20 bill.

"Thanks," she said, and looked up at the clock. "This buys you till twenty past," she said, and tucked the bill into her bra. She didn't want to open her bag. She didn't want to risk him spotting the .44 in her bag, under the silk scarf. She was going to blow his brains out with that gun.

"Nothing for our friendly barkeep?" he asked.

"Huh?"

"I thought he got twenty percent."

"Oh. No, we have an arrangement."

"Well, good. I'd hate to think you were cheating him. You don't cheat people, do you, Linda?"

"I try to give good value," she said.

"Good. 'Cause you promised me a lot of fun, didn't you?"

"Show you a real good time," she said, and nodded.

Across the room, Annie was in conversation with the frizzied brunette who'd earlier partnered with Sheryl. The place was beginning to thin out a bit. There'd be a new shift coming in, Eileen guessed, the morning people, the denizens of the empty hours. He'd paid for twenty minutes of her time, but he'd dumped Sheryl without a backward glance, and she couldn't risk losing him to any of the other girls here. Twenty minutes unless he laid another bill on the bar. Twenty minutes to get him outside on the street, where he'd moved on the other three women. Show him a real good time, all right. Punish him for what he'd done. Make him pay for the three women he'd killed. Make him pay, too, for what a man named Arthur Haines had done to her face…and her body…and her spirit.

"So where are all the jokes?" she asked.

"Jokes?"

"Sheryl said you're full of jokes."

"No, Sheryl didn't say that."

"I thought she said—"

"I'm sure she didn't."

A mistake? No. Back off a bit, anyway.

"She said she'd settle for ten bucks, sit here with you, let you tell her some more jokes…"

"Oh. Yeah."

"So let me hear one."

"I'd rather talk about you right now."

"Sure," Eileen said.

" 'Cause I find that fun, you know. Learning about other people, finding out what makes them tick."

"You sound like a shrink," she said.

"Well, my father's a shrink."

"Really?"

"Yeah. Practices in LA. Lots of customers out there. You know what LA stands for?"

"What?"

"Lunatic Asylum."

"I've never been there, so I wouldn't—"

"Take my word for it. Every variety of nut in the—do you know the one about the guy who goes into a nut shop?"

"No."

"He stutters badly, he says to the clerk, 'I'd l-l-like to b-b-buy a p-p-pound of n-n-nuts.' The clerk says, 'Yes, sir, we have some very nice Brazil nuts at three dollars a pound.' The guy says, 'N-n-no, that's t-t-too high.' So the clerk says, 'I've also got some nice almonds at two dollars a pound.' The guy says, 'N-n-no, that's t-t-too high, t-t-too.' So the clerk says, 'I've got some peanuts at a dollar a pound,' and the guy says, 'F-f-fine.' The clerk weighs out the peanuts, puts them in a bag, and the guy pays for them. The guy says, 'Th-thank you, and I also w-w-want to th-thank you for n-n-not m-m-mentioning m-m-my im-p-p-pediment.' The clerk says, 'That's quite all right, sir, and I want to thank you for not mentioning my deformity.' The guy says, 'Wh-what d-d-deformity?' The clerk says, 'Well, I have a very large nose.' The guy says, 'Oh, is that your n-n-nose? Your n-n-nuts are so high, I th-thought it was your p-p-pecker.'"

Eileen burst out laughing.

The laughter was genuine.

For the briefest tick of time she forgot that she was sitting here at the bar with a man she felt reasonably certain had killed three women and would do his best to kill her as well if she gave him the slightest opportunity.

The laughter surprised her.

She had not laughed this heartily in a long time. She had not laughed since the night Arthur Haines slashed her cheek and forced himself upon her.

She could not stop laughing.

She wondered all at once if the laughter was merely a release of nervous tension.

But she kept laughing.

Tears were rolling down her cheeks.

She reached into her bag for a tissue, felt under the silk scarf, touched the butt of the .44, and suddenly the laughter stopped.

Dabbing at her eyes, she said, "That was very funny."

"I'm going to enjoy you," he said, smiling, looking into her eyes. "You're going to be a good one."

Alice was telling him that a lot of men got turned on by midgets, did he realize that?

Parker realized it. She was a perfect little doll, blond hair and blue eyes, beautifully formed breasts and well-shaped legs. She was wearing a green dress that hugged the womanly curves of her body, legs crossed, one foot jiggling in a high-heeled green slipper.

He said, "I read a lot of these men's magazines, you know…"

"Uh-huh," she said, nodding encouragement. Drink in her right hand, cigarette in her left.

"And there's all sorts of letters from men who get turned on by all sorts of women."

"Uh-huh."

"Like, for example, there are many men who are sexually attracted to women with back problems."

"Back problems?" Alice said.

"Yes. Women who wear braces."

"I see," she said.

"And there are men who enjoy one-armed women."

"Uh-huh."

"Or even double amputees."

"Uh-huh."

"Or women who are color blind."

"Color blind, right."

"But I've never seen any letters from men who find *midgets* sexually attractive. I wonder why. I mean, I find *you* very attractive, Alice."

"Well, thank you," she said. "But that's what I was saying. A *lot* of men get turned on by midgets."

"I can understand that."

"It's what's called the Snow White Syndrome."

"Is that what it's called?"

"Yes, because she was living with those seven dwarfs, you know."

"That's right, I never thought of that. I mean, if you look at it that way, it could be a dirty story, couldn't it?"

"Well, sure. Not that dwarfs are midgets."

"No, no. They *aren't*?"

"No. Midgets are perfectly proportioned little people."

"You certainly are perfectly proportioned, Alice."

"Well, thank you. But my point is, with so many men being attracted to female midgets…"

"Uh-huh."

"You think you'd see midgets in ads and all."

"I never thought of it that way."

"I mean, wouldn't you like to see me modeling lingerie, for example?"

"Oh, I would."

"But instead, if you're a midget, you have to join a circus."

"I never thought of it that way," he said again.

"Have you ever seen a midget working as a clerk in a department store?"

"Never," he said.

"Do you know why?"

"Because you can't see over the counter?"

"Well, that's one reason, of course. But the main reason is there's a lingering prejudice against little people."

"I'll bet there is."

"Short has become a dirty word," Alice said. "Have you ever seen a short movie star?"

"Well, Al Pacino is short."

"On my block, Al Pacino is a *giant*," she said, and giggled.

Parker loved the way she giggled.

"Have you ever seen a movie where there are midgets making *love*?" she asked.

"Never."

"We *do* make love, you know."

"Oh, I'll bet."

"Have you ever seen a midget fireman? Or a midget cop?"

He had not yet told her he was a cop. He wondered if he should tell her he was a cop.

"Well, they changed the requirements, you know," he said.

"What requirements?"

"The height requirements. It used to be five-eight."

"So what is it now?"

"You can be any height. I know cops you can fit them in your vest pocket."

"You mean a midget can become a cop?"

"Well, I don't know about *midgets*. But I guess…"

"Because I can shoot a gun as good as anybody else, you know. I used to do an Annie Oakley act in the circus. Little Annie Oakley, they called me. That was before I got to be Tiny Alice."

"You *are* tiny," he said. "That's one of the things I find very sexually attractive about you."

"Well, thank you. But what I'm asking, if I applied to the police department…to become a woman cop, you know…would they accept me? Or would they think *short*? Do you see what I mean?"

"I don't think of you as short," Parker said.

"Oh, I'm short, all right."

"I think of you as delicate."

"Well, thank you. There's this man Hans, he's one of the Flying Dutchmen, an aerial act, you know?"

"Uh-huh."

"He wrote me this very hot love letter, I memorized it. What made me think of it was your use of the word delicate."

"Well, you are delicate."

"Thank you. Would you like to hear the letter?"

"Well…sure," Parker said, and glanced over his shoulder to see where Peaches was. She was nowhere in sight. "Go ahead," he said.

"He said he wanted to disrobe me."

"Take off your clothes, you mean."

"Yes. He said he wanted to discard my dainty delicate under things…that's what made me think of it, delicate."

"Yes, I see."

"And pat my pubescent peaks…this is him talking now, in the letter."

"Yes."

"And probe my pithy pussy, and manipulate my miniature mons veneris and Lilliputian labiae…"

"Uh-huh."

"And caress my compact clitoris and crisp pauciloquent pubic patch. That was the letter."

"From one of the Flying Dutchmen, huh?"

"Yes."

"He speaks good English."

"Oh, yes."

"That isn't the guy you're with tonight, is it? The guy you came in with?"

"No, no. That's Quentin."

"He's not one of the Flying Dutchmen, huh?"

"No, he's a clown."

"Oh."

"A very good one, too."

"So how long have you been in town? I didn't even know the circus was here, I'll tell you the truth."

"Well, we're not here. We won't be here till the spring sometime. We go down to Florida next month to start rehearsing the new season."

"Oh, so you're just visiting then, is that it?"

"Yeah, sort of."

"You're not married or anything, are you?"

"No, no. No, no, no, no, no."

Shaking her head like a little doll.

"How long will you be in town?"

"Oh, I don't know. Why?"

"I thought we might get together," Parker said, and shrugged.

"How about the big redhead you're with?"

"Peaches? She's just a friend."

"Uh-huh."

"Really. I hardly know her. Alice, I've got to tell you, I've never met a woman as delicate and as attractive as you are, I mean it. I'd really like to get together with you."

"Well, why don't you give me a call?"

"I'd like that," he said, and took his pad from his pocket.

"That's *some* notebook," she said. "It's bigger than I am."

"Well, you know," he said, and wondered again if he should tell her he was a cop. Lots of women, you told them you were a cop, it turned them off. They figured all cops were on the take, all cops were crooks. Just because every now and then you accepted a little gift from somebody. "So where can I reach you?" he said.

"We're staying at Quentin's apartment. The four of us."

"Who's the four of us? Not the Flying Dutchmen, I hope."

"No, no, they went back to Germany, they'll be joining us in Florida."

"So who's the four of you?"

"Willie and Corky...they're married...and Oliver and me. And of course Quentin, whose apartment it is. Quentin Forbes."

"What's the address?" Parker asked.

"403 Thompson Street."

"Downtown in the Quarter," he said, nodding. "The Twelfth."

"Huh?"

He wondered if he should explain to her that in this city you didn't call the Twelfth the "One-Two." Any precinct from the 1st to the 20th was called by its full and proper designation. After that, it became the Two-One, the Three-Four, the Eight-Seven, and so on. But that would have meant telling her he was a cop, and he didn't want to chance losing her.

"What's the phone number there?" he asked.

"348..."

"Ex*cuse* me."

Voice as cold as the second day of February, hands on her hips, green eyes blazing.

"I'd like to go home now," Peaches said. "Did you plan on accompanying me? Or are you going to play house all night?"

"Uh…sure," Parker said, and got to his feet. "Nice meeting you," he said to Alice.

"It's in the book," Alice said, and smiled up sweetly at Peaches.

Peaches tried to think of a scathing midget remark, but nothing came to mind.

She turned and started for the door.

"I'll call you," Parker whispered, and ran out after her.

The house was a white clapboard building with a white picket fence around it. A matching white clapboard garage stood some twenty feet from the main structure. Both buildings were on a street with only three other houses on it, not too far from the turnpike. It was two minutes past midnight when they reached the house. The first day of November. The beginning of the Celtic winter. As if in accordance, the weather had turned very cold. As they pulled into the driveway, Brown remarked that all they needed was snow, the turnpike would be backed up all the way to Siberia.

There were no lights burning on the ground floor of the house. Two lighted windows showed on the second story. The men were inappropriately dressed for the sudden cold. Their breaths plumed from their mouths as they walked to the front door. Hawes rang the doorbell.

"Probably getting ready for bed," he said.

"You wish," Brown said.

They waited.

"Give it another shot," Brown said.

Hawes hit the bell button again.

Lights snapped on downstairs.

"Who is it?"

Marie's voice, just inside the door. A trifle alarmed. Well, sure, midnight already.

"It's Detective Hawes," he said.

"Oh."

"Sorry to bother you so late."

"No, that's all…just a minute, please."

She fumbled with the lock, and then opened the door. She *had* been getting ready for bed. She was wearing a long blue robe. Laced ruff of a nightgown showing in the V-necked opening. No slippers.

"Have you found him?" she asked at once.

Referring to Jimmy Brayne, of course.

"No, ma'am, not yet," Brown said. "Okay for us to come in?"

"Yes, please," she said, "excuse me," and stepped back to let them in.

Small entryway, a sense of near-shabbiness. Worn carpeting, scarred and rickety piece of furniture under a flaking mirror.

"I thought…when you told me who you were…I thought you'd found Jimmy," she said.

"Not yet, Mrs. Sebastiani," Hawes said. "In fact, the reason we came out here…"

"Come in," she said, "we don't have to stand here in the hall."

She backed off several paces, reached beyond the doorjamb for a light switch. A floor lamp came on in the living room. Musty drapes, a faded rug, a thrift-shop sofa and two upholstered armchairs, an old upright piano on the far wall. Same sense of down-at-the-heels existence.

"Would you like some coffee or anything?" she asked.

"I could use a cup," Brown said.

"I'll put some up," she said, and walked back through the hall and through a doorway into the kitchen.

The detectives looked around the living room.

Framed photographs on the piano, Sebastian the Great doing his act hither and yon. Soiled antimacassars on the upholstered pieces. Brown ran his finger over the surface of an end table. Dust.

Hawes poked his forefinger into the soil of a potted plant. Dry. The continuing sense of a house too run down to care about—or a house in neglect because it would soon be abandoned.

She was back.

"Take a few minutes to boil," she said.

"Who plays piano?" Hawes asked.

"Frank did. A little."

She'd grown used to the past tense.

"Mrs. Sebastiani," Brown said, "we were wondering if we could take a look at Brayne's room."

"Jimmy's room?" she said. She seemed a bit flustered by their presence, but that could have been normal, two cops showing on her doorstep at midnight.

"See if there's anything up there might give us a lead," Brown said, watching her.

"I'll have to find a spare key someplace," she said. "Jimmy had his own key, he came and went as he pleased."

She stood stock still in the entrance door to the living room, a thoughtful look on her face. Hawes wondered what she was thinking, face all screwed up like that. Was she wondering whether it was safe to show them that room? Or was she merely trying to remember where the spare key was?

"I'm trying to think where Frank might have put it," she said.

A grandfather clock on the far side of the room began tolling the hour, eight minutes late.

One...two...

They listened to the heavy bonging.

Nine...ten...eleven...twelve.

"Midnight already," she said, and sighed.

"Your clock's slow," Brown said.

"Let me check the drawer in the kitchen," she said. "Frank used to put a lot of junk in that drawer."

Past tense again.

They followed her into the kitchen. Dirty dishes, pots, and pans stacked in the sink. The door of the refrigerator smudged with handprints. Telephone on the wall near it. Small enamel-topped table, two chairs. Worn linoleum. Only a shade on the single window over the sink. On the stove, the kettle began whistling.

"Help yourselves," she said. "There's cups there, and a jar of instant."

She went to a drawer in the counter, opened it. Hawes spooned instant coffee into each of the cups, poured hot water into them. She was busy at the drawer now, searching for the spare key. "There should be some milk in the fridge," she said. "And there's sugar on the counter there." Hawes opened the refrigerator. Not much in it. Carton of low-fat milk, slab of margarine or butter, several containers of yogurt. He closed the door.

"You want some of this?" he asked Brown, extending the carton to him.

Brown shook his head. He was watching Marie going through the drawer full of junk.

"Sugar?" Hawes asked, pouring milk into his own cup.

Brown shook his head again.

"This may be it, I really don't know," Marie said.

She turned from the drawer, handed Brown a brass key that looked like a house key.

The telephone rang.

She was visibly startled by its sound.

Brown picked up his coffee cup, began sipping at it.

The telephone kept ringing.

She went to the wall near the refrigerator, lifted the receiver from its hook.

"Hello?" she said.

The two detectives watched her.

"Oh, hello, Dolores," she said at once. "No, not yet, I'm down in the kitchen," she said, and listened. "There are two detectives with me," she said. "No, that's all right, Dolores." She listened again. "They want to look at the garage room." Listening again. "I don't know yet," she said. "Well, they...they have to do an autopsy first." More listening. "Yes, I'll let you know. Thanks for calling, Dolores."

She put the receiver back on its hook.

"My sister-in-law," she said.

"Taking it hard, I'll bet," Hawes said.

"They were very close."

"Let's check out that room," Brown said to Hawes.

"I'll come over with you," Marie said.

"No need," Brown said, "it's getting cold outside."

She looked at him. She seemed about to say something more. Then she merely nodded.

"Better get a light from the car," Hawes said.

Marie watched them as they went out the door and made their way in the dark to where they'd parked their car. Car door opening, interior light snapping on. Door closing again. A moment later, a flashlight came on. She watched them as they walked up the driveway to the garage, pool of light ahead of them. They began climbing the steps at the side of the building. Flashlight beam on the door now. Unlocking the door. Should she have given them the key? Opening the door. The black cop reached into the room. A moment of fumbling for the wall switch, and then the light snapped on, and they both went inside and closed the door behind them.

The bullet had entered Carella's chest on the right side of the body, piercing the pectoralis major muscle, deflecting off the rib cage and missing the lung, passing through the soft tissue at the back

of the chest, and then twisting again to lodge in one of the articu-
lated bones in the spinal column.

The X-rays showed the bullet dangerously close to the spinal
cord itself.

In fact, if it had come to rest a micrometer further to the left,
it would have traumatized the cord and caused paralysis.

The surgical procedure was a tricky one in that the danger of
necrosis of the cord was still present, either through mechanical
trauma or a compromise of the arterial supply of blood to the
cord. Carella had bled a lot, and there was the further attendant
danger of his going into heart failure or shock.

The team of surgeons—a thoracic surgeon, a neurosurgeon,
his assistant, and two residents—had decided on a posterolateral
approach, going in through the back rather than entering the
chest cavity, where there might be a greater chance of infection
and the possibility of injury to one of the lungs. The neurosurgeon
was the man who made the incisions. The thoracic surgeon was
standing by in the event they had to open the chest after all. There
were also two scrub nurses, a circulating nurse, and an anesthesiologist in the room. With the exception of the circulating nurse
and the anesthesiologist, everyone was fully gowned and gloved.
Alongside the operating table, machines monitored Carella's
pulse and blood pressure. A Swan-Ganz catheter was in place,
monitoring the pressure in the pulmonary artery. Oscilloscopes
flashed green. Beeps punctuated the sterile silence of the room.

The bullet was firmly seated in the spinal column.

Very close to the spinal cord and the radicular arteries.

It was like operating inside a matchbox.

The River Dix had begun silting over during the heavy September
rains, and the city had awarded the dredging contract to a private
company that started work on the fifteenth of October. Because

there was heavy traffic on the river during the daylight hours, the men working the barges started as soon as it was dark and continued on through until just before dawn. Generator-powered lights set up on the barges illuminated the bucketsful of river slime scooped up from the bottom. Before tonight, the men doing the dredging had been grateful for the unusually mild weather. Tonight, it was no fun standing out here in the cold, watching the bucket drop into the black water and come up again dripping all kinds of shit. People threw everything in this river.

Good thing Billy Joe McAllister didn't live in this city; he'd have maybe thrown a dead baby in the river.

The bucket came up again.

Barney Hanks watched it swinging in wide over the water, and signaled with his hand, directing it in over the center of the disposal barge. Pete Masters, sitting in the cab of the diesel-powered dredge on the other barge, worked his clutches and levers, tilting the bucket to drop another yard and a half, two yards of silt and shit. Hanks jerked his thumb up, signaling to Masters that the bucket was empty and it was okay to cast the dragline out over the river again. In the cab, Masters yanked some more levers and the bucket swung out over the side of the barge.

Something metallic was glistening on the surface of the muck in the disposal barge.

Hanks signaled to Masters to cut the engine.

"What is it?" Masters shouted.

"We got ourselves a treasure chest," Hanks yelled.

Masters cut his engine, climbed down from the cab, and walked across the deck toward the other barge.

"Time for a coffee break, anyway," he said. "What do you mean a treasure chest?"

"Throw me that grappling hook," Hanks said.

Masters threw the hook and line to him.

Hanks tossed the hook at what appeared to be one of those aluminum cases you carried roller skates in, except that it was bigger all around. The case was half-submerged in slime, it took Hanks five tosses to snag the handle. He pulled in the line, freed the hook, and put the case down on the deck.

Masters watched him from the other barge.

Hanks tried the catches on the case.

"No lock on it," he said, and opened the lid.

He was looking at a head and a pair of hands.

Kling arrived in the Canal Zone at thirteen minutes past midnight.

He parked the car on Canalside and Solomon, locked it, and began walking up toward Fairview. Eileen had told him they'd be planting her in a joint called Larry's Bar, on Fairview and East Fourth. This side of the river, the city got all turned around. What could have been North Fourth in home territory was East Fourth here, go figure it. Like two different countries, the opposite sides of the river. They even spoke English funny over here.

Larry's Bar.

Where the killer had picked up his three previous victims.

Kling planned on casing it from the outside, just to make sure she was still in there. Then he'd fade out, cover the place from a safe vantage point on the street. Didn't want Eileen to know he was on the scene. First off, she'd throw a fit, and next she might spook, blow her own cover. All he wanted was to be around in case she needed him.

He had put on an old pea jacket he kept in his locker for unexpected changes of weather like the one tonight. He was hat-less and he wasn't wearing gloves. If he needed to pull the piece, he didn't want gloves getting in the way. Navy-blue pea jacket, blue jeans—too lightweight, really, for the sudden chill—blue socks and black loafers. And a .38 Detective Special in a holster at his waist. Left-hand side. Two middle buttons of the jacket unbuttoned for an easy reach-in and cross-body draw.

He came up Canalside.

The Beef Trust was out in force, despite the cold.

Girls huddled under the lampposts as though the overhead lights afforded some warmth, most of them wearing only short skirts and sweaters or blouses, scant protection against the cold. A lucky few were wearing coats provided by mobile pimps with an eye on the weather.

"Hey, sailor, lookin' for a party?"

Black girl breaking away from the knot under the corner lamppost, swiveling over to him. Couldn't be older than eighteen, nineteen, hands in the pockets of a short jacket, high-heeled ankle-strapped shoes, short skirt blowing in the fresh wind that came off the canal.

"Almos' do it for free, you so good-lookin'," she said, grinning widely. "Thass a joke, honey, but the price is right, trust me."

"Not right now," Kling said.

"Well, *when,* baby? I stann out here much longer, my pussy turn to ice. Be no good to neither one of us."

"Maybe later," Kling said.

"You promise? Slide your hand up under here, take a feel of heaven."

"I'm busy right now," Kling said.

"Too busy for *this*?" she said, and took his hand and guided it onto her thigh. "Mmmmm-*mmmmm,*" she said, "sweet chocolate pussy, yours for the takin'."

"Later," he said, and freed his hand and began walking off.

"You come on back later, man, hear?" she shouted after him. "Ask for Crystal."

He walked into the darkness. On the dock, he could hear rats rustling along the pilings. Another lamppost, another huddle of hookers.

"Hey, Blondie, lookin' for some fun?"

White girl in her twenties. Wearing a long khaki coat and high heels. Opened the coat to him as he went past.

"Interested?" she said.

Nothing under the coat but garter belt and long black stockings. Quick glimpse of rounded belly and pink-tipped breasts.

"Faggot!" she yelled after him, and twirled the coat closed as gracefully as a dancer. The girls with her laughed. Fun on the docks.

Made a right turn onto Fairview, began walking up toward Fourth. Pools of light on the sidewalk ahead. Larry's Bar. Two plate-glass windows, beer displays in them, entrance door set between them. He went to the closest window, cupped his hands on either side of his face, peered through the glass. Not too crowded just now. Annie. Sitting at a table with a black man and a frizzied brunette. Good, at least one backup was close by. There at the bar. Eileen. With a big blond guy wearing glasses.

Okay, Kling thought.

I'm here.

Don't worry.

From where Shanahan sat slumped behind the wheel of the two-door Chevy across the street, he saw only a big blond guy looking through the plate-glass window of the bar. Six feet tall, he guessed, give or take an inch, broad shoulders and narrow waist, wearing a seaman's pea jacket and blue jeans.

Shanahan was suddenly alert.

Guy was still looking through the window, hands cupped to his face, motionless except for the dancing of his blond hair on the wind.

Shanahan kept watching.

The guy turned from the window.

No eyeglasses.

Might not be him.

On the other hand…

Shanahan got out of the car. It was clumsy moving with the right arm in a cast, but he'd rather be made for a cripple than a cop. Guy walking up the street now. How come he wasn't going in the bar? Change of MO? Shanahan fussed with the lock of the car door, watching him sidelong.

Minute the guy was four car lengths away, Shanahan took off after him.

The bar was baited with Eileen, but there were plenty of other girls out here on the street. And if this guy was suddenly changing his pattern, Shanahan didn't want *any* of them dying.

Eileen didn't like the tricks her mind was beginning to play.

She was beginning to like him.

She was beginning to think he couldn't possibly be a murderer.

Like the stories you read in the newspapers after the kid next door shot and killed his mother, his father, and his two sisters. Nice kid like that? all the neighbors said. Can't believe it. Always had a kind word for everyone. Saw him mowing the lawn and helping old ladies across the street. This kid a killer? Impossible.

Or maybe she didn't *want* him to be a murderer because that would mean eventual confrontation. She knew that if this was the guy, she'd have to end up face to face with him on the street outside. And the knife would come out of his pocket. And…

It was easier to believe he couldn't possibly be the killer.

You're tricking yourself, she thought.

And yet…

There really were a lot of likable things about him.

Not just his sense of humor. Some of his jokes were terrible, in fact. He told them almost compulsively, whenever anything in the conversation triggered what appeared to be a vast computer-bank memory of stories. You mentioned the tattoo near his thumb, for example—the killer had a tattoo near his thumb, she reminded herself—and he immediately told the one about the two girls discussing the guy with the tattooed penis, and one of them insisted only the word Swan was tattooed on it, whereas the other girl insisted the word was Saskatchewan, and it turned out they were both right, which took Eileen a moment to get. Or you mentioned the sudden change in the weather, and he immediately reeled off Henry Morgan's famous weather forecast, "Muggy today, Toogy tomorrow," and then segued neatly into the joke about the panhandler shivering outside in the cold and another panhandler comes over to him and says, "Can you lend me a dime for a cup of coffee?" and the first guy says, "Are you kidding? I'm standing here bare-assed, I'm shivering and starving to death, how come you're asking *me* for a dime?" and the second guy says, "Okay, make it a nickel," which wasn't very funny, but which he told with such dramatic flair that Eileen could actually visualize the two panhandlers standing on a windy corner of the city.

Outside, the city beckoned.

The night beckoned.

The knife beckoned.

But inside, sitting here at the bar with the television set going, and the sound of voices everywhere around them, the world seemed safe and cozy and warm, and she found herself listening intently to everything he said. Not only the jokes. The jokes were a given. If you wanted to learn about him, you had to listen to his jokes. The jokes were some sort of defense system, she realized, his way of keeping himself at arm's distance from anyone. But scattered in among the incessant jokes, there were glimpses of a shy and somewhat vulnerable person longing to make contact—until another joke was triggered.

He had used up his first $20 five minutes ago, and was now working on the second $20, which he said should take them through to 12:40.

"After that, we'll see," he said. "Maybe we'll talk some more, or maybe we'll go outside, depends how we feel, right? We'll play this by ear, Linda, I'm really enjoying this, aren't you?"

"Yes," she said, and guessed she meant it.

But he's the killer, she reminded herself.

Or maybe not.

She hoped he wasn't.

"If you add up these twenties," he said, "a dollar a minute, you'll be getting a third of what my dad gets in LA, he gets a hundred and fifty bucks for a fifty-minute hour, which ain't bad, huh? For listening to people tell you they have bedbugs crawling all over them? Don't brush them on me, right? Well, I guess you know that one, I guess I've already told that one."

He hadn't told that one. But suddenly, as he apologized for what he'd mistakenly thought was repetition, she felt oddly close to him. Like a married woman listening to the same jokes her husband had told time and again, and yet enjoying them each time as if he were telling them for the first time. She knew the "Don't-brush-them-on-me" joke. Yet she wished he would tell it, anyway.

And wondered if she was stalling for time.

Wondered if she was putting off that eventual moment when the knife came out of the pocket.

"My father was very strict," he said. "If you have any choice, don't get raised by a psychiatrist. How's your father? Is he tough on you?"

"I never really knew him," she said.

Her father. A cop. On the beat, they used to call him Pops Burke. Shot to death when she was still a little girl.

In the next instant, she almost told him that her *uncle* and not her father was the one who'd had the most telling influence on her life. Uncle Matt. Also a cop. Whose favorite toast was, "Here's to golden days and purple nights." An expression he'd heard repeated again and again on a radio show. Recently, Eileen had heard Hal Willis's new girlfriend using the same expression. Small world. Even smaller world when your favorite uncle is sitting off-duty in his favorite bar making his favorite toast and a guy walks in with a sawed-off shotgun. Uncle Matt drew his service revolver and the guy shot him dead. She almost told Bobby she'd become a cop because of her Uncle Matt. She almost forgot in that instant that she herself was a cop working undercover to trap a killer. The word "entrapment" flashed into her mind. Suppose he isn't the killer? she wondered. Suppose I blow him away and it turns out—

And realized again that her mind was playing tricks.

"I grew up in a world of don't do this, don't do that," Bobby said. "You'd think a shrink would've known better, well, I guess it was a case of the shoemaker's children. Talk about repression. It was my mother who finally helped me to break out. I make it sound like a prison, don't I? Well, it was. Do you know the one about the lady walking along the beach in Miami?"

She shook her head.

She realized she was already smiling.

"Well, she sees this guy lying on the sand, and she goes up to him and she says, 'Excuse me, I don't mean to intrude, but you're very white.' The guy looks up at her and says, 'So?' The lady says, 'I mean, most people they come down to Miami, they lie in the sun, they get a nice tan. But you're very white.' The guy says, 'So?' The lady says, 'So how come you're so white?' The guy says, 'This is prison pallor, I just got out of prison yesterday.' The lady shakes her head and says, 'How long were you in prison?' The guys says, 'Thirty years.' The lady says, 'My, my, what did you do, they put you in prison for thirty years?' The guy says, 'I killed my wife with a hatchet and chopped her up in little pieces.' The woman looks at him and says, 'Mmmm, so you're single?' "

Eileen burst out laughing.

And then realized that the joke was about murder.

And then wondered if a murderer would tell a joke about murder.

"Anyway, it was my mother who broke me out of prison," Bobby said, "and she had to die to do it."

"What do you mean?"

"Left me a lot of money. Do you know what she said in her will? She said, 'This is for Robert's freedom to risk enjoying life.' Her exact words. She always called me Robert. 'Robert's freedom to risk enjoying life.' Which is just what I've been doing for the past year. Kissed my father off, told him to shove it, told him I'd be happy if I never saw him again, and then left LA forever."

She wondered if there were any warrants out on him in LA.

But why would there be any warrants?

"Went to Kansas City, had a good time there…got the tattoo there, in fact, what the hell, I'd always wanted a tattoo. Then on to Chicago, lived it up there, too, plenty of money to take risks, Linda. I owe that to my mother." He nodded thoughtfully, and then said, "He's the one who killed her, you know."

She looked at him.

"Oh, not literally. I mean he didn't stick a knife in her or anything. But he was having an affair with our housekeeper, and she found out about it, and it broke her heart, she was never the same again. They said it was cancer, but stress can induce serious illness, you know, and I'm sure that's what caused it, his fooling around with Elga. The money my mother eventually left me was the money she'd got in the divorce settlement, which I think was poetic justice, don't you? I mean, him raising me so strictly—while he's fooling around with that Nazi hooker, mind you—and my mother giving me *his* money so I could lead a richer life, so I could risk enjoying life. I think that was the key word, don't you? In the will? Risk. I think she wanted me to take risks with the money, which is what I've been doing."

"How?" Eileen asked.

"Oh, not by investing in hog bellies or anything," he said, and smiled.

"By living well. Living well is the best revenge, isn't it? Who said that? I know *somebody* said that."

"Not *me*!" Eileen said, and backed away in mock denial.

"Don't brush them on me, right?" he said, and they both laughed.

He looked at the clock.

"Five minutes left," he said. "Maybe we'll go outside then. Would you like to go outside then? When the five minutes are up?"

"Whatever you want," she said.

"Maybe that's what we'll do," he said. "Have a little fun. Do something new and exciting, huh? Risks," he said, and smiled again.

He had a very pleasant smile.

Transformed his entire face. Made him look like a shy little boy. Blue eyes soft, almost misty, behind the eyeglasses. Shy little kid sitting in the back row, afraid to raise his hand and ask questions.

"In a way, you know," he said, "it *has* been a sort of revenge. What I've been doing with the money. Traveling, having a good time, taking my risks. And getting even with him, in a way, for Elga. Our housekeeper, you know? The woman he tricked my mother with. Deceiving her all those years. A shrink, can you imagine? Holier than thou, and he's laying the goddamn housekeeper.

I mean, my mother was the one who put him through medical school. She was a schoolteacher, you know, worked all those years to put him through school, do you know how long a psychiatrist has to go to school? It's very difficult to believe that women can be so callous toward other women. I find that very difficult to believe, Linda. I mean, Elga behaving like a common hooker… excuse me, I don't mean any offense. Excuse me, really," he said, and patted her hand. "But, you know, you hear all this talk about sisterhood, you'd think she might have had some sense of concern for my mother, I mean the woman was married to him for forty *years*!" He grinned suddenly. "Do you know the one about this man who comes to his wife, they've been married forty years, he says to her, 'Ida, I want to do it like dogs.' She says, 'That's disgusting, Sam, doing it like dogs.' He says, 'Ida, if you won't do it like dogs, I want a divorce.' She says, 'Okay, Sam, we'll do it like dogs. But not on our block.' "

Eileen nodded.

"Didn't like that one, huh?"

"Mezz' a mezza," she said, and seesawed her hand on the air.

"I promise we won't do it like dogs, okay?" he said, smiling. "How would you like to do it, Linda?"

"You're the boss," she said.

"Have you ever seen a snuff movie?" he asked.

"Never," she said.

Here it comes, she thought.

"Does that scare you?" he said. "My asking about a snuff movie?"

"Yes," she said.

"Me, too," he said, and smiled. "I've never seen one, either."

Explore it, she thought.

But she was afraid to.

"Think you might like that?" she asked.

Her heart was suddenly pounding again.

"Killing someone while you were laying her?"

He looked deep into her eyes as though searching for something there.

"Not if she knew it was going to happen," he said.

And suddenly she knew for certain that he was their man, and there was no postponing what would happen tonight.

He looked up at the clock.

"Time's up," he said. "Let's go outside."

The call to the squadroom came at twenty minutes to 1:00. The call came from Monoghan, who was in a phone booth on the edge of the River Dix. He asked to talk to either Brown or Genero. Willis told him Brown and Genero were both out.

"So who's this?" Monoghan asked.

"Willis."

"What I got here," Monoghan said, "is a head and a pair of hands. These guys dragging the river turned up this aluminum case, like it's big enough to hold a man's head. And his hands. So that's what I got here. A head cut off at the neck, and a pair of hands cut off at the wrists."

"Uh-huh," Willis said.

"So earlier tonight I was with Brown and Genero back out behind this restaurant the Burgundy, and what we had there was the upper part of a torso in a garbage can, is what we had. And now I got a head and a pair of hands, and it occurred to me this might be the same body here, this head and hands."

"Uh-huh," Willis said.

"So what I want to know, does Brown or Genero have a positive make on the stiff? 'Cause otherwise we now got a head to look at, and also some hands to print."

"Let me take a look at Brown's desk," Willis said. "I think he left some stuff here."

"Yeah, go take a look," Monoghan said.

"Hold on," Willis said.

"Yeah."

"Hold on, I'm putting you on hold."

"Yeah, fine," Monoghan said.

Willis pressed the hold button, and then went over to Brown's desk. He riffled through the papers there, and then stabbed at the lighted extension button, and picked up the receiver.

"Monoghan?"

"Yeah."

"From what I can gather, the body was identified as someone named Frank Sebastiani, male, white, thirty-four years old."

"That's what I got here, a white male around that age."

"I've got a picture here, too," Willis said.

"Whyn't you run on over with it?" Monoghan said. "We see we got the same stiff or not."

"Where are you?"

"Freezing my ass off on the drive here. Near the river."

"Which river?"

"The Dix."

"And where?"

"Hampton."

"Give me ten minutes," Willis said.

"Don't forget the picture," Monoghan said.

The apartment over the garage was perhaps twelve feet wide by twenty feet long. There was a neatly made double bed in the room, and a dresser with a mirror over it, and an upholstered chair with a lamp behind it. The wall surrounding the mirror was covered with pictures of naked women snipped from men's magazines banned in 7-Eleven stores. All of the women were blondes. Like Marie Sebastiani. In the bottom drawer of the dresser, under a stack of Brayne's shirts, the detectives found a pair of crotchless black panties. The panties were a size five.

"Think they're Brayne's?" Hawes asked drily.

"What size you think the lady wears?" Brown asked.

"Could be a five," Hawes said, and shrugged.

"I thought you were an expert."

"On *bras* I'm an expert."

Men's socks, undershorts, sweaters, handkerchiefs in the other dresser drawers. Two sports jackets, several pairs of slacks, a suit, an overcoat, and three pairs of shoes in the single small closet. There was also a suitcase in the closet. Nothing in it. No indication anywhere in the apartment that Brayne had packed and taken off in a hurry. Even his razor and shaving cream were still on the sink in the tiny bathroom.

A tube of lipstick was in the cabinet over the sink.

Brown took off the top.

"Look like the lady's shade?" he asked Hawes. "Pretty careless if it's her, leavin' her OCPs in the dresser and her…"

"Her *what*?"

"Her open-crotch panties."

"Oh."

"You think she was dumb enough to be makin' it with him right here in this room?"

"Let's see what else we find," Hawes said.

What else they found was a sheaf of letters rubber-banded together. They found the letters in a cardboard shoe box on the top shelf of the closet. The letters were inside lavender-colored envelopes, but none of the envelopes had been stamped or mailed. The name "Jimmy" was scrawled on the front of each envelope.

"Hand-delivered," Hawes said.

"Mmm," Brown said, and they began reading the letters.

The letters were written in purple ink.

The first letter read:

> Jimmy,
> Just say when.
> *Marie*

It was dated July 18.

"When did he start working for them?" Brown asked.

"Fourth of July."

"Fast worker, this lady," Brown said.

The second letter was dated July 21. It described in excruciatingly passionate detail all the things Marie and Jimmy had done together the day before.

"This is dirty," Brown said, looking up.

"Yes," Hawes said. He was reading over Brown's shoulder.

There were twenty-seven letters in all. The letters chronicled a rather active sex life between the lady and the sorcerer's apprentice, Marie apparently having been compulsive about jotting down everything she had done to Jimmy in the recent past, and then outlining everything she hadn't yet done to him but which she planned to do to him in the foreseeable future, which—if the chronology was faithful—she did indeed get around to doing to him.

She did a lot of things to him.

The last letter was dated October 27, four days before the murder and dismemberment of the lady's husband. She suggested in this last letter that one of the things she wanted to do to Jimmy on Halloween night was tie him to the bed in his black silk under-shorts and spread herself open over him in her black crotchless panties and then—

"You see any black silk undershorts in the dresser there?" Brown asked.

"No," Hawes said. "I'm reading."

"A celebration, do you think?" Brown asked. "All this stuff she planned to do to him on Halloween?"

"Maybe."

"Do hubby in, chop him up in little pieces, then come back here and have a witch's sabbath."

"Where does she call it that?"

"Call it what?"

"Witch's sabbath."

"*I'm* calling it that," Brown said. "Black silk undershorts, black OCPs…"

"So where's Brayne?" Hawes asked. "If they were planning a celebration…"

"Did you look under the bed?" Brown asked, and then turned suddenly toward the window.

Hawes turned at exactly the same moment.

An automobile had just pulled into the driveway.

At ten minutes to 1:00—ten minutes after Bobby had suggested that they go outside—Eileen excused herself and went to the ladies' room. Annie, sitting at a table with an Italian sailor who was having difficulty making his needs understood, watched her as she crossed the room and made a left turn at the phone booths.

"Excuse me," Annie said.

By the time she got to the ladies' room, Eileen was already in one of the stalls. Annie did a quick check for feet. The other stalls were empty.

"Yes or no?" she asked.

"Yes," Eileen said.

Her voice from behind the closed door sounded odd.

"Are you sure?"

"I think so."

"You okay?"

"Fine. Checking out the hardware."

The door opened. Eileen looked pale. She went to the sink, touched up her lipstick, blotted it.

"You going out now?" Annie asked.

"Yes."

The same odd voice.

"Give me three minutes to get on the street," Annie said.

"Okay."

Annie went to the door.

"I'll be there," she said simply.

"Good," Eileen said.

Annie took one last look at her, and then went out.

"What I'm talking about is decency and honor," Peaches said.

It was very cold and they were walking along the street rapidly.

"I'm talking about a person's responsibility to another person," Peaches said, clinging to Parker's arm for warmth and nothing else.

Parker was beginning to feel married.

"You went to that party with *me*," Peaches said, "and not with Little Miss Muffet."

"If a person can't have a simple conversation with another person…"

"That wasn't a conversation," Peaches said. "That was a person-and-a-half exchanging deep sighs and meaningful glances."

"I don't think it's nice of you to make midget jokes," Parker said.

"Oh, was she a midget?" Peaches said. "I thought maybe she'd shrunk in the wash."

"That's just what I mean," Parker said.

"I thought maybe she was ET in drag."

"I'm sorry if you're upset," he said.

"I am upset."

"And I'm sorry."

He *was* sorry. He was thinking it was getting to be a very cold night after a lovely day in the tropics, and he would much prefer spending the winter in Peaches's probably warm and generous bed here in town instead of in his own narrow, mean bed in his grubby little apartment away the hell out in Majesta. He was also thinking tomorrow was time enough to give Alice a call.

"What bothers me is I thought we were having such a good time together," Peaches said.

"We were. We still are. The night is young," he said.

"I thought you sort of liked me."

"I do like you. I like you a lot."

"I like you, too," Peaches said.

"So where's the problem? There's no problem. I don't see any problem. What we'll do," Parker said, "is we'll go back to your place, and we'll have a drink, and maybe watch some television…"

"That sounds nice," she said, and hugged his arm.

"It does, doesn't it?" he said. "It does sound nice."

"And we'll forget all about Eeansie-Beansie Spider."

"Who?" Parker said.

"Your little friend," Peaches said.

"I already forgot about her," Parker said.

They were just passing one of those subway-kiosk newsstands on the corner. The blind owner was kneeling over a stack of newspapers on the pavement, cutting the cord around them. Parker came up beside him. The blind man knew he was there, but he took his good sweet time cutting the cord. Parker waited; he prided himself on never having hassled a blind man in his life. The blind man finally hefted the papers up onto the newsstand and then walked around to the little door on the side of the stand and went in behind the counter.

"So?" he said.

Parker was looking down at the headline.

"You want a paper?" the blind man said.

The headline read:

2 COPS SHOT

4 MIDGETS SOUGHT

The car in the driveway of the Sebastiani house was a 1979 Cadillac Seville, silver-sided with a black hardtop, still in seemingly excellent condition. The woman who got out of the Caddy was in excellent condition herself, tall and leggy and wearing a black cloth coat the color of her hair. Hawes and Brown watched her from the upstairs window of the garage as she went directly to the front door of the house and rang the bell.

Hawes looked at his watch.

A few minutes before 1:00 in the morning.

"Who the hell is that?" he said.

They came out of Larry's Bar at exactly 1:00 A.M., twenty minutes after Bobby had first suggested they leave. A strong wind was blowing off the canal. He had insisted that she continue wearing his jacket, and she still had it draped over her shoulders. She hoped it wouldn't get in the way when she yanked the gun. Her hand hovered over the open top of her bag, seemingly resting there close to the shoulder strap. But close to the butt of the gun, too.

Bobby had his right hand in his pants pocket.

On the knife, she thought.

He had slashed his first victim in a doorway two blocks from the bar.

The second one in an alleyway on East Ninth.

The third on Canalside itself, heavily trafficked with hookers.

"Pretty cold out here," he said. "Not exactly what I had in mind."

Annie was the first of the three detectives to spot them coming out of the bar.

She had hit the street the moment she'd left Eileen in the ladies' room, and had taken up position in the darkened doorway of a closed Chinese noodle factory. It was very cold out here on the street, and she wasn't dressed for it. Skirt too damn short, blouse too flimsy. Eileen came out of the bar like a flare, red hair blowing on the wind, the guy's jacket draped over her shoulders, made an immediate left turn, walking on the guy's right, her own right hand on the curb side and resting on her bag. The guy's right hand was in his pants pocket.

Two of the lampposts on Fairview had been vandalized, and there were wide stretches of darkness between the light on the corner and the third one up. On the distant corner, a traffic light turned to red as flaming as Eileen's hair. The red hair was a plus. Easy to keep her in view. Annie gave them a twenty-yard lead, and then fell into step behind them, keeping close to the buildings on her left, the guy's blind side because he was turned to the right as he walked and talked. She cursed the hooker heels she was wearing because they made such a clatter on the sidewalk, but the guy seemed unaware of her presence behind them, just kept chatting up Eileen as they dissolved into the darkness between the lighted lampposts.

Eileen's red hair was the beacon.

Kling, scanning the street from a vantage point diagonally across from the bar, was the second detective to spot them.

The street was dark where he waited in the shadow of an abandoned tool works, the lamppost globe shattered, but the woman was unmistakably Eileen. Never mind the red hair, he'd have known her if she was wearing a blond wig. Knew every nuance of her walk, the long stride, the swing of her shoulders, the rhythmic jiggle of her buttocks. He was about to move out, cross the street and fall in behind them, when he saw Annie.

Good, he thought, she's in place.

He stayed on the opposite side of the street, ten feet behind Annie who was working hard to keep up without showing herself. Eileen and the guy were walking very fast, up toward the traffic light on the corner, which changed now, throwing a green wash onto the roadway. The formation could have been a classic tailing triangle—one cop behind the quarry, another cop ahead of them on the same side of the street, a third cop on the opposite side of the street—except that it was lacking the third cop.

Or so Kling thought.

Shanahan was the third cop.

He had been tailing Kling from the moment he'd spotted him peering through the plate-glass window of the bar. Pacing the street impatiently, always circling back to the bar, checking out the front door from across the street, then drifting off again, and back again, behaving very much like a person waiting for somebody to come out of there. When Eileen finally came out of the bar with a *second* blond guy, Shanahan's blond took off after them. Annie was up ahead, she had Eileen and *her* blond covered and in sight. But this other blond guy was still showing too much interest. Shanahan gave him a lead, and then fell in behind him again.

Up ahead, Eileen and her blond turned left at the traffic light, and disappeared around the corner.

Shanahan's blond hesitated only a moment.

Seemed undecided whether to make his move or not.

Then he pulled a gun and started across the street.

Annie recognized Kling at once.

He had a gun in his hand.

She didn't know whether she was more surprised by his presence here or by the gun in his hand. Too many thoughts clicked through her mind in the next three seconds. She thought, He's going to blow it, the guy hasn't made his move yet. She thought, Does Eileen know he's here? She thought—

But Eileen and her man were already around the corner and out of sight.

"Bert!" she shouted.

And in that instant Shanahan came thundering up yelling, "Stop! Police!"

Kling turned to see a man pointing an arm in a plaster cast at him.

He turned the other way and saw Annie running across the street.

"Mike!" Annie shouted.

Shanahan stopped dead in his tracks. Annie was waving her arms at him like a traffic cop.

"He's on the job!" she shouted.

Shanahan had earlier told Eileen that he and Lou Alvarez were just full of tricks. He hadn't realized, however, that Alvarez had sent another man to the Zone without telling him about it. That tricky, he didn't think Alvarez was. Shanahan's own little trick was a .32 revolver in his right hand, his finger inside the trigger guard, the gun and the hand encased in the plaster cast. He felt like an asshole now, the plaster cast still pointed at a guy Annie had just identified as a cop.

The realization came to all three of them in the same instant.

The traffic light on the corner turned red again as though signaling the coming of their mutual dawn.

Without a word, they looked up the street.

It was empty.

Eileen and her man were gone.

A minute ago, she'd had three backups.

Now she didn't have any.

Dolores Eisenberg was Frank Sebastiani's older sister.

Five feet ten inches tall, black hair and blue eyes, thirty-eight, thirty-nine years old. Hugging Marie to her when Brown and Hawes came over from the garage. Tears in the eyes of both women.

Marie introduced her to the cops.

Dolores seemed surprised to see them there.

"How do you do?" she said, and glanced at Marie.

"We're sorry for your trouble," Brown said.

An old Irish expression. Hawes wondered where he'd picked it up.

Dolores said, "Thank you," and then turned to Marie again. "I'm sorry it took me so long to get here," she said. "Max is in Cincinnati, and I had to find a sitter. God, wait'll he hears this. He's crazy about Frank."

"I know," Marie said.

"I'll have to call him again," Dolores said. "When Mom told me what happened, I tried to reach him at the hotel, but he was out. What time was that, when you called Mom?"

"It must've been around eleven-thirty," Marie said.

"Yeah, she called me right afterward. I felt like I'd been hit by a locomotive. I tried to get Max, I left a message for him to call me, but then I left the house around midnight, as soon as the sitter got there. I'll have to call him again."

She was still wearing her overcoat. She took it off now, revealing a trim black skirt and a crisp white blouse, and carried it familiarly to the coatrack. They were still standing in the entrance hall. The house seemed exceptionally still at this hour of the morning. The heater came on with a sudden whooosh.

"Would anyone like some coffee?" Dolores asked.

A take-charge lady, Hawes thought. Tragedy in the family, here she is at 1:00 in the morning, ready to make coffee.

"There's some on the stove," Marie said.

"Officers?" Dolores said.

"Thank you, no," Brown said.

"No, thanks," Hawes said.

"Marie? Honey, can I get a cup for you?"

"I'm all right, Dolores, thank you."

"Poor baby," Dolores said, and hugged her sister-in-law close again. Her arm still around her, she looked at Brown and said, "My mother told me you think Jimmy did it, is that right?"

"That's a strong possibility," Brown said, and looked at Marie.

"You haven't found him, though?"

"No, not yet."

"It's hard to believe," Dolores said, and shook her head. "My mother said you have to do an autopsy. I wish you wouldn't, really. That's really upsetting to her."

It occurred to Brown that she did not yet know her brother's body had been dismembered. Hadn't Marie told the family? He debated breaking the news, opted against it.

"Well, ma'am," he said, "an autopsy's mandatory in any trauma death."

"Still," Dolores said.

Brown was still looking at Marie. It had further occurred to him that on the phone with Dolores not an hour ago, she herself advised her sister-in-law about the autopsy. Yet now Dolores sounded as if the information had come from her mother. He tried to remember the exact content of the phone conversation. Marie's end of it, anyway.

Hello Dolores, no, not yet, I'm down in the kitchen.

Which meant her sister-in-law had asked her if she was in bed, or getting ready for bed, or whatever, and she'd told her, No, I'm down here with two detectives. Which meant that Dolores *knew* there were two detectives here, so why had she looked so surprised to *find* them here?

They want to look at the garage room.

So you had to figure Dolores had asked her what two detectives were doing there. And she'd told her. And then the business about the autopsy. Which Dolores had just now talked about as if it had come from her mother. But if Dolores had called here just before leaving the house…well, wait a minute.

On the phone, Marie hadn't said anything about expecting her, nothing like "See you soon then," or "Hurry on over," or "Drive safely," just "I'll let you know," meaning about the autopsy, "Thanks for calling."

Brown decided to play it flat out.

He looked Dolores dead in the eye and said, "Did you call here about an hour ago?"

And the telephone rang.

Brown figured there had to be a god.

Because if the earlier ringing of the phone had visibly startled Marie, this time the ringing caused an immediate look of panic to flash in her eyes. She turned toward the kitchen as if it had suddenly burst into flames, made an abortive start out of the entrance hall, stopped, said, "I wonder…" and then looked blankly at the detectives.

"Can't be Dolores again, can it?" Brown said.

"What?" Dolores said, puzzled.

"Better go answer it," Brown said.

"Yes," Marie said.

"I'll go with you," he said.

In the kitchen, the phone kept ringing.

Marie hesitated.

"Want me to get it?" Brown asked.

"No, I'll…it may be my mother-in-law," she said, and headed immediately for the kitchen, Brown right behind her.

The phone kept ringing.

She was thinking, You goddamn fool, I *told* you the cops were here!

She reached out for the receiver, her mind racing.

Brown was standing in the doorway to the kitchen now, his arms folded across his chest.

Marie lifted the receiver from the hook.

"Hello?" she said.

And listened.

Brown kept watching her.

"It's for you," she said, sounding relieved, and handed the receiver to him.

Parker felt like a real cop again.

A working detective.

The feeling was somewhat exhilarating.

The newspaper story accompanying the headline told him everything he needed to know about the liquor-store holdups tonight. The story extensively quoted Detective Meyer Meyer who had been interviewed in his room at Buenavista Hospital. Meyer had told the reporter that the heists and subsequent felony murders had been executed by four midgets being driven by a big blonde woman in a blue station wagon. One of the holdup victims had described the thieves as midgets. She had further told the police that one of the midgets was named Alice.

Parker did not have to be a detective to know that there couldn't be too many midgets named Alice in this city. But making the connection so quickly made him feel like a real cop again.

He put Peaches in a taxi—even though they were only four blocks from her apartment—told her he'd try to call her later, and then hailed a cruising patrol car. The two uniformed cops in the car advised Parker they were from the Three-One—which Parker knew anyway since the number of the precinct was on the side of the car—and they didn't know if they had authority to provide transportation for a detective from the Eight-Seven.

Parker said, "This is a homicide here, open the fucking door!"

The two uniformed cops looked at each other by way of consultation, and then the cop riding shotgun unlocked the back door for him. Parker sat in the back of the car like a common criminal, a metal grille separating him from the two cops up front.

"403 Thompson Street," he told the driver.

"That's all the way down the Quarter," the driver complained.

"That's right, it should take you fifteen, twenty minutes."

"Half hour's more like it," the shotgun cop said, and then got on the walkie-talkie to tell his sergeant they were driving a bull from the Eight-Seven downtown.

The sergeant said, "Let me talk to him."

"He's in back," the shotgun cop said.

"Stop the car and let me talk to him," the sergeant said. He sounded very no-nonsense. Parker had met sergeants like him before. He loved trampling on sergeants like him.

They stopped the car and opened the back door. The shotgun cop handed the walkie-talkie in to Parker.

"What's the problem?" Parker said into it.

"Who's this?" the sergeant said.

"Detective Andrew Lloyd Parker," he said, "87th Squad. Who's this?"

"Never mind who this is, what's the idea commandeering one of my cars?"

"The idea is homicide," Parker said. "The idea is two cops in the hospital. The idea is I gotta get downtown in a hurry, and I'd hate like hell for the media to find out a sergeant from the Three-One maybe stood in the way of a timely arrest. That's the idea. You think you got it?"

There was a long silence.

"Who's your commanding officer?" the sergeant asked, trying to save face.

"Lieutenant Peter Byrnes," Parker said. "We finished here?"

"You can take the car downtown, but I'll be talking to your lieutenant," the sergeant said.

"Good, you talk to him," Parker said, and handed the walkie-talkie to the shotgun cop. "Let's get rolling," he said.

They closed the back door again. The driver set the car in motion.

"Hit the hammer," Parker said.

The blues looked sidelong at each other. This kind of thing didn't seem to warrant use of the siren.

"Hit the fucking hammer," Parker said.

The driver hit the siren switch.

They were sitting in the living room when Brown got off the phone. Marie and her sister-in-law side by side on the sofa, Hawes in an easy chair opposite them.

Brown walked in looking very solemn.

"Hal Willis," he said to Hawes.

"What's up?" Hawes said.

Brown tugged casually at his earlobe before he started talking again. Hawes picked up the signal at once. Little dog-and-pony act on the way.

"They found the rest of the body," Brown said.

Marie looked at him.

"Head and the hands," Brown said. "In the river. I'm sorry, ma'am," he said to Dolores, "but your brother's body was dismembered. I hate to break it to you this way."

"Oh my *God*!" Dolores said.

Marie was still looking at Brown.

"Guys dredging the river pulled up this aluminum case, head and the hands in it," he said.

Hawes was trying to catch the drift. He kept listening intently.

"Did you know this?" Dolores asked Marie.

Marie nodded.

"You knew he'd been…?"

"Yes," she said. "I didn't tell Mom because I knew what it would do to her."

"Monoghan responded," Brown said to Hawes, "phoned the squad. Willis went on over with the stuff on my desk."

The stuff on his desk, Hawes thought. The reports, the positive ID, the poster he'd taken from the high school bulletin board.

"I hate to have to go over this another time, Mrs. Sebastiani," Brown said, "but I wonder if you can give me a description of your husband again. So we can close this out."

"I have it right here," Hawes said. He was beginning to catch on. Nobody closed out a case while the murderer was still running around loose. He took his notebook from the inside pocket of his jacket, flipped through the pages. "Male, white, thirty-four years old…" he said.

"That right?" Brown asked Marie.

"Yes," she said.

"Five-eleven," Hawes said, "one-seventy…"

"Mrs. Sebastiani?"

"Yes."

Eyes flashing with intelligence now. Hawes figured she was beginning to catch on, too. Didn't know exactly what was coming, but was bracing herself for it. Hawes didn't know exactly what was coming, either. But he had a hunch.

"Hair black," he said, "Eyes…"

"Why do we have to go over this again?" she said. "I identified the body, you have everything you—"

"My brother's hair was black, yes," Dolores said softly, and patted Marie's hand.

"Eyes blue," Hawes said.

"Blue eyes, yes," Dolores said. "Like mine."

"Will I have to come into the city again?" Marie asked. "To look at…at what they…they found in the…?"

"Mrs. Sebastiani," Brown said, "the head we found in the river doesn't match your husband's photograph."

Marie blinked at him.

Silence.

Then:

"Well…does…does that mean…what does that mean?"

"It means the dead man isn't your husband," Brown said.

"Has someone made a mistake then?" Dolores asked at once. "Are you saying my brother isn't dead?"

"Mrs. Sebastiani," Brown said, "would you mind very much if I read you this description you gave me of Jimmy Brayne?"

"I really don't see why we have to go over this a hundred times," she said. "If you were doing your job right, you'd have *found* Jimmy by now."

Brown had already taken out his notebook.

"White male," he read, "thirty-two years old. Height, six feet. Weight, a hundred and eighty…"

"Yes," she said impatiently.

Eyes alert now. Hawes had seen those eyes before. Desperate eyes, trapped eyes. Brown was closing in, and she knew it.

"Hair black, eyes brown."

"Yes," she said again.

"Mrs. Sebastiani, the eyes were brown."

"Yes, I just told you…"

"On the head in the river. The eyes were brown." He turned to Dolores. "Does your brother have an appendectomy scar?" he asked.

"A what?"

"Did he ever have his appendix removed?"

"No. I don't understand what you—"

"Was he ever in a skiing accident? Did he ever tear the cartilage on his—"

"He never skied in his life," Dolores said.

She looked extremely puzzled now. She glanced at Marie.

"The techs printed the fingers and thumbs on both hands," Brown said. "We're running a comparison check right this minute. Was your brother ever in the service?"

"Yes. The Army."

"Would you know if Jimmy Brayne was ever in the service?"

"I don't know."

"Or in any security-sensitive job? How about you, Mrs. Sebastiani? You seem to know a lot about Jimmy Brayne, maybe you know whether he's ever been fingerprinted."

"All I know about him…"

"Right down to his beauty spot," Brown said, and snapped the notebook shut.

"Marie, what is he talking about?" Dolores asked.

"I think she knows what I'm talking about," Brown said.

Marie said nothing.

"If the prints come up blank," Brown said, "we've still got the head. Someone'll identify him. Sooner or later, we'll get a positive ID."

She still said nothing.

"He's Jimmy Brayne, isn't he?" Brown asked.

Silence.

"You and your husband killed Jimmy Brayne, didn't you?" he said.

She sat quite still, her hands folded on the lap of her robe.

"Mrs. Sebastiani," Brown said, "would you like to tell us where your husband is?"

Parker opened the door with a skeleton key.

On the sofa bed in the living room, a male midget and a female midget were asleep. They jumped up the minute the door opened.

"Hello," Parker said softly, and showed them the gun.

Wee Willie Winkie was one of the midgets. He was wearing striped pajamas. He looked cute as a button, but his face went pale the moment he saw the gun. His wife, Corky, was wearing panties and a baby-doll nightgown. Pink. She grabbed a pillow and hugged it to her breasts as Parker approached the bed. Light from the hallway spilled illumination into the room. It glinted on the gun in Parker's hand. Corky's brown eyes were opened wide. She kept holding the pillow to her breasts. Parker thought she looked a little bit like Debbie Reynolds.

"Are the others asleep?" he whispered.

Willie nodded.

"Where?"

Willie pointed to a pair of closed doors.

"Up," Parker whispered.

They got out of bed. Corky looked embarrassed in only her nightgown and panties. She kept holding the pillow to her in front, but her back was exposed. Parker gestured with the gun.

"We're going to wake them up," he whispered. "Don't yell or I'll shoot you both."

In one of the bedrooms, Oliver Twist was asleep with a full-sized woman. The woman was very fat and very blonde. Parker remembered the old joke about the midget marrying the circus fat lady and running around the bed all night yelling, "Mine, all mine!"

He nudged the midget.

The midget popped up in bed.

Red hair all mussed, blue eyes wide.

"Shhhh," Parker said. "It's the police."

Oliver blinked. So did Willie. This was the first he was hearing of this. Up to now, he'd thought they were dealing with a burglar, which was bad enough. Now he knew it was a cop in here, his worst nightmare realized. He glanced at Corky, his eyes blaming his wife for her goddamn friendship with Little Annie Oakley and her trigger-happy finger.

"Wake up your lady," Parker said to Oliver.

Oliver nudged the fat blonde.

She rolled over.

He nudged her again.

"Go away," she said.

Parker pulled the blanket off her. She was wearing a long granny nightgown. She tried to pull the blanket back over her again, grasped futilely at only thin air, and then sat up, annoyed and still half-asleep.

"Police," Parker said, smiling.

"What?" she said, blinking.

"You the one did the driving?" he said.

"What driving?" she said.

"She don't know what driving," Parker said to Oliver, still smiling.

"Quentin did the driving," Oliver said. "This lady had nothing to do with any of it."

"Any of what?" the blonde said.

Quentin, Parker thought. The guy at the party.

"Where is he?" he asked.

"In the other room," Oliver said.

"Let's go tell him the party's over," Parker said. "Get out of bed. Both of you."

They got out of bed.

"Is this a joke?" the blonde whispered to Oliver.

"I don't think it's a joke," Oliver whispered back.

Parker herded the four of them into the other bedroom. The radiator was hissing, and the room was suffocatingly hot. Parker snapped on the lights. Quentin Forbes was in bed with Alice. Neither of them stirred. They had thrown back the covers in their sleep, and they were both naked. Alice looked as pretty as a little doll, her blonde hair fanned out over the pillow.

"Police!" Parker shouted, and they both jumped up at the same time. "Hello, Alice," he said, and smiled.

"Hello, Andy," she said, and smiled back.

"We have to get dressed now," he said, as if to a child.

"Okay," she said, and reached under the pillow.

Parker said it even before he saw the gun in her hand.

"Don't."

She hesitated.

"Please, Alice," he said. "Don't."

She must have discerned something in his eyes. She must have known she was looking into the eyes of a cop who had seen it all and heard it all.

"Okay," she said, and put down the gun.

Forbes said, "This is an outrage."

"It is, I know," Parker said.

"Let me see your badge," the blonde said.

Parker showed her his shield.

"What is this?" she asked.

"Let's get dressed now," he said, and went to the window and yelled down for the two uniformed cops from the Three-One.

There were only three pairs of handcuffs among them, and six people to cuff. This was a problem in the law of supply and demand. One of the blues went downstairs again and radioed for assistance, making it clear this wasn't a 10-13, they just needed some more handcuffs. The sergeant at the Twelfth wanted to know what two blues from the Three-One and a detective from the Eight-Seven were doing on his turf, but he sent a car around with the extra cuffs. By the time the cuffs arrived, Parker had personally searched the apartment. He'd found a valise full of money. He'd found a trunk with costumes and masks and wigs in it. He'd found four .22-caliber Zephyr revolvers and a Colt .45-caliber automatic.

He figured he had a case.

When they put the cuffs on her, Alice was wearing a pair of tailored gray slacks, a long-sleeved pink blouse, a double breasted navy-blue jacket with brass buttons, blue patent leather shoes with French heels, and a little navy-blue overcoat. She looked adorable.

As they went out of the apartment together, she said, "It didn't have to happen this way, you know."

"I know," Parker said.

Willis hoped there wasn't a gun in the room here. He hoped there wouldn't be shooting. With O'Brien along…

"Police," O'Brien said, and knocked on the door again.

Silence inside the room there.

Then the sound of a window scraping open.

"He's moving!" Willis said.

He was already backing away from the door and raising his right leg for a piston-kick. Arms wide for leverage, he looked like a football player going for the extra point. His leg lashed out, the sole and heel of his shoe hitting the door flat, just above the knob. The latch sprang, the door swung inward, O'Brien following it into the room, gun extended. Don't let there be another gun in here, Willis thought.

A man in his undershorts was halfway out the window.

"That's a long drop, mister," O'Brien said.

The man hesitated.

"Mr. Sebastiani?" Willis said.

The man still had one leg over the windowsill. There was no fire escape out there, Willis wondered where the hell he thought he was going.

"My name is Theo Hardeen," he said.

"So your wife mentioned," Willis said.

"My wife? I don't know what you're talking about."

They never knew what anyone was talking about.

"Mr. Sebastiani," Willis said, "at this very moment, your wife is driving in from Collinsworth with two detectives from the 87th Squad, upon whose instructions and advice we're—"

"I don't have any wife in—"

"They also have a chain saw in the car," O'Brien said.

"They found a chain saw in your garage," Willis said.

"There's a lot of blood on the saw," O'Brien said.

"Sir, we're arresting you for the crime of murder," Willis said, and then began reeling off Miranda-Escobedo by rote. Sebastiani listened to the recitation as though he were being lectured. He still had one leg over the windowsill.

"Mr. Sebastiani?" Willis said. "You want to come in off that window now?"

Sebastiani came in off the window.

"She blew it, huh?" he said.

"You both did," Willis said.

This time is for real, Carella thought.

No tricks this time.

This time I go west.

Swirling darkness, blinking lights, aurora borealis, murmuring voices, beeping sounds, everything so fake and far away, but everything so real and immediate, it was funny. Floating somewhere above himself, hovering above himself like the angel of death, "Wear this garlic around your neck," Grandma used to say, "it'll keep away the angel of death," but where's the garlic now, Grandma? Crisp white sheets and soft feather pillows, tomato sauce cooking on the old wood stove in the kitchen, your eyeglasses steaming up, the time Uncle Jerry ate the rat shit, thinking it was olives, everyone gone now, is Meyer dead, too?

Jesus, Meyer, don't be dead.

Please don't be dead.

Floating on the air above himself, looking down at himself, the big hero, some hero, open to the world, open to the hands and eyes of strangers, an open book, don't let Meyer be dead, let me hold you, Meyer, let me hold you, friend. Let's go in now, did someone say that years and years ago? Open him up now, open up the hero, big editorial conference out there, but no last-minute editorial decisions this time, no one here to say you can't kill the hero, big hero, some hero, cold-cocked by midgets, bang-bang, gotcha, close the book.

Exit.

But...

Please save that for later, okay? Save the final curtain for somewhere down the line, I'm a married man, give me a break. He almost laughed though nothing was funny, tried to laugh, wondered if he was smiling instead, heard someone say something through the fog rolling in off the water, heavy storm brewing out there, I never even learned to sail, he thought, I never had a yacht.

All the things I never did.

All the things I never had.

Well, listen, who's…?

All the treasures.

$37,500 a year doesn't buy treasures.

Ah, Jesus, Teddy, I never bought you treasures.

All the things I wanted to buy you.

Forgive me for the treasures, bless me father for I have sinned, A is for amethyst and B is for beryl, C is for coral and D is for diamonds, F is for furs and G is for gold and H is for heaven and I is for…

E is missing.

E is for exit.

But…

Please don't get ahead of me, please don't rush me, just give me a little time to finish the rest of the alphabet, I beg of you, please.

I is for me.

"Careful," someone said.

There's one hot-bed hotel the girls use, plus fifty or sixty rented rooms all over the Zone.

Shanahan talking.

Too many hours ago.

She had lost her backups, she knew that.

She didn't know what had happened on the street outside, but they were gone, that was for sure.

So here we are, she thought.

Alone at last.

You and me.

Face to face.

Not in that single hot-bed hotel, where there was a chance they might find her before the crack of dawn, but in one of those fifty or sixty rented rooms. Lady downstairs taking the money from him, looking at it on the palm of her hand as if she expected a tip besides, up the stairs to the third floor, the smells of cooking permeating the hallways, terrific spot for a honeymoon, key in the door, the door opening on a room with a bed and a dresser and a wooden chair and a lamp and a tattered window shade, and a small door at the far end leading into a bathroom with only a toilet bowl and a soiled sink.

"It's small, but it's cheerful," he'd said, grinning, and then he'd locked the door behind them and put the key into the same pocket with the knife.

That was almost an hour ago.

He'd been talking ever since.

She kept reminding him that time was money, wanting him to make his move, get it over with, but he kept laying $20 bills on her, "A dollar a minute, right?" he said, and the empty minutes of the night kept ticking away, and he made no move to approach her.

She wondered if she should bust him, anyway. Here we go, mister, it's the Law, run a lineup for the pair of hookers who'd described him, run the risk of them either chickening out or not remembering, run the further risk—even *with* a positive ID— that he'd talk his way out of it, walk away from it. Two hookers claiming they saw him chatting up the victims didn't add up to a conviction. No. If he was their man, he had to move on her before she could bust him. Come at her with the knife. No easy way out of this one, she thought. It's still him and me, alone together in this room. And all I can do is wait. And listen.

She was learning a lot about him.

He was lying on the bed with his hands behind his head, looking up at the ceiling, and she was sitting in the wooden chair across the room near the dresser, her bag on the floor near her dangling hand, and she felt like a psychiatrist listening to a patient. The room was warm enough, she had to say that for it. Sizzling hot radiator throwing heat, she was almost getting drowsy, that's all she needed. His jacket draped over the back of the wooden chair now, his voice droning into the room. She sat with both feet planted firmly on the floor, legs slightly apart, gun strapped to her ankle inside the right boot. She was ready for anything. But nothing came. Except talk.

"…that maybe *she* was partly to blame for what happened, you know?" he said. "My mother. Listen, I love her to death, don't get me wrong, she's the one who made my freedom possible, may she rest in peace. But when you think of it another way, was it all my *father's* fault? Can I just hold him responsible? For laying Elga? I mean, isn't my *mother* partly to blame for what happened?"

Elga again.

Hardly a sentence out of his mouth without some mention of the housekeeper.

"She was a schoolteacher, you know, my mother, did I tell you that?"

Only a hundred times, Eileen thought.

"Put him through medical school, left me with Elga all the while I was growing up, well, listen, I don't blame her for that. She was teaching to support the family, you know, that was a lot of responsibility. Do you know the one about the kindergarten teacher who gets the obscene phone call? She picks up the phone, she says, 'Hello?' and the voice on the other end says, 'Doo-doo, pee-pee, ca-ca,' well, that's an old one, you probably heard it. My mother didn't teach kindergarten, she was a high school teacher, worked in a tough school, long, hard hours, sometimes didn't get home till six or seven, had to correct papers all night long, I *hated* Elga. But what I'm saying, responsibility is a two-way street. If my father was laying Elga, maybe part of the fault was my mother's, do you see what I mean? She always said she hated teaching, but then why did she take it so seriously? Her sense of responsibility, sure. But shouldn't she have been responsible to her husband, too? To her son? Shouldn't she have taken care of *our* needs, too? I mean, shit, teaching didn't have to become an *obsession* with her, did it?"

I don't want to be your shrink, Eileen thought. I don't want to hear anything else about you, make your goddamn move!

But he wouldn't stop talking.

"Children sense things, don't you think?" he said. "I must have *known* something was wrong in that house. My father yelling at me all the time, my mother never there, there was tension in that house, you could cut it with a knife."

Silence.

She watched him on the bed.

Hands behind his head, staring up at the ceiling.

"I'll tell you the truth, I sometimes felt like killing her."

More silence.

Here it comes, Eileen thought.

"When I was a kid," he said.

And the silence lengthened.

"Fucking dedicated schoolteacher," he said.

She watched him.

"Ignoring the people who loved her."

Kept watching him. Ready. Waiting.

"I tried to make sense of it later, after she died. Left me all that money. This is for Robert's freedom to risk enjoying life. That was guilt talking, wasn't it? That was her guilt for having ignored us both."

Silence again.

"Do you know what she did once? Elga?"

"What did she do?"

"I was eight years old."

"What did she do?"

"She took off her bloomers."

Bloomers. A child's expression.

"Showed herself to me."

Silence.

"I ran away from her and locked myself in the bathroom."

Silence.

"My mother found me in there when she got home from school. Elga said I'd been a bad boy. Told my mother I'd locked myself in the bathroom and wouldn't come out. My mother asked me why I'd done that. Elga was standing right there. I said I was afraid of the lightning. It was raining that day. Elga smiled. The next time we were alone together, she…she…forced me to…"

He sat up suddenly.

"Do you know the one about the guy who goes into a sex shop to buy a merkin? The clerk says, 'Did you want this sent, sir, or will you take it with you?' The guy says, 'No, I'll just eat it here.'" He laughed harshly and abruptly and then said, "How would you like me to eat *your* pussy?"

"Sure," she said.

"Then take off your bloomers."

He swung his legs over the side of the bed.

"Come over here and take off your bloomers."

"You come here," Eileen said.

He stood up.

He put his right hand in his pocket.

She thought, Yes, take out the knife, you son of a bitch.

And then she thought, No, don't, Bobby.

And was suddenly confused again.

"Bobby," she said wearily, "I'm a cop."

"Sure," he said, "a cop."

"I don't want to hurt you," she said.

"Then don't bullshit me!" he said angrily. "I've had enough bullshit in my life!"

"I'm a cop," she said, and took the gun out of her bag, and leveled it at him. "Let's go find some help for you, okay?"

He looked at her. A smile cracked over his face.

"Is this a trick?" he said.

"No trick. I'm a cop. Let's go, okay?"

"Go where? Where do you want to go, baby?" He was still smiling.

But his hand was still in his pocket.

"Find some people you can talk to," she said.

"About what? There's nothing I have to say to—"

"Put the knife on the floor, Bobby."

She was standing now, almost in a policeman's crouch, the gun still leveled at him.

"What knife?" he said.

"The knife in your pocket, Bobby. Put it on the floor."

"I don't have a knife," he said.

"You have a knife, Bobby. Put it on the floor."

He took the knife out of his pocket.

"Good, now put it on the floor," she said.

"Suppose I don't?" he said.

"I know you will, Bobby."

"Suppose I lock myself in the bathroom instead?"

"No, you won't do that, Bobby. You're going to put the knife on the floor…"

"Like a good little boy, huh?"

"Bobby…I'm not your mother, I'm not Elga, I'm not going to hurt you. Just drop the knife on the floor…"

"Listen to the shrink," he said. "You're a fucking *hooker* is what you are, who the fuck do you think you're kidding?"

"Bobby, please drop the knife."

"Say pretty please," he said, and the blade snicked open.

The gun was in her hand, she had him cold.

"Don't move," she said.

The policeman's crouch more defined now, more deliberate.

He took a step toward her.

"I'm warning you, don't move!"

"Do you know the one about the guy who goes into a bank to hold it up? He sticks the gun in the teller's face and says, 'Don't muss a moovle, this is a fuck-up!' "

Another step toward her.

"This isn't fun anymore," he said, and sliced the knife across the air between them.

"Whoosh," he said.

And came at her.

Her first bullet took him in the chest, knocking him backward toward the bed. She fired again almost at once, hitting him in the shoulder this time, spinning him around, and then she fired a third time, shooting him in the back, knocking him over onto the bed, and then—she would never understand why—she kept shooting into his lifeless body, watching the eruptions of blood along his spine, saying over and over again, "I gave you a chance, I gave you a chance," until the gun was empty.

Then she threw the gun across the room and began screaming.

Some people never change.

Genero didn't even seem to know she couldn't hear him.

He was there at the hospital to tell Carella what a hero he'd been, shooting four teenagers who'd firebombed a building.

He sat in the hallway talking to Teddy, who was praying her husband wouldn't die, praying her husband wasn't already dead.

"...and all at once they came running out," he said, "Steve would've been proud of me. They threw the firebomb at me, but that didn't scare me, I..."

A doctor in a green surgical gown was coming down the hallway.

There was blood on the gown.

She caught her breath.

"Mrs. Carella?" he said.

She read his lips.

At first she thought he said, "We shot him."

A puzzled look crossed her face.

He repeated it.

"We got it," he said.

She let out her breath.

"He'll be okay," the doctor said.

"He'll be okay," Genero repeated.

She nodded.

And then she cupped her hands to her face and began weeping.

Genero just sat there.

Annie talked to him in the hallway of the Seven-Two.

"The landlady called 911 because somebody was screaming upstairs," she said. "She caters to hookers, she wouldn't have called unless she thought it was very serious."

Kling nodded.

"She quieted down just a little while ago. She's down the hall in Interrogation. I'm not sure you ought to talk to her."

"Why not?" Kling said.

"I'm just not sure," Annie said.

He went down the hall.

He opened the door.

She was sitting at the long table in the Interrogation Room, the two-way mirror behind her. Just sitting there. Looking at her hands.

"I'm sorry if I screwed it up," he said.

"You didn't."

He sat opposite her.

"Are you okay?" he asked. "No," she said.

He looked at her.

"I'm quitting," she said. "What do you mean?"

"The force."

"No, you're not."

"I'm quitting, Bert. I don't like what it did to me, what it keeps doing to me."

"Eileen, you—"

"I'm quitting this city, too."

"Eileen..."

"This fucking city," she said, and shook her head.

He reached for her hand. She pulled it away.

"No," she said.

"What about me?" he said.

"What about me?" she said.

The phone rang at a little past 2:00 in the morning.

She picked up the receiver.

"Peaches?" the voice said. "This is Phil Hendricks at Camera Works, we talked earlier tonight."

Him again!

"What I want you to do," he said, "I want you to take off your blouse and go look at yourself in the mirror. Then I want you to—"

"Listen, you creep," she said, "if you call me one more time—"

"This is Andy Parker," he said. "I'm in a phone booth on the corner. Is it too late to come up?"

"You dope," she said.

It was the last trick of the night.

ABOUT THE AUTHOR

Ed McBain was one of the many pen names of the successful and prolific crime fiction author Evan Hunter (1926–2005). Born Salvatore Lambino in New York, McBain served aboard a destroyer in the US Navy during World War II and then earned a degree from Hunter College in English and psychology. After a short stint teaching in a high school, McBain went to work for a literary agency in New York, working with authors such as Arthur C. Clarke and P.G. Wodehouse, all the while working on his own writing on nights and weekends. He had his first breakthrough in 1954 with the novel *The Blackboard Jungle*, which was published under his newly legal name Evan Hunter and based on his time teaching in the Bronx.

Perhaps his most popular work, the 87th Precinct series (released mainly under the name Ed McBain) is one of the longest running crime series ever published, debuting in 1956 with *Cop Hater* and featuring over fifty novels. The series is set in a fictional locale called Isola and features a wide cast of detectives including the prevalent Detective Steve Carella.

McBain was also known as a screenwriter. Most famously he adapted a short story from Daphne Du Maurier into the screenplay for Alfred Hitchcock's *The Birds* (1963). In addition to writing for the silver screen, he wrote for many television series, including *Columbo* and the NBC series *87th Precinct* (1961–1962), based on his popular novels.

McBain was awarded the Grand Master Award for lifetime achievement in 1986 by the Mystery Writers of America and was the first American to receive the Cartier Diamond Dagger award from the Crime Writers Association of Great Britain. He passed away in 2005 in his home in Connecticut after a battle with larynx cancer.

Made in the USA
Charleston, SC
02 April 2012